Fuzzy Nation

Also by John Scalzi

Old Man's War
The Ghost Brigades
The Android's Dream
The Last Colony
Zoe's Tale
Your Hate Mail Will Be Graded

Edited by John Scalzi

Metatropolis

Fuzzy Nation

John Scalzi

A Tom Doherty Associates Book

New York

This is a work of fiction. All of the characters, organizations, and events por-
trayed in this novel are either products of the author's imagination or are used
fictitiously.

FUZZY NATION

Copyright © 2011 by John Scalzi

Published by arrangement with the Berkley Publishing Group, a member of
Penguin Group (USA) Inc.

Edited by Patrick Nielsen Hayden

A Tor Book
Published by Tom Doherty Associates, LLC
175 Fifth Avenue
New York, NY 10010

Tor® is a registered trademark of Tom Doherty Associates, LLC.

ISBN 978-0-7653-2854-0

Printed in the United States of America

Fuzzy Nation is dedicated to the following:

To Mary Robinette Kowal, a good friend and even better writer;

and

To Ethan Ellenberg, who did more work to make this happen than either of us expected. His efforts are greatly appreciated.

The author additionally bows deeply in the direction of H. Beam Piper, for the most obvious of reasons.

Fuzzy Nation is a reimagining of the story and events in *Little Fuzzy,* the 1962 Hugo-nominated novel by H. Beam Piper. Specifically, *Fuzzy Nation* appropriates the general story arc of *Little Fuzzy,* as well as character names and plot elements, and weds them to entirely new elements, characters, and events. Think of this as a "reboot" of the Fuzzy universe, not unlike the recent J. J. Abrams "reboot" of the *Star Trek* film series (but hopefully with better science).

Because *Fuzzy Nation* is a reimagining of, rather than a sequel to, *Little Fuzzy,* readers do not need to have read the Piper novel to enjoy this one. That said, it is the author's sincere hope that those of you who have not read *Little Fuzzy* will be inspired to do so; it's a wonderful book, well worth the reading. *Fuzzy Nation* is not intended to supplant or improve upon *Little Fuzzy,* which would be impossible to do. It is simply a variation on the story, events, and characters established by Piper a half century ago.

—JS

Fuzzy Nation

Jack Holloway set the skimmer to HOVER, swiveled his seat around, and looked at Carl. He shook his head sadly.

"I can't believe we have to go through this again," Holloway said. "It's not that I don't value you as part of this team, Carl. I do. Really, I do. But I can't help but think that in some way, I'm just not getting through to you. We've gone over this how many times now? A dozen? Two? And yet every time we come out here, it's like you forget everything you've been taught. It's really very discouraging. Tell me you get what I'm saying to you."

Carl stared up at Holloway and barked. He was a dog.

"Fine," Holloway said. "Then maybe *this* time it will stick." He reached down into a storage bin and hoisted a mound of putty in one hand. "This is acoustical blasting putty. What do we do with it?"

Carl cocked his head.

"Come on, Carl," Holloway said. "This is the first thing I taught you. We put it on the side of the cliff at strategic points," Holloway said. "Just like I already did earlier today. You remember. You were there." He pointed in the direction of Carl's Cliff, a massive outcropping of rock, two hundred meters high, with geological striations peeking out of the vegetation covering most of the rock face. Carl followed Holloway's finger with his eyes, more interested in the finger than in the cliff his master had named for him.

Holloway set down the putty and picked up another, smaller object. "And this is the remote-controlled blasting cap," he said. "Which we attach to the acoustical blasting putty, so we don't have to be near the acoustical blasting putty when we set it off. Because that's *boom*. How do we feel about *boom,* Carl?"

Carl got a concerned look on his doggy face. *Boom* was a word he knew. Carl was not fond of *boom.*

"Right," Holloway said. He set down the blasting cap, making sure it was nowhere near the blasting putty, and that the cap receiver was inactive. He picked up a third object.

"And this is the remote detonator," Holloway said. "You remember *this,* right, Carl?"

Carl barked.

"What's that, Carl?" Holloway said. "*You* want to set off the acoustical blasting putty?"

Carl barked again.

"I don't know," Holloway said, doubtfully. "Technically it is a violation of Zarathustra Corporation safe labor practices to allow a nonsentient species member to set off high explosives."

Carl came up to Holloway and licked his face with a whine that said *please please oh please.*

"Oh, all right," Holloway said, fending off the dog. "But this is the *last* time. At least until you grasp *all* the fundamentals of the job. No more slacking off and leaving all the hard work to me. I'm paid to supervise. Are we clear?"

Carl barked once more and then backed off, tail wagging. He knew what was coming next.

Holloway glanced down at the detonator's image panel and checked, for the third time since he placed the charges earlier in the day, that the detonator was keyed specifically to the blasting caps placed into the charges. He pressed the panel to answer YES to each of the automated safety questions and waited while the detonator confirmed by geolocation that it was, in fact, safely outside the blast radius of any charges. This could be overridden, but it took some hacking, and anyway, Holloway preferred not to blow himself up whenever possible. And Carl was not so fond of *boom*.

CHARGES SET AND READY, read the detonator panel. PRESS PANEL TO DETONATE.

"Okay," Holloway said, and set the detonator on the skimmer floor between him and Carl. Carl looked up expectantly.

"Wait for it," Holloway said, and swiveled around in his chair to face the cliff. He could hear Carl's tail thumping excitedly against a crate.

"Wait for it," Holloway said again, and tried to spy the places on the cliff he had drilled into earlier in the day, using the skimmer as a platform while he inserted and secured the charges into the drill holes.

Carl gave a little whine.

"Fire!" Holloway said, and heard the dog scramble forward.

The cliff puffed out in four spots, spewing rock and dirt and hurling vegetation for meters. The cliff face darkened as the birds (which is to say, the local flying animal equivalent to birds) that had been nesting in the cliff face's vegetation took to the air, alarmed by the noise and sudden eruptions. A few seconds later, four closely spaced *cracks* snapped the air in the skimmer's open cockpit, the sound of the explosions finally reaching Holloway and Carl—loud, but without the Carl-worrying *boom*.

Holloway glanced over to his right, where his information

panel lay, sonic imaging program up and running. The sonic probes he'd placed on and around the cliff were spewing their raw feed into the program, which was collating and combining the data, turning it into a three-dimensional representation of the internal structure of the cliff.

"All right," he said, and swiveled around to look at Carl, who still had his paw on the detonator, tongue lolling out of his mouth.

"Good boy!" Holloway said, and dug into the storage bin to pull out a zararaptor bone, still heavy with meat. He unwrapped it from its storage film and tossed it at Carl, who fell on it happily. That was the deal: Press the detonator, get a bone. It had taken Holloway more than a few tries to get Carl to press the detonator accurately, but it had been worth the effort. Carl had to come on the surveying trips anyway. Might as well have him be useful, or at least entertaining.

Now, it really *was* a violation of Zarathustra Corporation safe labor practices to let a dog blow things up. But Holloway and Carl worked alone, hundreds of kilometers from ZaraCorp's local headquarters on-planet and 178 light-years from its corporate headquarters on Earth. He wasn't technically a ZaraCorp employee anyway; he was a contractor, just like every other prospector/surveyor here on Zara XXIII. It was cheaper that way.

Holloway reached down and rubbed Carl's head affectionately. Carl, engrossed in the raptor bone, paid him not the slightest bit of mind.

An urgent beep came from Holloway's infopanel. He picked it up to see that the data feeds were suddenly spiking through their bandwidth.

A low rumble thrummed its way into the skimmer cockpit, getting louder the longer it lasted. Carl looked up from his bone and whined. This noise was perilously close to *boom*.

Holloway glanced up and saw a column of dust rising violently from the cliff wall, obscuring everything behind it.

"Oh, crap," he said to himself. He had a very bad, sinking feeling about this.

After a few minutes, the dust began to clear a bit, and his very bad, sinking feeling got worse. Through the indistinct haze, Holloway could see that a portion of the cliff wall had collapsed, the borders of the collapse roughly contiguous with where he had placed his explosive charges. Stark geological striations glared out from where vegetation had been before. Birds swooped into the area, looking for their nests, the remains of which were a couple hundred meters below them, the wreckage muddying and rerouting the river at the foot of the cliff.

"Oh, crap," Holloway said again, and reached for his binoculars.

ZaraCorp would be awfully pissed he'd just caused a cliff collapse. ZaraCorp had been working hard over the last few years to reverse the long-standing public image the company had as a rampant despoiler of nature—earned, to be sure, by actually despoiling nature on a number of planets it had operations on. The public was no longer buying the argument that uninhabited planets had higher ecological tolerances than inhabited ones, or that these ecosystems would quickly restore natural equilibriums once ZaraCorp had moved on. As far as they were concerned, strip-mining was strip-mining, regardless of whether you were doing it in the mountains of Pennsylvania or the hills of Zara XXIII.

Confronted with overwhelming public opposition to his company's ecological practices (or lack thereof), Wheaton Aubrey VI, Chairman and CEO of Zarathustra Corporation, said "fine" and ordered ZaraCorp and all its subsidiaries to exercise practices consistent with ecological guidelines suggested by the Colonial

Environmental Protection Agency. It was all the same to Aubrey. He was no friend to the various ecologies of the planets his company was on, but ZaraCorp's Exploration & Exploitation charter with the Colonial Administration specified that the company would receive tax credits when conforming to CEPA guidelines, so long as the incurred business costs were above a meager cost-of-development baseline formulated decades before anyone cared about the ecological despoilage of worlds they would never actually set foot on.

ZaraCorp's ostentatious new regime of ecological best practices, in other words, helped drive the company's tax indebtedness to something close to zero, a neat trick for an organization whose size and income were a nontrivial fraction of that of the Colonial Administration itself.

But it also meant that events that tarnished ZaraCorp's new eco-friendly PR campaign were looked at rather harshly. For example, collapsing an entire cliff wall. The whole point of using acoustic charges was to minimize the invasiveness of geologic exploration. Holloway didn't intend to make half the cliff fall away, but given ZaraCorp's reputation, the company would have a hard time getting anyone to believe that. Holloway had played fast and loose with regulations before and had mostly gotten away with it, but this was just the sort of thing that *would,* in fact, get Holloway booted off the planet.

Unless.

"Come on, come *on,*" Holloway said, still peering through his binoculars. He was waiting for the haze to settle enough to make out details.

The communication circuit on Holloway's infopanel fired up, showing the ID of Chad Bourne, Holloway's ZaraCorp contractor rep. Holloway swore and slapped the AUDIO ONLY option.

"Hi, Chad," he said, and put the binoculars back to his eyes.

"Jack, the geeks in the data room tell me there's something really screwy with your feeds," Bourne said. "They say everything was coming in clear and then it was like someone turned the feeds up to eleven." Chad Bourne's voice came in crystal clear and enveloping, thanks to the skimmer's one true indulgence: a spectacular sound system. Holloway had it installed when he realized he'd be spending almost all his working life in the skimmer. It was a wonder in many ways, but it didn't make Bourne sound any less adenoidal.

"Huh," Holloway said.

"They say it's the sort of thing you see when there's an earthquake. Or a maybe a rock slide," Bourne said.

"Now that you mention it, I think I felt an earthquake." Holloway said.

"Really," Bourne said.

"Yes," Holloway said. "Just before it happened, Carl was acting all strange. They say animals are always the first to know about these things."

"So the fact that the data geeks just told me there was absolutely no seismic event of any magnitude in your part of the continent doesn't bother you any," Bourne said.

"Who are you going to believe," Holloway said. "I'm here. They're there."

"They're here with roughly twenty-five million credits' worth of equipment," Bourne said. "You've got an infopanel and a history of bad surveying practices."

"*Alleged* bad surveying practices," Holloway said.

"Jack, you let your dog blow shit up," Bourne said.

"I do not," Holloway said. The dust at the cliff wall had finally begun to clear. "That's just a rumor."

"We have an eyewitness," Bourne said.

"She's unreliable," Holloway said.

"She's a trusted employee," Bourne said. "Unlike some people I could name."

"She had a personal agenda," Holloway said. "Trust me."

"Well, that's just the thing, isn't it, Jack?" Bourne said. "You have to earn that trust. And right now, you've got not so much of it with me. But I'll tell you what. I have a surveying satellite that's coming up over the horizon in about six minutes. When it gets there, I'm going to have it look at that cliff wall you probably just blew up. If it looks like it's supposed to, then the next time you get into Aubreytown, I'll buy you a steak at Ruby's and apologize. But if it looks like I know it's going to look like, I'm going to revoke your contract and send some security agents to bring you in. And not the ones you go drinking with, Jack. The ones who *don't* like you. I know, I'll send Joe DeLise. He'll be delighted to see you."

"Good luck getting him off his barstool," Holloway said.

"For you, I think he'd do it," Bourne said. "What do you think about that?"

Holloway didn't respond. He'd stopped listening several seconds earlier, because in his binoculars was a thin stratum of rock, sandwiched between two much larger striations. The stratum he was focused on was dark as coal.

And sparkled.

"Yes," Holloway said.

"Yes, what?" Bourne said. "Jack, are you even listening to what I'm telling you?"

"Sorry, Chad, you're breaking up," Holloway said. "Interference. Sunspots."

"Jesus, Jack, you're not even *trying* anymore," Bourne said. "Enjoy your next five minutes. I've already called up your contract on my infopanel. As soon as I get that satellite image, I'm pressing the delete button." Bourne broke contact.

Holloway looked over at Carl and picked up the detonator panel. "Crate," he said to the dog. Carl barked, picked up his bone, and headed for his crate, which would immobilize him in case of a skimmer crash. Holloway dropped the detonator into the storage bin, secured his infopanel, and strapped himself into his chair.

"Come on, Carl," he said, and goosed the skimmer forward. "We've got five minutes to keep ourselves from getting kicked off the planet."

Chapter Two

Five minutes thirty seconds later Holloway slapped open the communication circuit on his infopanel, sound only. "I suppose you're going to tell me my contract is deleted," he said to Bourne.

"It is so very deleted," Bourne said. "And I'm keying in the security retrieval order right now. Just stay where you are and someone will be along to pick you up in about an hour. They'll take you directly to the beanstalk. Pack light."

"No chance I can convince you otherwise," Holloway said.

"No way," Bourne said. "I've got six dozen contractors I supervise, Jack. Six dozen. Not one of them is as much of a pain in my ass as you are. I'm about to make my life that much easier."

"You're sure your satellite image is showing you what you need to see?" Holloway asked.

"The satellite takes images at a centimeter resolution, Jack," Bourne said. "Live images. I am at this very moment staring at the cliff wall you just blew up, and seeing you and your dog sitting on a ledge that up until a few moments ago was *inside* the cliff. Say hello to Carl for me."

Holloway turned to Carl. "Chad says hello." Carl blinked and lay down to rest.

"Carl's a nice dog," Bourne said. "Too bad he's yours."

"That's been noted before," Holloway said. "Chad, if the satellite can resolve to a centimeter, you should look at my hand."

"You're giving me the middle finger," Bourne said, after a second. "Nice. Have you always been twelve years old, or is this new?"

"Glad you noticed, but not that hand," Holloway said. "The other hand."

There was a moment's pause. Then, "Bullshit," said Bourne.

"No," Holloway said. "Sunstone."

"Bullshit!" Bourne said again.

"Big one, too," Holloway said. "This one's the size of the proverbial baby's fist. And there are three more just this big here on this ledge with me. I pulled them out of the seam like they were apples off a tree. This was the original jellyfish burial ground, my friend."

"Infopanel," Bourne said. "High-resolution imager. Now."

Holloway smiled and reached for his infopanel.

Zara XXIII was in most respects an unremarkable Class III planet: roughly Earth sized, roughly Earth mass, winging around its star in the "Goldilocks zone" that made liquid water possible and life therefore an inevitability. It lacked native sentient life, but most Class III planets did, otherwise they'd be Class IIIa and ZaraCorp's E & E charter would be void, the planet and its resources held in trust for the thinking creatures who lived on it. Because Zara XXIII lacked creatures with forebrains (or the forebrain equivalent), however, ZaraCorp was free to explore and exploit it, mining the metals and plunging depths for the petroleum that humans had long ago exhausted on their own world.

But for all that Zara XXIII was mostly unremarkable, it stood out from all the other ZaraCorp planets in one way: 100 million years previously, its oceans were dominated by an immense jellyfish-like creature that survived on algae and diatoms that themselves fed on the unusually mineral-rich waters of Zara XXIII's seas. When these jellyfish died, their fragile corpses sank downward into the oxygen-starved depths, covering the ocean floors in places for kilometers. These corpses were eventually covered in silt and mud, and in the course of time, weight and pressure compressed and transformed the jellyfish into something else.

They became sunstones: opal-like stones that did not just catch the light like filigreed fire but were in fact thermoluminescent. The body heat of someone wearing a stone was enough to make it glow from within. Not the garish glow of a light stick at a dance party or a glow-in-the-dark mood ring you'd give your kid, but a subtle and elegant incandescence that warmed skin tones and flattered the wearer. Because every person's skin temperature was ever so slightly different, even the same sunstone looked different on another person. It was the ultimate personalized gemstone.

ZaraCorp discovered them while excavating what it hoped was a coal seam and decided the funny rocks kicking up in the hopper were more promising than the coal. Since then the corporation had taken the lessons of the old diamond cartels to heart, positioning sunstones as the rarest of all possible gems: found only on one planet, strictly limited and therefore fetching the highest possible prices. The sunstone Holloway held in his hand was worth roughly nine months of income. Cut and shaped, it would be worth more than he'd likely make in three years as a contract surveyor.

Which he no longer was.

"Holy cow," Bourne said, glancing at the sunstone through the infopanel's camera. "That thing's like a jawbreaker."

"It sure is," Holloway said. "I could retire on this baby, and on the other sunstones I picked out of the seam here. And I guess I will, since now I own them and the entire seam."

"What?" Bourne said. "Jack, being out in the sun has made you delirious. You don't own a damn thing here."

"Sure I do," Holloway said. "You deleted my contract, remember? That makes me an independent prospector, not a contract prospector. As an independent prospector, anything I find is mine, and any seam I chart I have the right to exploit. That's basic Colonial Authority E and E case law. *Butters versus Wayland*, to be specific."

"Oh, come off it, Jack," Bourne said. "You know ZaraCorp doesn't allow independent prospectors on planet."

"I wasn't one when I came on planet," Holloway said. "You just made me one."

"And besides which, ZaraCorp owns this entire planet," Bourne said.

"No," Jack said. "ZaraCorp has an exclusive Explore and Exploit charter for the planet, granted by the Colonial Authority. De facto, ZaraCorp runs the planet. De jure, it's Colonial Authority territory."

"Are you having a problem with the word *exclusive*?" Bourne said. "An *exclusive* E and E charter means only ZaraCorp is allowed to explore and exploit."

"No," Holloway said. "It just means ZaraCorp is the exclusive *corporate* entity allowed on the planet. Single individuals are allowed E and E rights on any Class Three planet, so long as they conform to CEPA guidelines and allow chartered corporate entities right of first refusal on purchase of their prospected materials. *Buchheit versus Zarathustra Corporation*."

"You're pulling these so-called cases right out of your ass, Jack," Bourne said.

"They're real, all right," Holloway said. "Go ahead and look them up. I was a lawyer in my past life, you know."

Bourne's snort came loud and clear through the infopanel. "Yeah, and you were *disbarred*," he said.

"Not because I didn't know the law," Holloway said. Which was true, as far as it went.

"It's all immaterial anyway, because when you surveyed the seam, you were working for ZaraCorp," Bourne said. "I deleted your contract afterwards. Therefore discovery of the seam and the fruits of that discovery belong to us."

"They might, if I had used ZaraCorp equipment to do the survey," Holloway said. "But in fact, I used my own equipment, which I bought and paid for, as specified in that contract you deleted. Since I used my own equipment, legally the right to the find vested back to me when you dropped me. *Levensohn versus Hildebrand.*"

"Bullshit," Bourne said.

"Look it up," Holloway said. Actually, he hoped Bourne wouldn't look it up; unlike the other two cases he quoted, he'd made up *Levensohn v. Hildebrand* on the spot. He was about to get kicked off planet anyway. It was worth a shot.

"I *am* going to look it up," Bourne said. "Trust me."

"Good," Holloway said. "Do that. And while you're doing that, I'm going to get busy excavating this seam. And when your security goons show up and try to roust me from my seam, I'll be absolutely delighted, because then I can sue them, you and Zara-Corp under *Greene versus Winston.*"

Holloway couldn't see it, but he knew Bourne had stiffened in his chair. *Greene v. Winston* were fighting words at ZaraCorp because, among other things, the decision had sent Wheaton

Aubrey V, ZaraCorp's previous Chairman and CEO, to San Quentin for seven years.

"*Greene* was overturned, you hack," Bourne said, tightly.

"No," Holloway said. "A narrow and limited exception was carved out of *Greene* in *Mieville versus Martin*. That exception doesn't apply here."

"The hell it doesn't," Bourne said.

"Well, I guess we'll find out," Holloway said. "It'll probably take years to work through the courts, though, and ZaraCorp will get all sorts of bad publicity while it does. We all remember what happened the last time. Also, just so you know, I've been recording this little conversation of ours. Just in case you get it into your head to suggest to DeLise and his security goons that they should toss me off this ledge when they find me."

"I resent that implication," Bourne said.

"I'm glad to hear that, Chad," Holloway said. "But I'd rather be safe than sorry."

Bourne sighed. "Fine, Jack," he said. "You win. Your contract is undeleted. Happy?"

"Not in the least," Holloway said. "If you deleted the old contract, then I have the right to negotiate a new contract."

"You get the standard contract just like everyone else," Bourne said.

"You talk as if I'm not standing next to a billion-credit sunstone seam, Chad," Holloway said. "Which I *own*."

"I hate you," Bourne said.

"Don't blame me," Holloway said. "You're the one who deleted my contract. But my demands are simple. First, I don't want to be fined for this cliff collapse. It was an accident, and I know when you sift the data you'll see that for yourself."

"Fine," Bourne said. "Done."

"And I want a one percent finder's fee," Holloway said.

Bourne swore. Holloway was asking for four times the standard finder's fee. "No way," Bourne said. "No *way*. They'll fire me for even *thinking* about approving that."

"It's one lousy percent," Holloway said.

"You want ten million credits for blowing up a cliff side," Holloway said.

"Well, it might be more than that," Holloway said. "I can see six more sunstones in the seam from where I'm sitting."

"No," Bourne said. "Don't even think about it. The most I'm allowed to authorize myself is point four percent. Take it and we're done. Leave it and we're going to court. And I *swear* to you, Jack, if I get fired for all of this, I'm going to hunt you down and kill you myself. And steal your dog."

"That's just low, stealing someone's dog," Holloway said.

"Point four percent," Bourne said. "Final offer."

"Done," Holloway said. "Write this up as a rider to the contract neither you nor I contend was ever stupidly deleted by you. If it's a rider, I don't have to fly into Aubreytown to approve it."

"Already done," Bourne said. "Transmitting now." The MAIL icon on Holloway's infopanel came to life. He picked up the infopanel, scanned the rider, and approved it with his security hash.

"Pleasure doing business with you, Chad," Holloway said, setting down the infopanel.

"Please die in a fire, Jack," Bourne said.

"Does this mean you're not taking me for a steak at Ruby's?" Holloway asked, but Bourne had already cut the connection.

Holloway smiled to himself and held up the sunstone in his hand, turning it in the sun. Even in its uncut, dirty state it was beautiful, and Holloway had held it long enough that his own ambient heat had worked into the heart of the stone, making its filaments glow like lightning trapped in amber.

"You're coming with me," Holloway said to the stone. Zara-Corp could have the rest of them, and would. But this was the stone that had just made him a very rich man. It was a lucky stone, indeed. And he had someone in mind to give it to. By way of apology.

Holloway stood up and slipped the sunstone into his pocket. He looked over at Carl, who was still lying on the ledge. Carl crooked an eyebrow at him.

"Well," Holloway said. "We've done all the damage we're going to do around here for today. Let's go home."

Chapter Three

Holloway's skimmer was roughly halfway back to his home when his infopanel alerted him that his house was being broken into; the emergency alert system's movement alarm had been tripped.

"Crap," Holloway said. He jabbed the AUTOPILOT function on the skimmer; the skimmer skewed momentarily as it acquired signal and pathing from Holloway's home base. There was no traffic here—Holloway's survey territory was deep inside a continent-wide jungle, far away from any population centers, or indeed any other humans—so the course was more or less a straight line to home over the hills and treetops. Autopilot engaged, Holloway picked up his infopanel and clicked through to the security camera.

Which showed nothing; Holloway had the camera on his work desk and generally used it as a hat stand. His view of his house—and whoever was currently inside it—was being blocked by a stained porkpie hat he'd worn for amusement's sake during his second year of law school at Duke.

"Stupid *hat*," Holloway said. He kicked up the gain on the

security camera's microphone and held the infopanel speaker against his ear, on the chance the interloper might talk.

No luck. There were no voices, and what little else he could hear was being washed out by the sound of the skimmer engines and wind rushing through the open cockpit.

Holloway clicked his infopanel back into its cradle and looked down at his skimmer instrument panel. The skimmer was moving along at a leisurely eighty kilometers an hour, a safe speed in the jungle, in which birds were liable to burst out of the trees and smash themselves into the vehicle. Home was another twenty klicks out; Holloway knew that without checking the GPS data because he could see Mount Isabel off to his right. The hill's eastern face was chewed away and the four square klicks in front of it fenced off and stripped bare of vegetation where ZaraCorp was doing what it euphemistically called "Smart Mining"—strip-mining but with an ostensible commitment to minimizing toxic impact and to restoring the area to its pristine state when the mining operations ceased.

At the time ZaraCorp started mining Mount Isabel, Holloway had idly wondered how an area could be restored to a pristine state once ZaraCorp had mined everything of value out of it, but this was not the same thing as him exhibiting actual concern. He'd been the one who did the original survey of Mount Isabel; the small sunstone patch that first drew his attention was exhausted in a matter of weeks, but the mount was a good source of anthracite coal, and the relatively rare rockwood tree grew on the mount and down its sides toward the river. He'd gotten his quarter of a percent out of the find—a decent-enough sum—and had moved on.

Holloway's critical eye guessed that Mount Isabel had another year or two left in her before she was mined down to a molehill, at which time ZaraCorp would airlift out its equipment and drop in a clutch of terrified summer interns, who would hurriedly strew bags of rockwood seeds on the ground—this counted as "restoring the area to a pristine state"—and who would also pray that the fence winding around the perimeter of the mining area held up while they did it.

The fences usually held. It was rare these days to lose an intern to a zararaptor. But fear was a fine motivator.

A loud crash came out of the infopanel. Whoever was in Holloway's house just dropped something breakable. Holloway swore and pressed the button that would enclose the skimmer cockpit, and then opened the throttle. They'd be home in five minutes; the birds in the treetops would just have to take their chances.

●   ●   ●

As the skimmer approached his home, Holloway dropped it into CONSERVE mode, which dropped its speed significantly but also made the skimmer almost silent. He stop-hovered the craft a klick out and reached for his binoculars.

Holloway's house was a tree house—or more accurately, a platform anchored across several very tall spikewoods, on the edges of which stood the modest prefabricated cabin that was his living quarters, and the two sheds in which Holloway kept his surveying and prospecting supplies. Power was supplied by solar panels held aloft by a turbine kite, connected to the compound's power plant, on which was also attached Holloway's moisture collector and waste incinerator. In the center of the platform was a parking space, with enough room for Holloway's skimmer and one other craft, provided it was small.

It was that space Holloway was looking at. It was empty.

Holloway relaxed a little. The only easy way into Holloway's compound was by skimmer. It was possible that someone could have approached by foot and then climbed up, but that person would've had to be either very lucky or very confident. The jungle floor belonged to zararaptors and the local versions of pythons and alligators, any of which looked at the soft and slow human animal as an easy-to-catch, easy-to-eat snack. Holloway lived in the trees because all the big predators were on the ground, save the pythons, and they didn't like spikewoods for reasons the name of the tree made obvious. The spikewoods also made climbing them a challenge if one were taller than half a meter, which any human would be.

Regardless, Holloway scanned the platform and through the foliage to look for climbing cables and the like. Nothing. The other option would be that someone dropped in from above, from a hovering skimmer, which then took off. But Holloway would have been pinged about any traffic within a hundred-klick radius when he set the autopilot. He hadn't been.

So: Either there was a super-awesome ninja assassin lurking in his cabin, knocking over pottery, or it was just some dumb animal. While Holloway wouldn't put it past Bourne to put a hit out on him, especially after today, he also doubted that Bourne could shake out a competent assassin on short notice. The best he would be able to do was some of the less intelligent ZaraCorp security types, such as the aforementioned Joe DeLise. They (and particularly DeLise) wouldn't have bothered with sneaking up on him.

Chances were excellent, then, that this was a dumb animal; probably one of the local lizards, in fact. They were the size of iguanas—just small enough to avoid impalement on the spikewoods—vegetarians, and dumber than rocks. They would get into absolutely everything if you gave them a chance. When Holloway first came to Zara XXIII and had his treetop compound built, the place was infested with them. He'd put up an electric fence at first, but discovered that waking up every morning to the sight and smell of barbecued lizard depressed the crap out of him. Then another prospector told him that the lizards were utterly terrified of dogs. Carl arrived shortly thereafter.

"Hey, Carl," Holloway said to his dog. "I think we got ourselves a lizard problem."

Carl perked up at this. He very much enjoyed his role as solver of lizard problems. Holloway smiled, took the skimmer off STOP-HOVER mode, and went in for a landing.

Carl was out of the skimmer as soon as Holloway turned off the engines and opened the cockpit. He sniffed happily and headed off in the direction of one of the storage sheds.

"Hey, dummy," Holloway said to Carl's tail, which was whipping back and forth. He walked over to his dog and whacked him gently on the flank. "You're going the wrong direction. The lizard's in the house." Holloway pointed in the direction of the cabin. He looked at the cabin at the same time, catching the image of the cat staring at him through the window over his work desk. Holloway stared back at the cat. It took him a second to remember that he didn't own a cat.

It took him a second after that to remember that cats didn't usually stand on two legs.

"What the hell *is* that?" Holloway said, out loud.

Carl turned at the sound of his master's voice and saw the cat thing in the window.

The cat thing opened its mouth.

Carl barked like a mad dog and bolted toward the cabin door. His lack of opposable thumbs would have brought him up short had Holloway not installed a dog door after he'd gotten tired of being woken up in the middle of the night to let Carl out to pee. The dog door's locking mechanism picked up the proximity signal from the chip in Carl's shoulder and unlocked the door roughly a quarter of a second before Carl jammed his head and body through it, bolting effortlessly into the cabin.

From his viewpoint, Holloway saw the cat thing fling itself away from the window. Less than a second after that, Holloway could hear the sounds of many things breaking.

"Oh, shit," Holloway said, and ran for the cabin door.

Unlike Carl, Holloway did not a have proximity chip implanted in his shoulder; he fumbled for the key to open the dead lock on the door, barking and crashing continuing nonstop as he did so. Holloway undid the bolt and cracked open the door just in time to see the cat thing running toward it.

The cat thing looked up, saw Holloway, and skidded, desperately trying to change its vector of direction. Carl, directly behind the cat thing, leapt up to avoid the braking creature and twisted midflight, connecting his flank with the cabin door, slamming it shut on Holloway's forehead and nose. Holloway cursed and dropped to his knees by the closed door, clutching his nose. There were more crashing noises inside.

After a few minutes, Holloway became aware of two things. The first was that his nose, while swollen, was not going to bleed out on him. The second was that all the crashing noises had stopped, replaced by the sound of Carl's constant bark. Holloway stood up, touched his nose one more time to make sure it wasn't going to spontaneously gush, and then very carefully opened the door to his cabin.

The cabin looked like one of Holloway's college dorm rooms at the end of a semester: an explosion of papers and objects on the floor, which should have been on a desk or shelf. Dishes previously in the cabin's tiny sink were shattered on the ground. Holloway's spare infopanel was likewise facedown on the floor. He couldn't bring himself to see whether it was still functional or not.

Carl was propped up against the cabin's sole bookcase, barking madly. A quick glance up established that he had treed the cat thing on top of the bookcase. Books and binders had been flung off the shelves as either the thing climbed up the shelf or Carl tried to get at it. The bookshelf was nowhere close to anything the cat thing could jump to; it seemed like it was too tall for the creature to jump down from, even if Carl weren't there. It was safe from Carl for the moment, but it was also well and truly stuck. It stared down at Carl and then over at Holloway, alternating between them, cat's eyes wide and terrified.

"Quiet, Carl!" Holloway said, but the dog was too out of his mind with the thrill of the chase to hear his master.

Holloway glanced around the room. Amid the mess he saw the creature's place of entrance: the small, tilting window in Holloway's sleeping alcove. He must have left it unlocked, and the creature must have been able to pry it open and get into the cabin. Once the cat thing got in, it wouldn't have been able to get back out; the window was easily accessible from the outside roof, but it looked like it would have been too high for the creature to get to from the cot or the floor.

He looked back at the cat thing, which was staring right at him. It stared at the window, and then back at him. It was as if the critter knew he'd figured out how it got in.

Holloway went to the tilting window in the alcove, closed it, and locked it. Then he walked over to his dog and grabbed him by the scruff of his neck. Carl stopped barking with a surprised *urk* and skidded his back paws ineffectually against the floor. Holloway maneuvered the dog to the cabin door, opened the door, and tossed the animal out. He pressed his leg against the dog door until he could secure its manual lock, and then stepped back. There were two thumps as Carl batted his head against the dog door. A few seconds later, his paws and head showed up in the window above Holloway's desk, alternately barking with in-dignity and whining to be let back in.

Holloway ignored his dog and turned to the cat thing, which looked at him, still terrified, but perhaps slightly less so now.

"Well, you little fuzzy thing," Holloway said. "Now it's just you and me."

f I were this thing, why would I be in here? Holloway thought. Animals weren't terribly complicated creatures; anywhere you went in the universe, they tended to want to do one of three things: eat, sleep, and have sex. Holloway concluded the last two of these were out. Food, then.

He glanced around the mess of his cabin; on the kitchen counter, next to the sink, was the plate he kept fruit on, covered by a plastic bell to keep out the local insects. In the rumpus, the plate had been moved but the bell had not been dislodged. Underneath it were two apples and a bindi, a local fruit that was shaped like a pear but tasted not too far off from a banana. Both apples and bindi kept well, which was why Holloway had them.

Holloway slowly walked back toward the kitchen area, keeping his eye on the cat thing, but taking it off momentarily to lift the plastic bell. He reached for an apple, but then thought better of it and took the bindi instead. The bindi was local fruit; the cat thing was a local animal. He'd never known an apple to kill an alien creature, but why take that chance.

Holloway opened a drawer and took out a knife. The cat

thing notably shifted at the sight of it. Holloway kept the knife low and quickly quartered the bindi, and got a reminder that bindi were sloppy fruit; juice and soft pulp ran through his fingers. He ignored this and conspicuously set the knife back into the drawer and closed it. He'd clean it off later.

The cat thing seemed to relax a bit, but then got more apprehensive as Holloway approached the bookcase again. The creature was at one corner of the top of the bookcase; Holloway pathed himself the long way around to stand by the other corner, too far away to grab the animal. The cat thing crouched there and stared at Holloway, unblinking.

Holloway took a quarter of the bindi and popped it in his mouth, chewing it slowly and obviously and with apparent satisfaction, watching the cat thing watch him. He swallowed and then placed another quarter of the bindi on the far top corner of the bookcase.

"That's yours," Holloway said, as if saying so would make the action any clearer to the animal. Then he placed the other two bindi quarters on his work desk and conspicuously turned his back on the cat thing, moving to pick up the mess in the cabin.

Holloway had no idea whether the thing would understand he was offering it food, or even if the creature would like bindi. If the thing really was like a cat, it'd be a carnivore. Well, Holloway had some lizard cutlets in the cooler. He could try those next.

One part of Holloway's brain, which fancied itself the sensible part, was currently yelling at him. *What the hell are you doing feeding a wild animal?* it was saying. *You should have opened the door and let Carl chase it out of the cabin. You never acted this way when the lizards got in.*

Holloway had no good answer for this, other than that for some reason, the creature interested him. Most of the land animals on

Zara XXIII were more reptilian than not; mammal-like creatures on the planet were few and far between. In fact, Holloway couldn't remember seeing one, either live or in a database, that was as large as this one was. He'd have to check the database again.

But what interested him the most was the way the creature was acting. The cat thing was obviously terrified, but it wasn't acting like a terrified animal. It seemed like it was smarter than the average wild animal, especially here on Zara XXIII, where the local fauna never struck Holloway as having developed an evolutionary premium on brains.

Also, the thing looked like a cat, and Holloway always liked cats. Holloway's internal sensible person smacked his virtual forehead at that.

Holloway took the papers he'd collected, tapped them together, and placed them on his work desk, glancing up at the cat thing. It was busily devouring the bindi slice as if it hadn't eaten in days. *That answers that,* Holloway thought. He reached down and turned over his spare infopanel, preemptively wincing as he did so, preparing for a cracked screen or something worse. To his surprise, it appeared unharmed. He powered it up and it came to life, fully functional. He breathed a sigh of relief and looked again at the cat thing, which had finished its fruit slice.

"You're lucky this thing still works," Holloway said to the creature. "If you broke it, I might have had to let Carl eat you."

The cat thing said nothing (of course) but kept glancing from Holloway to the two remaining bindi slices. The thing was obviously still hungry and trying to figure out how to get to the bindi without getting near Holloway. Holloway reached over, picked up one of the bindi slices, and slowly moved it toward the animal, holding the slice by pinching the smallest amount of the fruit possible with his thumb and index finger.

"Here you go," Holloway said.

Oh, smart, said his internal sensible person. *Now you're going to get the Zara XXIII equivalent of rabies.*

The cat thing likewise appeared dubious about this new development and shrank back from the proffered slice.

"Come on, now," Holloway said to the thing. "If I were going to kill you and eat you, I would have done it already." He jiggled the piece of fruit.

After a few seconds the cat thing cautiously moved forward, apparently hesitant, and then snatched at the slice, using both its hands. And they *were* hands; Holloway noted three fingers and a long thumb, riding lower on the palm than its human equivalent. Holloway blinked and the little hands were gone as the creature retreated to its far corner, never taking its eyes off Holloway as it began to devour its second bindi slice.

Holloway shrugged, turned away from the creature again, and then knelt and started shelving the books and binders strewn across the floor.

After a few minutes of this, he became aware he was being watched. He looked up and saw the cat thing peering down at him, blinking.

"Hello," he said to the thing. "Done with your food? Want more?" The thing opened its mouth as if to respond, but no noise come out. Holloway saw the thing's teeth, which were decidedly not catlike, and were more like human teeth than not. *Omnivore,* said a voice in his head that was not his own, but belonged to someone he used to know quite well. The voice gave him an idea.

Holloway stood up and moved over to his work desk. He took the porkpie hat off his security camera, which he then righted because it had been knocked over while Carl chased the creature. The camera featured an omnidirectional image sensor;

it could see in every direction except for directly below, where it was blocked by its own stand. He took his spare infopanel, clicked it into its own stand and turned it on, keying it to show the image feed from the security camera. Then he picked up the last slice of bindi and held it up to the cat thing. The creature, now substantially less afraid of Holloway, held out its hands to receive it.

"No," Holloway said, and placed the slice back on the work desk. Then he picked up the chair from the floor and positioned it so that if the cat thing were to work its way back down to the floor, it could use the chair to climb up and get the fruit. "You want it, come and get it," Holloway said. He put on the porkpie hat and then went to the cabin door, opening it just enough to let himself out without letting Carl in.

Carl was deeply displeased with this development and barked at Holloway in frustration. Holloway patted his dog's head and walked over to his skimmer. He reached in for his infopanel, powered it up and accessed the security camera feed.

"Let's see how smart you really are," he said. He adjusted the image to show a panorama view of the cabin.

For several minutes, the creature did nothing. Finally it started down the bookcase, taking rather more time to climb down the case than it had to fling itself up it. For a minute, Holloway couldn't see the cat thing, because the work desk blocked the floor. Then the chair moved slightly and the catlike head popped up, scanning for the piece of fruit.

It spied the fruit, and then suddenly gave a look of alarm and disappeared. Holloway grinned; the creature had just caught the image of itself in the infopanel he'd set the fruit in front of. Holloway had wondered whether the thing would recognize itself in a mirror, or in this case a video feed acting like a mirror. The immediate answer seemed to be that it did not, but then Holloway could remember times he'd been startled by his own reflection. What would be interesting was what would happen next.

The cat thing's head poked up again, more slowly this time, watching the "other" cat thing. Eventually it hauled itself up on the desk and walked over to the infopanel. It crouched down to peer at it, and then tapped on it. It moved a hand and appeared to watch its doppelganger do the same thing. After a few minutes of this, satisfied, it turned away from the infopanel, grabbed the bindi slice with both hands, and then sat down on the edge of the desk, feet dangling, to eat the fruit. It had recognized itself.

"Congratulations, you are now officially as smart as a dog," Holloway said. Carl looked up at the word *dog*. Holloway knew it was only his imagination that the dog appeared somewhat offended at the comparison.

Holloway rewound the images of the cat thing, recorded them, and kept the security camera on RECORD. He put the infopanel back down and went back into the cabin, once again slipping through the door to keep the increasingly annoyed Carl on the outside.

The cat thing noted Holloway's entrance but didn't move, or even stop kicking its feet leisurely as its legs dangled. It had apparently decided that Holloway wasn't a threat. Carl appeared at the window behind the desk and barked at the creature. It looked over casually but didn't stop eating its fruit. It had figured out that Carl couldn't get through the window and, for the moment at least, represented no threat.

Carl barked again.

The cat thing set its fruit down, pulled its legs up from the edge, grabbed its fruit and then walked over to the window. Carl stopped barking, confused by what the creature was doing. The cat thing sat down, millimeters away from the windowpane, stared at Carl, and then very deliberately started eating its fruit

in front of the dog. Holloway could have sworn it was intentionally chewing with its mouth open.

Carl went nuts barking. The cat thing stayed there, eating
and blinking. Carl dropped from the window; two seconds later,
there was a thump as Carl's head hit the dog door. The manual
lock was still on. Carl showed back up in the window a few seconds after that, no longer barking but clearly annoyed at the cat
thing.

"Now you're just getting cocky," Holloway said, to the cat
thing. The cat thing glanced back at Holloway, and then went
back to staring at Carl, finishing up its fruit.

Holloway decided to push his luck. He walked over to the
work desk and opened one of its drawers. The cat thing watched
with interest but didn't move. Holloway retrieved a dog collar
and a leash from the drawer. He almost never put them on Carl,
but sometimes they were necessary when the two of them went
to Aubreytown. He closed the drawer and then went back to the
cabin door, slipping out before Carl could change his position
from the window. Holloway went over to the dog and in full view
of the creature slipped the collar around Carl's neck and latched
the leash onto the collar.

Carl took in the collar and the leash and glanced up at Holloway, as if to say, *What the hell?*

"Trust me," Holloway said to Carl. "Heel!"

Carl was frustrated, but he was also well trained; any dog that
could wait for an order to detonate explosives was one that knew
how to listen to its master. He reluctantly came down from the
window and stood next to Holloway.

"Stay," Holloway said, and walked back the length of the
leash. Carl stayed. Holloway glanced over at the cat thing, which
seemed to be taking this all in with interest.

"Sit," Holloway said to his dog. Carl actually glanced over to the cabin window and then back at Holloway, as if to say *Dude, you're embarrassing me in front of the new guy*. But he sat, an almost inaudible whine escaping as he did so.

"Down," Holloway said. Carl lay down, dejectedly. His humiliation was complete.

"Heel," Holloway said again, and Carl got up and stood by his master. Holloway was still looking at the cat thing, which had watched the whole event. Holloway slid his hand along the leash so that Carl was close by his side, and started walking toward the door of the cabin. The cat thing stared but didn't move.

Holloway opened the door to the cabin but stayed outside with Carl for a minute. Carl got ready to burst through the doorway but Holloway cinched him close, compelling him to heel. Carl whined but then quickly calmed down. He had figured out how this was going to go.

The two of them walked slowly through the doorway. The cat thing remained on the desk, eyes wide but not making any panicky movements.

"Good dog," Holloway said to Carl, and walked him right in front of the desk. "Sit." Carl sat.

"Down," Holloway said. Carl lay.

"Roll over," Holloway said.

Holloway swore he heard his dog sigh. Carl rolled on his back and lay there, paws up, looking at the cat thing.

The cat thing sat there for a moment, looking at the open door and then back at the dog. Then it walked over to the edge of the desk and slid itself down into the chair. Carl made to move himself into an upright position, but Holloway laid his hand on his dog's chest. "Stay," he said. Carl stayed.

The cat thing slid off the chair and onto the floor less than a foot from Carl's muzzle. The two animals regarded each other curiously; the cat thing glanced up and down Carl's prone form while Carl, for his part, snuffled madly, trying to process every last particle of the cat thing's scent.

The cat thing edged closer and then oh-so-very-carefully reached out a hand toward Carl's muzzle. Holloway surreptitiously put a little more pressure on Carl's chest with one hand and tightened his grip on the leash with his other, ready if Carl overreacted.

The cat thing touched Carl's muzzle, withdrew its hand slightly, and then touched it again, stroking it softly. It did this for several seconds. From the other side of Carl, his tail thumped lightly.

"There it is," Holloway said. "See, that's not so bad."

Carl turned his head a bit, flicked out his tongue, and gave the cat thing a very wet slurp across the face. The creature backed up, sputtering indignantly, and tried to wipe off its face. Holloway laughed. Carl's tail thumped more.

The cat thing's head snapped up suddenly, as if hearing something. Carl squirmed at the movement, but Holloway held him down. The cat thing opened its mouth and wheezed for a moment, as if having trouble catching its breath. It looked at Holloway, then at the door. It bolted and was out of the cabin and gone.

After a minute, Holloway took the collar off Carl. The dog leapt up and raced out the door. Holloway stood and followed at a more leisurely rate.

The dog had stopped at the edge of the platform, looking up into the foliage of one of the eastern spikewoods, tail wagging lazily. Holloway suspected their guest had made its way off the platform in that direction.

Holloway called Carl to him, headed back into the cabin, and gave his dog a biscuit once the animal came through the door.

"Good dog," Holloway said. Carl thumped his tail and then lay down to focus on his treat.

Holloway walked over to his desk, picked up the infopanel, and watched the video of their guest. By now he was sure that he had been the first human ever to see a creature like it; if someone else had found one, they'd almost certainly be pets by now, given their intelligence and friendliness. There'd already be breeders and pet shows and advertisements for Little Fuzzy Food, or whatever. Holloway felt fortunate his own strain of avarice didn't run in that direction. Breeding pets was more work than he would want.

Be that as it may, the find of a previously unknown mammal that large was significant. Not for Holloway, who would be hard-pressed to make any money off it, nor for ZaraCorp, whose own interest in the local flora and fauna was largely limited to when their remains turned into oily and exploitable sludge. But Holloway knew one person who would be very interested in this cat thing. Strange cat things were right up her alley.

Holloway saved and closed the video file, and smiled. Yes, she would be very happy to see this video.

The only real question was whether she'd be happy to see *him*.

t any one time, there were perhaps 100,000 people on Zara XXIII. More accurately, 100,000 humans; there might be an occasional Urai or Negad, brought in by ZaraCorp in a minor, mid-level management capacity to show that the company was committed to sapient diversity in its hiring and staffing practices. But they rarely stayed long, and neither ZaraCorp nor its human employees did much to convince them to stay. Zara XXIII was a "man shop" all the way through.

Sixty thousand of the people on Zara XXIII worked directly at the few hundred E & E camps, in crews ranging in number from fifteen to two thousand, depending on the size and complexity of the exploit site. The majority of these people were laborers—the men and some women who operated the mining or harvesting machinery, hauled the product off of mountains or out of mines or up from wells—and a few managers and supervisors. But each site also had its support roles, including cooks, IT, janitorial, medical teams, and "happy staff" of both sexes.

These E & E camps dotted the planet from equator to poles; they sent raw materials to Aubreytown, the planet's sole city, located on a high equatorial plateau to save the cost of a few miles of beanstalk construction. Aubreytown sent back supplies, relief crews, and coffins for some of those whom the relief crews were relieving. One could spend an entire life working at Zara-Corp E & E camps, and some did.

Twenty thousand of the people on Zara XXIII worked the beanstalk in Aubreytown, taking the raw materials shipped in from the E & E camps and preparing them for transport, first up the beanstalk and then to the ships docked at the 'stalk shipping terminal, at geostationary distance from the planet. The ships represented the massive and inequitable transfer of raw material wealth from Zara XXIII to Earth—or would, if there were any native sapient species on the planet to recognize the inequity. There weren't, so it was all good from the point of view of Zara-Corp and the Colonial Authority.

Fifteen thousand people on Zara XXIII were contracted prospectors/surveyors, like Holloway. These contractors paid an annual franchise fee of several thousand credits to ZaraCorp and were given a territory to survey for the company. If they found anything exploitable, and ZaraCorp landed an E & E camp to exploit it, the contractor shared the wealth to the tune of one quarter of 1 percent of the gross market value of the materials extracted.

If your territory included rich seams of sunstones, you could get wealthy, as Holloway was about to. If it included ores or rare woods, you could make a comfortable amount. If like most surveyors you worked a territory that included no raw materials in a high enough concentration for ZaraCorp to bother extracting, you'd go broke, fast. Most survey contractors lasted a year or two before they shipped earthside, flat busted. ZaraCorp required every contractor to prepay the return trip. Independent survey-ors were not tolerated planetside.

The remaining five thousand people were miscellaneous: construction and maintenance crews for Aubreytown buildings and structures. ZaraCorp executives and white collar staff stationed planetside to keep track of materials and profits, and support staff for said execs. A Colonial Authority Judge and her two clerks. A well-armed if not hugely well-trained security detail, whose primary job was to break up the fights in the Aubreytown bars (that is, when they were not the ones starting the fights themselves). The owners and staffs of Aubreytown's sixteen bars, three restaurants, and one combination general store/brothel. The medical staff at Aubreytown's twelve-bed hospital. And finally, the single and somewhat lonely clergyman operating the ecumenical chapel at the edge of Aubreytown, which ZaraCorp had placed next to the waste incinerator. There were no spouses who did not themselves have jobs. There were no children at all.

The astute observer will have noticed that among the enumerated staff there were none engaging in pure science. This was by design. ZaraCorp's charter was for exploration and exploitation; of the two of these, the company preferred to focus on the second whenever possible. Exploration was farmed out to the mostly hapless contract surveyors, on whom the company turned a profit regardless of whether they discovered anything useful or not. Trained scientists were not needed for this sort of exploration, merely people willing to set acoustical charges, take samples, and then feed the data into specialized machinery, which did all the hard work of science. Exploitation required engineers and other workers with expertise of a technical nature, not lab guys.

Nevertheless ZaraCorp staffed three scientists at Zara XXIII, primarily to satisfy CEPA E & E charter requirements. They numbered one geologist, one biologist, and one despairing xenolinguist, who was supposed to be assigned to Uraill but through bureaucratic snafus had been sent to Zara XXIII instead. He was obliged to remain until the paperwork could be cleared up, a process that had now consumed two standard years and showed no sign of resolution. The xenolinguist, paid but useless, spent his time reading detective novels and drinking.

Jack Holloway had met the xenolinguist once at a ZaraCorp function he'd been forced to attend. He learned from the somewhat lubricated man everything he'd ever possibly need to know about the phonological complexities of the various branches of the Urai language tree and how the Urai's three ancillary tongues had an impact on each. He told his date for the function that after an hour of *that,* she had damn well better make it up to him. She had. She was the biologist.

And the person whom Holloway was looking at now.

Isabel Wangai didn't see Holloway. She was staring down at her infopad as she stepped out of her office block, and he was across the street anyway, standing there with Carl on his leash. Carl had seen Isabel, and immediately his tail started thumping like mad. Holloway checked both ways down the street; there was nothing but foot traffic. He unhooked Carl from his leash, and the dog went bounding across the street to Isabel.

Isabel looked momentarily confused as a dog leapt at her, but when she recognized the animal she let out a cry of delight and knelt to receive her daily recommended allowance of canine face licking. She was playfully tugging on Carl's ears as Holloway walked up.

"He's happy to see you," Holloway said.

"I'm happy to see him," Isabel said, and kissed the dog on the nose.

"Are you happy to see me?" Holloway asked.

Isabel looked up at Holloway and smiled that smile of hers. "Of course I am," she said. "How else would I get to see Carl?"

"Cute," Holloway said. "I'll just be taking my dog now, then."

Isabel laughed, stood up, and gave Holloway a friendly peck on the cheek. "There," she said. "All better."

"Thanks," Holloway said.

"You're welcome," Isabel said. She turned to the dog, clapped, and held her hands out. Carl jumped up and put his paws in her hands for a double-handshake. "Are you in town for a reason, or did you just travel six hundred klicks so I could see Carl?"

"I have business with Chad Bourne," Holloway said.

"That should be fun," Isabel said, glancing over at Holloway. "You two still antagonizing each other?"

"We get along great now," Holloway said.

"Uh-huh," Isabel said. "I've heard you lie enough to know you're doing it now, Jack."

"Let me put it another way, then," Holloway said, and drew out the sunstone he'd brought with him. "I've recently given him reason to get along with me."

Isabel saw the stone, released Carl from his double hand-shake, and then held out her hand to Holloway. He placed the stone in it. She held it up in the sunlight, letting the crystals in-side it glimmer.

"It's big," she said, finally.

"Not as big as some of the others," Holloway said.

"Hmmm," Isabel said, considering the stone again. She closed her hand around it and faced Holloway. "So you finally hit your big score."

"Looks like," Holloway said. "The acoustic image has the sunstone seam a hundred meters wide, and the seam kept going past the image. And it's more than four meters thick in places. It could be the mother lode of sunstone finds."

"Well, congratulations, then, Jack," Isabel said. "It's what you've always wanted." She moved to return the stone, which was now glowing faintly in her hand.

"It's yours," Holloway said. "A gift. By way of an apology."

Isabel arched an eyebrow, slightly. "An apology. Really. And for what are we apologizing today?" she asked.

"You know," Jack said, uncomfortably. "All of it."

"Right," Isabel said.

"I'm admitting I screwed up," Holloway said.

"You just can't say *how*," Isabel said. "That's actually an important part of any apology, Jack."

Jack pointed at the sunstone. "Big rock," he said.

Isabel gave a small laugh at that and handed it back to him. Holloway took it reluctantly.

"It's worth a lot," Holloway said. "If nothing else, you could sell it."

"And go crazy at the company store?" Isabel said.

"Or the other part of that edifice," Holloway said.

"I think not," Isabel said. "In either part. Anyway, if I were that motivated by money, I wouldn't be a biologist. I'd do what you do."

"Ouch," Holloway said.

"Sorry," Isabel said. "It's a lovely sunstone. And I do appreciate the apology attempt. But I don't think it suits me."

"The apology or the rock?" Holloway said.

"Either," Isabel said. "I'd like a better apology, when you can manage to say it. And you know how I feel about sunstones in general."

"The jellyfish are long past caring," Holloway said.

"Maybe," Isabel said. "On the other hand, watching ZaraCorp take that hill you named after me and strip every single living thing off it because there might be some of *these* in it"—she pointed at the stone that was now in Holloway's hand—"sort of killed the attraction for me."

"They didn't do it just because of the sunstones," Holloway said. "They wanted the rockwood, too."

Isabel stared at Holloway.

"That was a joke," Holloway said.

"Really," Isabel said, with that flatness in her voice Holloway had learned to dread, and ultimately, to hide from. "You've told better ones."

"I suppose I could get you another gift to make up for it," Holloway said.

"What, another rock? Thanks, no," Isabel said. "I liked that you named a living hill for me, once upon a time. *That* was a thoughtful gift. A shame what happened to it." She turned, bent to give Carl a kiss on the head, and headed off down the street.

"There's something else," Holloway said.

Isabel stopped and took a second before turning back to face Holloway. "Yes?" she said. Her tone indicated he'd already used up all his time with her for the day.

Holloway fished out a data card from his pocket. "I got a visitor to the cabin a few days ago," he said. "Some sort of creature. Something I hadn't seen before. I don't think anyone's seen it before. I thought you might be interested."

She was, despite herself. "What kind of animal?" she asked.

"I think you probably should just see the video for yourself," Holloway said.

"If it's another lizard, ZaraCorp won't care," Isabel said. "Not unless it's poisonous to humans or urinates pure petroleum."

"It's not a lizard," Holloway promised. "Is the company telling you what to research?"

"Of course it is," Isabel said. "More accurately, it's telling me what *not* to research. Unfortunately, if I'm not cataloging lizards on this planet, I'm not doing much of anything else. I'm going to end up like Chen." Chen was the xenolinguist.

Holloway moved his head, motioning to the data card. "This will keep you busy," he said. "I guarantee it."

Isabel looked at the card doubtfully but walked forward and extended her hand. "I'll take a look at it," she said, taking the card. "You'd better not be wasting my time, Jack."

"I'm not," he said. "I've learned not to do that, at least."

"Good," Isabel said. "It's nice that you got something out of the relationship."

"It's not currently much use to me on a day-to-day basis," Holloway said. "Seeing that you're in town all the time now."

"Well, life is like that sometimes," Isabel said. "We learn things too late, and then we don't get to use them." She looked at Holloway.

"I *am* sorry," Holloway said.

"I know," Isabel said. "Thank you, Jack." She gave him another peck on the cheek, friendly again, but no more than that. "And now I really do have to go. You've made me late for my lunch appointment." She patted Carl again and walked off, hurrying.

Holloway watched her go for a few minutes and then reached down and clicked the leash back on Carl's collar. "I think that went well," he said to Carl. "All things considered."

Carl looked up at Holloway with what he judged was a fair amount of dubiousness.

"Oh, shut up," Holloway said. "It wasn't *all* my fault."

Carl and Holloway turned their eyes back down the street just in time to watch Isabel turn the corner and disappear.

Chapter Six

Y ou're late," Bourne said on the steps of ZaraCorp's administrative building. Holloway came alone; he'd taken Carl back to the skimmer, gave him a zararaptor bone, and turned on the air circulator.

"I was catching up with someone," Holloway said.

"Saw Isabel, did you," Bourne said. "You two still antagonizing each other?"

"Funny, she asked me the same question about you," Holloway said.

"I bet," Bourne said. "You know, Jack, I'm not one for reading too much into things, but even I can see that when you name a hill for your girlfriend, and then you have that hill strip-mined down to rubble, it's not a good sign for the relationship."

"There's a reason I don't come to you for advice about my love life," Holloway said.

"Fair enough," Bourne said. "I hear she's seeing someone new."

"I wouldn't know about that," Holloway said.

"Yeah, one of the new administrative group that transferred planetside a few months ago," Bourne said. "A lawyer. Assistant general counsel. If you and I had gone to court, he'd probably have been the one that would have gutted your claim like a fish."

"Sounds like a nice guy," Holloway said.

"Well, you know," Bourne said. "The general consensus is that Isabel traded up."

"I thought we were late," Holloway said, changing the subject.

"*You're* late," Bourne said. "But I figured you'd be late, because that's just the sort of antagonistic prick you are. So I told you to come twenty minutes earlier than I needed you here. *We're* right on time. Now come on." He walked up the steps.

"This place is as lovely as ever," Holloway said, once they were inside the building. On Earth, the Zarathustra Corporation's headquarters in Dayton, Ohio, were considered to be one of the major architectural achievements of the last century. On Zara XXIII, light-years from the need for public relations and corporate gamesmanship, the local headquarters were a nondescript block of cheap and durable building components designed to house staff efficiently and without undue expense.

"I love what you've done with the cubicles," Holloway said. "I didn't know you could still get fluorescent lights."

Bourne ignored this and kept walking, forcing Holloway to follow. "Listen, Jack," he said, glancing back at his guest. "I know you and I have our problems, but if you can, I want you to behave yourself at this meeting."

"Why this particular meeting?" Jack said.

"That seam you found," Bourne said. "It's big."

"I know that, Chad," Holloway said. "I found it, remember?"

"No," Bourne said. They had arrived at the door of a meeting room. "You think you know. But it's bigger than even *you* think it is. It's attracted a lot of attention here and back home already. It's become a *priority*."

"What does that mean?" Holloway said.

"Promise me, Jack," Bourne said. "As the contractor who found the seam, you have a vested interest, and we're required by the E and E charter to keep you in the loop with everything. And I will. But you have to promise me that you're going to behave yourself."

"Or what?" Holloway said, genuinely curious.

"There's no 'or what,' Jack," Bourne said. "This isn't just you and me sticking each other with pins to see who screams first anymore. I'm not threatening you. I'm not making demands. I'm *asking*. Please. Behave."

Holloway was quiet for a minute. "You say this find is big," he said, to Bourne.

"Yeah," Bourne said.

"How big?" Holloway asked.

"So big that if I didn't happen to be your ZaraCorp handler, the only way I'd even get to be *near* this meeting is if I was told to bring in some sandwiches," Bourne said.

"This is different from your daily life how?" Holloway asked.

"Jesus, Jack," Bourne said. "Are you even listening to me?"

"It was a joke," Holloway said.

"You've told better ones," Bourne said, and then noticed the sudden smile on Holloway's face. "What?"

"That's the second time I've heard *that* today, too," he said.

"Jack," Bourne said.

"Relax, Chad," Holloway said. "I hear you. I'll behave. I promise."

"Thank you," Bourne said.

"But after all that, this meeting better live up to the billing," Holloway said.

"Well, you tell me," Bourne said. He opened the door to the meeting room. Inside was the entire upper echelon of the local ZaraCorp management.

"Okay, that *is* impressive," Holloway muttered to Bourne. Bourne didn't respond.

"And here is the man who just made Zarathustra Corporation's annual report that much brighter this year," said Alan Irvine, ZaraCorp VP and Planetary Director for Zara XXIII. He smiled and got up from his chair to shake Holloway's hand, and gave him a too-hearty slap on the back. "Mr. Holloway. You are most welcome here."

"Thanks," Holloway said.

"Please, sit," Irvine motioned to an empty chair at the table. There was only one; Bourne, apparently, would spend the meeting standing, along with a series of other underlings who unobtrusively lined the walls. "I assume you're familiar with the rest of the crew here."

"Yes," Holloway said, and nodded generally down the table. "I've been to the ZaraCorp holiday parties."

"Of course you have," Irvine said. "I seem to recall you on the arm of that biologist of ours. Warner?"

"Wangai," Holloway said.

"That Indian?" Irvine asked.

"Kenyan," Holloway said. "By way of Oxford."

"Right," Irvine said. "Still seeing her?"

"Saw her earlier today," Holloway said.

"Wonderful," Irvine said. He turned and motioned to one person in particular. "Here's someone you *don't* know, though. Mr. Holloway, this is Wheaton Aubrey the Seventh. He's doing a tour of the ZaraCorp divisions and properties and happened to be here when you called in this claim. You may recognize the name."

"Sure. One very much like it is on all my checks," Holloway said. He could sense Bourne stiffening up behind him. This was very close to not behaving. Fortunately a small ripple of laughter went around the table at the comment.

"So it is," Irvine said. "And likely not too far in the future, it'll be *his* signature there."

"Hopefully later rather than sooner," Aubrey said in a tone that to Holloway did not suggest that the former was in fact all that much more preferable than the latter. Aubrey turned in his seat to face Holloway. "I see from your file you went to Duke."

"Law school, yes," Holloway said.

"I was there for undergrad," Aubrey said. "Class of '18."

"We missed by three years," Holloway said.

"It's not every Duke JD that ends up in the wilds of a Class Three planet," Aubrey said.

"It's a long story," Holloway said.

"I would think so, considering it apparently involves disbarment," Aubrey said. "That's never a quick thing to explain, is it?"

Holloway looked at Aubrey, with his pleasant, sun-tousled features, notwithstanding the famously beakish Aubrey nose, which Holloway guessed had never once been punched in for its owner being a smug dick. "No, it's not," he said. "But inasmuch as this particular long story ends up with me getting rich and you and your family getting even richer, I don't suppose either of us can complain about it too much." He smiled at Aubrey.

After a moment, Aubrey smiled back. "Indeed not," he said. He turned toward Irvine, who had watched the exchange between Aubrey and Holloway with some consternation. "And it's one story that we can skip to the end of, since I believe we were about to discuss just how *much* richer we are all going to be."

"Right," Irvine said, and tapped the infopanel on the table in front of him. The wall directly behind him woke up and displayed a presentation slide. "Johan, I think you're going to walk us through what we're seeing."

"Yes," said Johan Gruber, Director of Exploitation for Zara XXIII. He turned to the wall. "After Mr. Holloway established the claim and forwarded the data from the initial survey, it became clear that the sunstone seam was likely larger than we had originally estimated. We sent an additional survey team to the area—"

"Excuse me?" Holloway said. All surveys of a contracted surveyor's land had to be performed or supervised by the surveyor. To do otherwise was to risk loss of a claim or subsequent profits from finds stemming from the original claim. "I wasn't made aware of that."

"Exigent circumstances," said Janice Meyer, ZaraCorp's General Counsel on Zara XXIII. "If you look in your contract, you'll see that ZaraCorp may, in certain pressing circumstances, operate in a contractor's territory to expedite the collection of information or materials."

"What's the pressing circumstance?" Holloway said.

"I am," said Aubrey. "This is a significant find, and I wanted to be able to report on it to the chairman and the rest of the board. I was scheduled to leave Zara Twenty-three tomorrow, so I authorized the exigent circumstances clause."

"You needn't worry, Mr. Holloway," Meyer said. "In the event of the exigent circumstances clause being triggered, all additional finds are automatically appended to the original find and the surveyor additionally compensated."

"How so?" Holloway said.

Meyer looked over to Irvine, who nodded. "We feel an additional tenth of a percent is appropriate," he said.

"That sounds fine," Holloway said.

"Congratulations on your point-three-five percent," said Aubrey, with the sort of casual condescension that comes from knowing that one's own share of the pie is immeasurably greater. He motioned at Gruber to continue.

Holloway debated saying anything but then realized that if he didn't, he'd be forced to take a cut. "Half a percent, actually," he said.

"I beg your pardon?" Aubrey said, annoyed to be interrupted.

Holloway glanced over to Bourne, who looked appalled to be noticed. "Tell him," he said.

"Uh," Bourne said, and then caught himself. "Mr. Holloway recently renegotiated his contract for point-four percent of the gross," he said. "So this bonus does take him to half a percent."

"I see," Aubrey said. "And was there a reason for this sudden renegotiation of a standard ZaraCorp contract?"

"Exigent circumstances," Holloway said.

Aubrey did not appear to find the joke amusing. "Fine," he said. "But your bonus doesn't apply until *after* we factor in the cleanup cost of your cliff collapse. CEPA is already processing the fine for that. You share in the profits, you share in the cost."

What a penny-ante little prick, Holloway thought, and glanced again to Bourne. Bourne glared back at him with a *stop picking on me* expression on his face. Holloway ignored the look. "Chad?" he said.

"What?" Aubrey snapped, shifting his attention to Bourne. "Does his contract get him out of *that,* too?"

Bourne tried to get the "trapped animal" look out of his eyes. He sighed. "Yes, it does," he said.

"Who are you?" Aubrey asked.

"Chad Bourne," Bourne said. "Contractor representative."

"You must be a very popular rep, Mr. Bourne," Aubrey said, "considering how lavishly you treat your contractors. Are there any *other* special favors we need to know about in Mr. Holloway's contract? Additional hidden points on the backend? Free nights at the brothel? Are you required to hand-wash his skimmer whenever he comes into town?"

"No," Bourne said. "That's all there is."

"You'd better hope so," Aubrey said. "Who is your director here?"

"I am," said Vincent D'Abo, Director of Staffing, raising his hand.

"After this meeting, you and I are going to have a talk," Aubrey said.

"Yes, sir," D'Abo said, and shot a poisonous look at both Bourne and Holloway.

"Now that we've wasted several minutes on contracts, let's get back to the actual *point* of this meeting, if that's not too much trouble," Aubrey said. Gruber, caught by surprise, cleared his throat and started over.

Holloway glanced back at Bourne, who looked pale. *Sorry,* Holloway said, mouthing the word silently. Bourne was resolute in ignoring him.

Holloway turned his attention back to the slides on the wall, and to the drone of Gruber's voice, describing the methodology of the additional surveys as well as the difficulty of doing the additional surveys on the jungle floor, that is, in places where the surveyors, if unwary, might be consumed by large predators. "In short, our survey teams are still sounding the extent of the seam," Gruber said. "But the data we do have are compelling. The next slide should make this clear."

The image flicked over to the next slide, which showed

topographical maps from the side and from above. The seam was featured in green on both images.

"Holy *crap*," Holloway said. The massive seam he'd found in the cliff was in fact just a tendril; it curled out of the cliff and branched like an alluvial flow into what looked like a wide river of rock that extended for kilometers north of the cliff, petering out only a klick south of Mount Isabel. Holloway looked at the width and breadth of the seam and tried to figure out how much it might be worth. His brain wasn't keeping up with the numbers.

Apparently he wasn't the only one. "What's this going to be worth to us?" asked Aubrey.

"It depends on how dense the seam is with sunstones," Gruber said. "The portion Mr. Holloway here excavated seems unusually dense, but for our models, I think it would be wise to employ standard sunstone density, based on the data from previous excavations."

"Fine," Aubrey said curtly. "Give me a number."

"Somewhere between eight hundred billion and one-point-two trillion credits," Gruber said.

It took a moment for the magnitude of the number to sink in. Someone at the table let out a low whistle. Holloway was pretty sure it wasn't him.

"A trillion-credit seam," Aubrey said, finally.

"Yes," Gruber said. "That is, provided we can extract the entire seam."

Aubrey snorted. "Christ, man," he said. "This thing is worth more than this company's last sixty years of revenue. Do you really think we're *not* going to extract the whole thing?"

"No, sir," Gruber said. "But there are practical and environmental issues—"

"Which we will solve one way or another," Aubrey said, interrupting Gruber.

"Yes, sir," Gruber said, pressing on. "Even so, it will present challenges, particularly in accessing the main seam in the lowland jungle areas. Challenges that will at present take us right to the line of CEPA regulations regarding mining and deforestation."

"CEPA regulations aren't written in stone," Aubrey said.

"No, sir," Gruber agreed. "But per your father's orders, they still have to be followed."

"Yes, of course," Aubrey said, with the same tone of voice he'd earlier used to opine about the desirability of his father's continued health. Holloway looked around the table to see if anyone evidenced any concern about this. The faces of the Zara-Corp executives were very carefully blank. Holloway smirked in spite of himself.

Aubrey looked around the table. "Gentlemen, I want to be clear about this," he said. "This seam of sunstones could be of enormous benefit to the Zarathustra Corporation. I don't need to remind you that our company's preeminence in the Exploration and Exploitation segment of the economy has been under attack, both from increased regulatory interference by the Colonial Authority, and by other E_i and Es, primarily BlueSky, whose revenues exceeded ours last year for the first time in history. This sunstone seam, fully exploited, could put ZaraCorp in an unassailable profit position for decades. *Decades*. So we *will* exploit it fully.

"Therefore, gentlemen: The excavation of this seam is now the top priority of your planetary organization," Aubrey said. "You need to go through your organization and find what resources you can commit on an immediate basis, and which resources you can shift to it thereafter. I have decided to stay on planet to personally supervise the start-up of this effort. If we're not exploiting this seam in a month—and I mean exploiting it in a serious, focused way—then you all are going to be looking for new jobs.

Which I will make it my personal business to ensure you never find. Are we clear?"

No one said anything. Wheaton Aubrey VII held no official executive title at Zarathustra Corporation, but then neither had Wheaton Aubrey VI before he became Chairman and CEO, nor his father before him. No one was under any illusion Aubrey VII was not next in line to the throne. No one was under any illusion Aubrey VII couldn't bury them and their careers under six miles of shit.

"Good," Aubrey said. "Then let's get to it." He grinned and thumped the table. "Damn! This is good news." He looked down the table again at Holloway. "Now I really *am* glad you were disbarred, Holloway."

"Thanks," Holloway said, dryly.

Chapter Seven

Holloway woke up to his nose being poked.

He swatted his hand in front of his face without opening his eyes. "Quit it, Carl," he said. He immediately dropped back into sleep.

Poke.

Holloway grunted and turned in his cot, away from his offending and offensive poking dog.

Poke.

This time the poke was on the back of his head. Holloway grunted and attempted a swat but ended up mostly just waving his arm around.

Poke.

This poke to the head occurred roughly at the same time a thought penetrated the fuzzy cotton batting in Holloway's brain: *Since when does Carl, face-licker extraordinaire, poke?* It took another moment or two for the implications of that thought to settle in.

At which point, Holloway hollered and levitated himself as far off his cot as possible, coming down badly into the space between the cot and the cabin wall. The half of his body still on the cot leveraged the thing down, toppling it and swinging the cot forward into his face. Only his flying pillow kept him from a gash on his forehead.

The cat thing, standing to the side of where the cot used to be, watched all of this with interest. When the carnage was done, it looked over at Holloway and blinked.

"Jesus!" Holloway said, to the creature. "How did *you* get in?"

How *did* it get in? Holloway glanced up at the window above where his cot should be; it was firmly closed, as were all the other windows in the cabin. The door was likewise closed. There was no way that fuzzy little bastard could get in, unless . . .

"Carl!" Holloway called, and looked out into the cabin from the sleeping alcove.

Carl peeked his head around the work desk, his best *oh crap I better not make eye contact* look on display.

"You let this thing in, didn't you?" Holloway said. "You went to your dog door and let him walk right through. Admit it."

Carl offered an apologetic tail thump and hid.

"Unbelievable," Holloway said. He glanced down at the cat thing again, which appeared serenely unconcerned about the entire domestic drama unfolding around it.

There was a *ping.* Holloway looked around the chaos of his sleeping alcove and found his infopanel on the floor next to his small nightstand. He'd been reading survey reports on it before he went to sleep. Now someone was calling him on it. Holloway picked up the infopanel and slapped it to life, audio only.

"What?" he said.

"Jack?" Isabel said. "Sorry. Did I wake you?"

"I was up," Holloway said, looking at the cat thing.

"Jack, that video you gave me," Isabel said. "Is it real?"

"What?" Holloway said.

"I mean, this is video you took, right? It's not something you found on the network somewhere," Isabel said.

"It's mine," Holloway said. "You should recognize the cabin, Isabel."

"I know, sorry," Isabel said. "It's just . . . well. Jack. Whatever this thing is on the video, no one's seen it before."

"You don't say," Holloway said. By this time the cat thing, bored with watching him, had started walking around the cabin like it owned the place.

"There's nothing like it in the archives, even," Isabel said. "Which is admittedly not saying much; it's not as if ZaraCorp ever does anything more than the absolute minimum required by an E and E charter, and they're focused on sapience detection anyway."

"Uh-huh," Holloway said. The cat thing had wandered over to Carl and put a hand on Carl's muzzle, stroking it. Carl thumped his tail and then glanced over guiltily to Holloway.

"That's right, you *traitor*," Holloway said.

"What?" Isabel said.

"Sorry," Holloway said. "Talking to Carl."

"What I'm saying is that even in the archives there's no evidence of a creature like this," Isabel said, continuing on. "We have data on a few mammal-like creatures, basically rodents, and one of the flying creatures here is mostly mammal-like. But nothing even comes close to this. How big was this creature, Jack?"

Holloway looked at the creature, which had made its way into the kitchen area. "It's about the size of a cat, I'd say," he said. "A big cat. Like a Maine Coon. If you stood the cat up on its hind legs."

"So it was primarily bipedal," Isabel said. "I mean, so far as you observed it."

The cat thing was climbing up one of the chairs at the kitchen nook table. "I'd say so."

"That's unusual too," Isabel said. "All the other mammal-like creatures here are quadrupeds. Except the flying one. Did you see it use its hands? Did it show any significant manual dexterity?"

The cat thing, by now on the seat of the chair, flung itself toward the kitchen counter, grabbed it at the edge, and deftly pulled itself up.

"Some," Holloway said.

"Do you know how unusual this creature is, Jack?" Isabel said.

"I'm getting the idea," Holloway said. The cat thing had by now reached its destination, which was the plastic bell Holloway kept his fruit under. Holloway maneuvered himself out of his sleeping alcove and walked toward his kitchen. "It sounds like you're pretty excited about it, at least."

"I am," Isabel said. "A new, large mammal like this in a fauna-sphere that's primarily reptilian in nature is a significant find. *Really* significant. It just doesn't happen that often."

"Looks like you finally hit your big score," Holloway said, intentionally echoing the words Isabel used with him the last time they'd seen each other. He'd reached the kitchen. The cat thing was looking at him, and then looking at the fruit bell, as if to say, *Get that for me, would you.*

"No," Isabel said. She hadn't noticed Holloway's choice of words. "No offense, Jack, but your security camera video could easily be faked."

"I didn't fake it," Jack said. He lifted the bell off the fruit.

"I know you didn't," Isabel said. "That's not what I'm saying. What I'm saying is I can't use it as evidence or proof. Video is too easy to tamper with or change. This isn't a secure-grade recording. If I submitted this as evidence, I'd get laughed at."

The cat thing reached into the fruit plate and lifted out the bindi, using both hands. "So what are you saying?" Holloway asked.

"Jack, do you think the creature is still in the area?" Isabel asked. "Somewhere close by, I mean."

The cat thing walked the bindi over to Holloway and set it down in front of him.

"Probably," Holloway said.

"I want to come out," Isabel said.

"Excuse me?" Holloway said. This statement distracted him completely away from the cat thing. "For a second there it sounded like you actually said you wanted to come out here."

"Yes," Isabel said.

"You," Holloway said. "Out *here.* Near *me.*"

Isabel sighed. "Jack," she began.

"Wait, scratch that," Holloway said. "Not *near* me. *With* me. Because you'd have to stay with me. Unless you fancied camping with the raptors."

"Are you enjoying yourself, Jack?" Isabel said.

"Maybe," Holloway said.

The cat thing reached over and poked Holloway in the side to get his attention. Holloway looked over. *What?* He mouthed silently to the creature.

The cat thing lifted the bindi again and set it down again, and then looked at Holloway with a look that betrayed impatience. Holloway suddenly remembered that the last time he'd given the thing some bindi, he'd sliced up the fruit. The animal was waiting for its slices.

"Pushy thing, aren't you," Holloway said. He reached into his drawer to retrieve a knife.

"I thought you might want to help me, Jack," Isabel said. "Considering you gave me the video in the first place."

Holloway realized Isabel thought that last comment was

directed at her. "Sorry," he said. "I didn't mean that the way you took it." He set down the infopanel and reached for the bindi.

"Look, Jack," Isabel said. "I know we ended things badly, and I know you're still upset with me about it. And I admit I didn't help things at the end. But I thought we'd gotten over that enough that we can be friends. Actual friends, as opposed to the 'polite in public' sort of friends. Right? So I'm asking you as a friend if you'll help me out with this."

"As a friend," Jack said. He quartered the bindi and offered the cat thing a slice, then set the rest of the fruit on the counter and washed his hands in the sink. The cat thing watched and seemed fascinated by the faucet.

"If it's not too much to ask," Isabel said. "This could be a really important find. And somewhat less importantly, it could be good for me. I'd like to think that still means something to you."

While Isabel spoke, Holloway reached into his cupboard, pulled out a small bowl, and filled it with water from the sink. He presented it to the cat thing, which crouched down and drank from it, pursing its lips like a human, rather than lapping from it like a cat or dog.

"Well, they are definitely interesting creatures," he said.

"So," Isabel said.

Holloway directed his attention back to the infopanel. "Of course you can come out, Isabel," he said. "I'll be happy to see you. I don't know where I'll *put* you, but I'll be happy to see you."

"Thank you, Jack," Isabel said. "Don't worry. You won't even notice I'm there."

Holloway cracked a smile. *I doubt that,* he thought to himself.

He glanced back over to the cat thing, which had finished its drink. Holloway had expected the creature to be eating its fruit, but what it was doing was taking a second slice of bindi and hefting it and the first slice under an arm. Then it sat, used its legs and feet to drag its fuzzy butt over to the edge of the kitchen counter, and jumped off. One of the bindi slices fell out of its grip when it landed; the cat thing collected it and then set off for the door.

"When do you want me?" Isabel asked.

"What?" Holloway said. He had been distracted by the cat thing.

"When do you want me to show up?" Isabel said. "I don't want to get in the way of your schedule."

"When do you *want* to show up?" Holloway asked. By now the cat thing had completed its journey to the door, and stood by it, as if waiting for someone to open it. It coughed. Holloway picked up the infopanel and started to move to the door, but then Carl got up from where he was sitting by the work desk.

"I'd like to be there this afternoon, to be honest," Isabel said. "But I have things I need to do here first."

"I thought you said you didn't have any work these days," Holloway said. Carl had walked to the dog door and stepped through. As he went through, the cat thing slipped under Carl and out the door, the dog's hindquarters following.

"I *didn't* have any work," Isabel said. "And then someone apparently found a huge sunstone deposit, and I've been told to prepare a biological impact report, double time."

"Sorry," Holloway said. He walked over to door.

"You should be," Isabel said. "Because the biological and ecological impact is going to be huge. The exploitation office here has filed an ecological exception request with CEPA. They want to tear out that seam as fast as they can get to it. It's going to make a huge mess of things, and they want me to sign off on it."

"Are you going to?" Holloway asked.

"I don't think I have much choice," Isabel said. "The jungle flora and fauna in the area they want to exploit aren't significant or unique. The biome scans and the robotic sampling I've done in the area don't show any unusual species. ZaraCorp can argue that it's not tearing up anything that can't be replanted or couldn't move back in from other parts of the jungle when they're done. That it will still wreak havoc with the area regardless is sort of an aside."

Holloway stepped through the door of his cabin and walked outside. Carl was sitting near the door, lazily thumping his tail. Holloway walked over to him and patted his head. The cat thing had walked over to the spikewood Holloway had seen it leave by on its last visit.

"Anyway, an eco exception request means extra work," Isabel continued. "I'm getting through it as fast as I can, but I don't see me being able to get out there for three more days at least, and more likely four."

"Four days works for me," Holloway said.

"All right," Isabel said. "I'll see you then, then. Don't make any more major biological discoveries until then, okay?"

The cat thing looked up into the spikewood and opened its mouth. It gave another little coughing sound, as it had at the door. The leaves of the spikewood moved slightly, and out of the foliage four forms emerged, small, furry, catlike. They looked down at the cat thing and then slowly descended.

"I promise nothing," Holloway said.

"You always were difficult," Isabel said.

"I thought you liked that about me," Holloway said.

"Not really," Isabel said.

"You could have told me that earlier," Holloway said.

"I'm pretty sure I did," Isabel said.

"Oh," Holloway said. "Sorry."

By this time the first of the new cat things had made its way over to the creature Holloway knew. The two animals appeared to bump foreheads gently, and then Holloway's cat thing took one of the bindi slices, broke it, and offered half of it to the new creature. It did the same to each of the creatures when they came up to it. Soon all the new creatures were munching quite contentedly on the fruit.

"I'll forgive you this time because you're being so nice to me," Isabel said.

"Thanks," Holloway said.

"I'll give you a call when I'm ready to head your way," Isabel said.

"Sounds good," Holloway said.

"I know you bought supplies when you came to town, but is there anything you need from here?" Isabel said. "Something you forgot?"

By now the creatures had finished their food and were looking at Holloway and Carl curiously. Carl was waving his tail furiously at the new arrivals. *Traitor,* Holloway thought again. Carl's mind-reading powers seemed to be suppressed for the moment.

"I could use some more bindi," Holloway said.

"All right," Isabel said. "How many do you want?"

"Oh, I don't know," Holloway said, staring at his new guests. "You might as well bring a lot."

Chapter Eight

They were fuzzy, and it seemed like they were family, so for lack of a better description, Holloway called his five visitors "the Fuzzy Family." And over the next couple of days he got to know them very well, because the Fuzzys decided they were moving in. There were five of them in total, and Holloway gave them names based on what they did and how they reacted to one another.

His original visitor was Papa Fuzzy, because it was obvious he was the leader of the little clan, the one who did the initial foraging and exploring and who had given the rest of the family the "all clear" to come down out of the trees and meet the human and the dog.

Holloway knew that if Isabel were already there, she would gently upbraid him about his patriarchal assumptions, starting with the assumption that Papa Fuzzy was in fact male. Holloway admitted to himself that Papa Fuzzy could very well be female, or something else entirely. Not every life system or life-form tracked precisely with the sexual divisions humans were used to. Hell, they didn't even on Earth; Holloway recalled Isabel lecturing him about sea horses, and how the males had a "brood pouch" which female sea horses deposited eggs into, which the male then fertilized and carried around until birth.

It was informative in its way, but fundamentally Holloway hadn't cared much about sea horses and brood pouches and whatever. He feigned interest because it had been early on in his relationship with Isabel, and he was hoping that after the lecture, there might be study hall. Eventually Isabel would figure out his *I'm not actually listening* look. That was one of their earlier problems, which never did get resolved satisfactorily. Which was, Holloway supposed, why he was now alone.

Well, alone with a dog and five little creatures he was now willy-nilly assigning gender and social roles. Holloway figured there was a way to check to see who was male and who was female, but he didn't figure that was actually *his* job. A biologist would be on-site in a few days. He could wait. And if he had guessed wrong, he could change his mind. Just ask Carl about that. He'd originally been named Carla, after Holloway's aunt, until someone pointed out his new puppy's plumbing in greater detail. Carl had been Holloway's first dog. This was the excuse he gave when people pointed and laughed.

So: Papa (for now) Fuzzy, leader and patriarch. Holloway watched him interact with the other fuzzys and wondered again at the thing's intelligence. He was damn smart, as far as animals went. Definitely smarter than Carl, whom he had apparently entirely coopted, given that the dog had now taken to following Papa around the treetop compound, tail wagging. It takes a certain kind of dog to willingly demote himself from alpha dog, and that dog was Carl. Holloway would have to speak to him about it, for what little good it would do, Carl being a dog and all.

Holloway rummaged through his brain to find an equivalently smart animal. If he had to guess, he'd say that Papa Fuzzy was about as smart as a capuchin monkey, a comparison Holloway was qualified to make because he had an acquaintance with one when he'd first landed on Zara XXIII. A "cap" had been the pet of Sam Hamilton, another surveyor, who worked the territory directly next to Holloway's. The rumor was the monkey might have been smarter than Hamilton, who was rumored to have children's reading primers on his infopanel so as to catch up for a lifetime of functional illiteracy.

Whether that was true or not, the monkey was clever as hell and also a little thief; Sam was repeatedly and apologetically handing back people's keys and wallets, although the latter were often missing the printed ZaraCorp credit scrip that surveyors used to buy supplies and to gamble with. Credit cards were also occasionally found to have balances lightened. No one believed the monkey was responsible for that. Holloway had had to have a talk with Sam about it at one point.

Now Sam and the monkey were gone: Sam hadn't taken care of his skimmer very well and had made an unscheduled hard landing on the jungle floor after one of his rotors flamed out. Sam had never bothered to get himself an emergency perimeter fence; by the time a neighboring surveyor had gotten to his location, the only thing left of Sam and his monkey had been a trail of blood leading into the jungle. Sales of emergency perimeter fences doubled in the next week.

The more Holloway thought about it, the more he figured that Papa Fuzzy might actually be smarter than that monkey. For one thing, he and his family were still alive in the same jungle that ate that monkey whole. He was also smart enough to realize that hanging out with Holloway might be an easier life than avoiding the predators in the trees and down on the jungle floor.

Next in the Fuzzy Family hierarchy had been the fuzzy who had first come down out of the trees to greet Papa. This fuzzy was slightly smaller than Papa, and lighter—golden-haired where Papa Fuzzy was more of a deep tortoiseshell coloring, but with a darker face. She (another assumption, Holloway realized) reminded Holloway of a Siamese or Himalayan breed of cat. This fuzzy was clearly Papa Fuzzy's companion; the two of them were often close together and seemed openly affectionate, petting and nuzzling each other frequently. Holloway was mildly concerned that it might go further than that and then he would be an unwilling witness to fuzzy sex, or something. But the two kept it in their metaphorical pants, at least when he was around.

In any event, this fuzzy seemed friendly and trusting of Holloway and Carl, mostly, Holloway assumed, because Papa Fuzzy was friendly and trusting with them. Holloway, in a burst of no creativity whatsoever, called this one Mama Fuzzy.

Next up in the fuzzy hierarchy was the gray fuzzy who was as large as Papa Fuzzy, but was a bit more stout and perhaps a step or two slower, both in speed and, it seemed to Holloway, in the brains department. This fuzzy was affectionate toward Mama Fuzzy but in a different way from Papa Fuzzy. If Holloway had to guess, he'd say that this fuzzy was Mama Fuzzy's own father, given how they acted and responded to each other. Again, a complete supposition on Holloway's part; it might be that he used to be Mama Fuzzy's mate before Papa Fuzzy came around, and now he was accepting some sort of secondary role. The ways of fuzzy society were a blank to Holloway, truth be told. Regardless, he found himself tagging this third animal as Grandpa Fuzzy.

Part of the reason Holloway found himself referring to Grandpa Fuzzy that way revolved around what appeared to be Grandpa's primary job, which was herding the final two fuzzys and keeping them in line. These two fuzzys were smaller and acted younger—more impulsive and heedless, as exemplified by the tendency of one of them to go up to Carl and jump on his back, attempting to ride the dog like a noble steed. Carl did not appreciate this and at one point nipped the fuzzy. The fuzzy batted the dog on the nose and then ran squealing, thrilled, as Carl tried to eat him. Holloway figured this one had to be the fuzzy equivalent of a teenage boy. His fur was blotchy patches of gray and black on white. Holloway called him Pinto.

The final fuzzy, golden and color-pointed like Mama Fuzzy, was as high spirited as Pinto but less obnoxious about it. Rather than trying to ride Carl, she would pet him and groom him and try to hug him whenever possible. Carl was a good sport about this but found it only slightly less trying than being ridden; it appeared that even this most gregarious of dogs eventually needed his own space. When that happened, Carl would gently shake off this last fuzzy and retreat to the cabin; his dog door was still keyed to his radio transmitter, so the fuzzys couldn't get through without his permission. He'd slip through the door and hide for an hour or two.

This littlest fuzzy did not seem offended or upset by the abandonment. She would simply turn her attentions to Holloway and whatever it was he was doing at the moment. She was not as affectionate to Holloway as she was to Carl but would stand close to him and pick up the objects he was working on or with. Holloway made a note to himself never to try to do a jigsaw puzzle with this particular creature around. For all that, he found her pleasant company and, frankly, adorable. He started to call her Baby Fuzzy.

Papa, Mama, Grandpa, Pinto, and Baby—they made a cozy little family unit. Holloway couldn't decide whether he had adopted them or whether it was the other way around. Actually he suspected that the family had adopted *Carl,* and that he was just sort of a bonus: the best darn butler a little fuzzy ever had.

Holloway found this idea unaccountably amusing, which was perhaps one of the reasons he had accepted the invasion of his home and life by the little creatures in the first place.

Which was not to say there were not adjustments.

Holloway experienced the first of these the morning after the Fuzzys had climbed down out of the trees. Holloway had woken up with a monumental backache; after a few seconds he realized it was because he was twisted like a pretzel in his cot.

The cause for this was four of the five fuzzys unequally distributed across his blanket, including one Grandpa, much to his consternation, hogging his pillow and snoring lightly in his face. While he was asleep, Carl had let the Fuzzys into the house and they had climbed into bed with him, and Holloway shifted in his sleep to give them room, resulting in his current contortionist position.

Holloway raised his head off the pillow and saw Carl lying on the floor next to the cot. Baby Fuzzy had nuzzled into his side and was sighing contentedly in her sleep. Carl didn't look terribly comfortable, either. He noticed Holloway looking at him and gave him a look with his eyebrows that said, *Sorry, man. I didn't know.*

"Idiot," Holloway said, and then dropped his head back down on the pillow.

Later Holloway was trying to work out the kinks in his muscles with a hot shower in the cabin's tiny lavatory when Baby Fuzzy pulled aside the curtain and got her first glimpse of naked, soap-covered man.

"Do you *mind*," Holloway said, mildly. He was not an exhibitionist, but being watched by a fuzzy while he showered didn't trigger any modesty concerns. It was like your cat watching you while you got dressed.

Baby turned her head and squeaked. Five seconds later, four

other heads peeked into the shower, watching the funny hairless thing doing its incomprehensible water ritual. *Now* Holloway felt vaguely uncomfortable.

"Are you taking notes?" Holloway said, to his audience. "You could all use one of these, you know. You don't smell as adorable as you look. Especially *you*," he said, motioning to Grandpa. "I woke up smelling your furry ass. You need an *intervention*, my friend."

Carl poked his head into the shower, as if to see what he was missing. Holloway turned the nozzle on the lot of them and smirked as they scattered.

Breakfast was likewise an experience. The Fuzzys, sitting on the kitchen table, appeared to be bored with their bindi and were far more interested in the massive sandwich Holloway was making for himself.

"Don't even *think* it," Holloway said to them, as he spread the mayo and mustard on his bread slices. He held up a slice to show them. "You see this? In a week it'll be gone. Then I get no more bread until I go back into town a month from now. Therefore: My bread. Not yours."

They all stared at the bread, entranced, including Carl.

"Besides, this is an all-Earth sandwich," Holloway continued, not caring that they couldn't understand him any more than Carl could when he spoke to him. "Wheat bread. Mayonnaise. Mustard. Smoked turkey." He placed said turkey on the bread, and then reached for the cheese. "Swiss cheese. It would probably kill you or rupture your intestines or something else absolutely horrible. Trust me, I'm doing you a favor eating it myself. That's the sort of selfless person I am." He closed the sandwich on itself and turned to put the ingredients back into the storage cooler.

When he turned back, Pinto was standing in front of him, eyes imploring.

"Nice try," Holloway said. "But you're not the cute one." He picked up the sandwich.

Baby got up, walked over next to Pinto, and employed that same look.

"Oh, come *on,*" Holloway said. "That's *completely* not fair."

Baby walked over to Holloway and lightly touched his arm, eyes wide and pleading.

"Stop that," Holloway said. "Your evil mystic cuteness has no effect on me."

Baby wrapped her tiny fuzzy arms around Holloway's arm and sighed, piteously and hungrily.

Two minutes later the sandwich had been sliced into six equal pieces, and each of the Fuzzys was enjoying its first smoked turkey and Swiss on wheat, chittering in delight with each bite. Holloway glumly looked down at his drastically reduced sandwich segment.

"Well, this sucks," he said after a minute.

Sensing weakness, Carl walked up to his master, eyes full of hope.

"Jesus," Holloway said. "Fine. Here." He handed over the miniature meal, which went down Carl's gullet in a single gulp. "I hope you choke on it. You're all fur-bearing pains in my ass, you know that."

Carl looked up, wagged his tail, and licked his lips happily.

●　●　●

Three days later a small, familiar skimmer landed next to Holloway's larger one, and an equally familiar person stepped out of it, bearing a netted bag full of fruit.

"Hello," Isabel said, to Holloway.

"Hello," Holloway said. "Is that a huge bag of bindi, or are you just happy to see me?"

"Quite obviously, it's a huge bag of bindi," Isabel said, unslinging the bag. "You said to bring a lot."

"I did at that," Holloway said, taking the bag.

"I also brought a week's worth of personal supplies and a tent," Isabel said. "To make good on the promise that you won't know I'm here."

"You are allowed to sleep in the cabin, you know," Holloway said. "The rainy season is about to start around here."

"Modern tents are often waterproof," Isabel said.

"I've heard," Holloway said. "The offer stands if you change your mind."

Isabel looked at him levelly. "You know I'm seeing someone," she said.

"I heard," Holloway said. "A lawyer or some such."

"Yes," Isabel said. "Just so we're clear about that."

"I said you could sleep in the cabin, not that you could sleep in the cot," Holloway said. "Anyway, we can set Carl up as a watchdog. You'd be perfectly safe."

Isabel looked around. "Where *is* Carl?" she asked.

"He's in the cabin," Holloway said.

"Are you keeping him in there so he doesn't scare away those creatures?" Isabel asked.

Holloway smiled. "Not exactly," he said. "Come on."

He walked her over to the cabin window. "Look inside," he said. "But move slowly and as quietly as possible."

Isabel looked at him quizzically and peered through the window to see the Fuzzy Family on the floor, looking at an infopanel propped up by the books on the bottom shelf of the bookcase. Carl was lying next to Baby, dozing.

She drew back quickly, putting her hand to her mouth to muffle a gasp. Then she turned to Holloway. "Oh my god," she said. "There's an entire family of them."

"Yeah," Holloway said.

"Well, it *might* be a family," Isabel said. "It could be some other sort of social structure. . . . What are you smirking about?"

"Nothing," Holloway said.

Isabel carefully peered into the cabin again and frowned. "What are they doing?" she asked.

"I put on a movie to keep them occupied," Holloway said.

"Do I want to know which one?" Isabel asked.

"An old science fiction movie called *Return of the Jedi,*" Holloway said, and shrugged. "It's got some little furry creatures in it. Ewoks. I figured, what the heck."

"Uh-huh," Isabel said.

A small flurry of noises came from the cabin. The Fuzzys were hopping about excitedly.

"What's that about?" Isabel asked.

"They like the scene where the Ewoks drop rocks on the bad guys," Holloway said.

"You're not at all concerned about teaching them bad habits, are you?" Isabel asked.

"They're animals, Isabel," Holloway said. "Really smart animals, but animals. I don't think they're going to make the leap from watching movement on an infopanel to dropping rocks on me from above."

"It's probably not a great idea for you to be domesticating them like this, either," Isabel said. "You're not going to be here forever, Jack. When you go, it's not like you're going to be taking them with you."

"You say that as if you think I had a choice," Holloway said. "I'd like for them to be a little *less* domesticated, actually. Then I might get a good night's sleep."

"They're sleeping on the cot?" Isabel asked.

"Now you know why I'm not inviting you to it," Holloway

said. "It's crowded enough. Last night I actually got up and slept in the skimmer. Anyway, they might be domesticating themselves, but at least this way you won't have to wait to make their acquaintance."

"How do you suggest we do that, incidentally?" Isabel said. "Have me meet them, I mean. I don't want to frighten them or scare them off."

"I wouldn't worry about that," Holloway said. "They're awfully friendly."

"That's not necessarily a good thing either," Isabel said. "Animals that have no fear of humans have a very sad tendency to go extinct. Ask the dodo about that."

"I understand that," Holloway said. "But it's not like I made them that way."

"But what you're doing isn't helping them either, Jack," Isabel said. "That's all I'm saying."

"Tell them that," Holloway said, and pointed to the window. Baby was there, looking out.

"God, that's cute," Isabel said.

Baby turned her head and opened her mouth. A few seconds later the entire Fuzzy Family was peeking out the cabin window.

"It's like they were evolutionarily designed for adorability, isn't it?" Holloway said.

"It really is," Isabel said.

The dog door opened and Carl walked halfway through. Isabel called to him, but he stayed put.

"Is he stuck?" Isabel asked, puzzled.

"Wait for it," Holloway said.

The Fuzzy Family piled through the door. When the last of them were out, Carl walked the rest of the way through and started toward Isabel, tail wagging furiously.

Isabel turned and looked at Holloway curiously. He shrugged.

"I didn't teach him that," he said. Then Carl and the Fuzzy Family reached Isabel, and she was distracted by cute.

Holloway smiled and took the opportunity to head to the cabin for a beer. As he went in, he noticed the infopanel was still showing the movie. The Fuzzys might be smart, but apparently they hadn't figured out how to turn the thing off. Holloway picked up the panel, paused the movie, and then cleared it off the screen, returning the infopanel to the default screen. It noted a voice message from Chad Bourne. Holloway opened it.

"Hi, Jack," the message said. "Before I say anything else, I want to say this was not my idea. We have our problems, but I think you know I wouldn't try to hold up what's yours. All right?"

What the hell? Holloway thought.

"That said, I've been ordered to suspend payments to your contractor account," the message continued. "The order came from Wheaton Aubrey the Seventh himself. I told him that suspending your payments was a violation of our contract with you, but he said before you received any initial payment on the sunstone seam, he wanted to talk to you. He said he's got a business proposition for you. He says he needs to discuss it with you personally."

Chapter Nine

Wheaton Aubrey VII was unavailable to meet Holloway immediately. He was on the planet's southwestern continent, touring some of the mining projects there, or so Holloway was told. He was also told that, while legally he had the right and obligation to do further surveying of the sunstone seam, he was to hold off on that as well until Aubrey could schedule him in. A nominal sum would be credited to his contractor account to compensate him for these further "exigent circumstances."

Of course, as Aubrey had ordered payments held pending further discussion, Holloway couldn't access the sum. He swore and remarked to Isabel that it was a good thing she'd brought the bindi, or else he'd starve. Isabel, occupied with the Fuzzys, barely looked up for the comment.

Two days later Holloway aimed his skimmer toward Carl's Cliff and his sunstone discovery. Aubrey would be there, surveying the initial site buildout. Holloway saw evidence of the activity long before he came close to it: a streamy cloud of particles marking a smeared line in the sky, evidence of industrial-grade machinery. A few minutes later, he was circling the site, looking for a place to land.

Holy God, they got busy fast, Holloway thought. At the foot of the cliff was a small but growing site, its perimeter marked by a high modular predator fence. On the inside of the fence, machines clear-cut the area, shaving the ground down to the dirt to serve as a foundation for permanent structures. Outside the area, robots were drilling holes to expand the fence line, their operators on the safe side of the barrier. When the holes were drilled, another set of robots would place the additional modular fencing and link it to the existing fence, pushing out the perimeter in steps until there was enough room for whatever structures Zara-Corp needed. Holloway looked around at the nature on display around him; it wouldn't be there for much longer.

"Skimmer, identify," came a message through Holloway's infopanel.

Holloway arched his eyebrows at this. "The hell you say," he replied. "Identify yourself first, pal."

"Skimmer, identify yourself now or you will be shot down," the voice said.

"Shoot at me and I'll land this thing on your skull," Holloway said. "And I'd get away with it, too, because *you* are on *my* claim. Now, you identify yourself or we'll see each other in court, and you'll be wearing a body cast."

There was silence for a minute, then "Skimmer, you are cleared to land at the beacon." An image materialized on the info panel, showing a beacon and a landing circle a small distance from one of the larger structures. "Mr. Aubrey is expecting you."

Damn right he is, Holloway thought. Holloway set the auto-approach to the beacon. He was on the ground a minute later, and as he climbed out of his skimmer, he noted two men approaching. He recognized one as Joe DeLise, part of the ZaraCorp security detail from Aubreytown. He was one of the security guys Holloway rather emphatically didn't drink with.

"Oh, it's *you*," Holloway said. "Figures. You never bothered to identify yourself, Joe. That's a violation of ZaraCorp regulations. I could have you written up."

"The next time you don't identify yourself, Holloway, I *will* have your skimmer shot down," DeLise said. "I've got my orders."

"And I have my stake contract," Holloway said.

"It's not your stake anymore," DeLise said.

Holloway cracked a smiled at that. "I don't think 'exigent circumstances' will go quite that far in a court of law, Joe. Not that I wouldn't mind hauling your fat ass in front of a judge to find out."

"Gentlemen, please," said the other man, who had watched the exchange of pleasantries between Holloway and DeLise with a bemused look on his face. "Mr. Holloway, Mr. DeLise does indeed have orders to ground any approaching skimmer that will not identify itself, by force if necessary. Mr. DeLise, Mr. Holloway's claim to this find is still very much in effect. So you're both right, and now you both may stick your dicks back into your pants."

DeLise audibly ground his teeth at this but said nothing. Holloway crooked his head at the second man, amused. "And you are?" he said.

"Brad Landon," the man said. He walked up to Holloway and held out his hand. "I'm Mr. Aubrey's personal assistant. I'm here to take you to him."

"He's too busy to greet me himself?" Holloway joked.

"Of course he is," Landon said, in a tone that told Holloway that his response, while a joke in return, was also in fact completely serious. Landon turned to DeLise. "Thank you, Mr. DeLise. I will take it from here. You may go back to your post."

"I want the skimmer waxed before I get back," Holloway said. DeLise shot him a look and stomped off.

"Do you always antagonize people when you meet them, Mr. Holloway?" Landon asked, as they set off across the base.

"I've met DeLise before," Holloway said. "Lots of times before. That's why I'm antagonizing him."

"I see," Landon said. "I thought perhaps it was one of those stereotypical hostility-to-authority things."

"I doubt Joe's an authority on much," Holloway said. "He's one of those guys who thinks the job description of 'cop' reads as 'professional thug.'"

"His service record is clean," Landon said. "I know. I saw it before I approved his being stationed here."

"I think it's interesting that you seem to be under the impression anyone's going to say anything bad about a company goon in a company town," Holloway said.

"Point taken," Landon said. "You think we should transfer him back, then."

"Hell, no," Holloway said. "Every night he's here is a night he's not beating up someone in a bar. You're doing the citizens of Aubreytown a favor."

Landon gave a slight smile at this.

The two men were approaching the area of fence Holloway had seen as he circled: Robots on one side of the fence were drilling holes, with the operators on the other side, maneuvering them from small stations bristling with levers. As they approached, Holloway was aware of an increasing sensation that felt like what happened to his ears if he climbed in altitude too quickly in his skimmer. He swallowed hard, to no use.

As Holloway got closer to the operators, he realized that one of them was Aubrey, wearing a ZaraCorp hard hat. Another man stood next to Aubrey's station; Holloway suspected it was the actual robot operator, politely and silently waiting for Aubrey to get done playing around so he could get back to work.

Landon pulled out a palm-sized infopanel and pressed it. "We're here," he said into the panel. From the robot station, Aubrey turned and motioned them over.

"Having fun?" Holloway asked, as they approached. He noticed Landon pursing his lips slightly in disapproval. Holloway had apparently forgotten that he was not supposed to speak until spoken to.

"Fun isn't the point," Aubrey said, climbing out of the station. He took off his hard hat. "One day I'll be running ZaraCorp. Dad always said that it was important for a leader to know what his people do and how they do it, and Grandpa said it to him, and so on. Every Aubrey does a tour of our businesses and tries his hand at the jobs our people do. Gives us a grounding."

"So twenty minutes with a fence-building robot makes you a better leader," Holloway said.

"It was a half hour, actually," Aubrey said, catching the sarcasm and returning it. "And maybe it does and maybe it doesn't, but even you might agree that coming out and participating in our operations is better than me simply being fed grapes in a country club, waiting for the old man to kick off."

"When you put it that way," Holloway said. The ear thing was getting worse. He swallowed again.

Aubrey watched Holloway with interest. "Feels like your ears are plugged, doesn't it?" he asked.

"Yeah," Holloway said.

Aubrey pointed to a large box on the fence line. "It's a speaker," he said. "Turns out zararaptors and other predators here hear higher frequencies than we do, and they hate loud noise. We're blasting twenty-five-kilohertz frequencies at about a hundred sixty decibels. They hear it and take off running in the other direction."

"Huh," Holloway said, and swallowed again.

"Used to be, we'd just shoot the things with automated sentries," Aubrey said. "But animal rights groups didn't like that much. Bad for our public relations. We figured we would give this a try."

"Very humane of you," Holloway said.

"Cheaper, too, as it happens," Aubrey said. "But it does have the side effect you're experiencing. You can't hear it, but you can *feel* it, all right. Stay here long enough and you'll get a migraine. Then you'll get a nosebleed."

"Lovely working conditions," Holloway said.

Aubrey pointed to his ears. "Noise-canceling in-ear headphones," he said. "Filters out the high end. No headaches."

"For you, maybe," Holloway said.

"All the fence workers have them," Aubrey said.

"Wonderful," Holloway said. "I don't."

"Oh, right," Aubrey said. "Well, come on, then." He started walking. Holloway and Landon followed.

"What do you think of the site?" Aubrey asked, as they walked.

"I'm amazed at how quickly you've built it up," Holloway said. "There was nothing here a week ago."

"I told you this is a priority for us," Aubrey said. "I commandeered airlifters to bring in the heavy equipment and stole the best crews from other sites. I had people here clearing land the same day you sat in on our meeting. When the site is finished it will be the largest single permanent site we'll have on Zara Twenty-three. It'll have to be in order to process that seam you found."

"I can't help but notice that you've been doing all of this without involving me," Holloway said.

"Well, it's—" Aubrey began.

"Exigent circumstances, yes, I know," Holloway said, and ignored that now both Aubrey and Landon were annoyed with him for his peremptory ways. He had stopped walking; they were far enough from the fence that his ears no longer hurt. "The problem is that exigent circumstances are by their very nature emergent and temporary. What you're doing here is systematic and permanent. If I'm not involved, then ZaraCorp has a very good case for eventually voiding my claim. I checked both ZaraCorp regulations and Colonial law on the matter. There's prior case law here: *Teppo versus Miller*. Teppo lost millions of credits because Miller showed he wasn't properly involved in the exploitation of his own claim. Now, you may or may not be intending to be pushing me into a *Teppo*-style situation, but that's what I see happening."

Aubrey looked at Holloway for a minute. "God save us from amateur lawyers," he said, eventually.

"I'm not an amateur," Holloway said.

"That's not what the Bar of the State of North Carolina says," Aubrey said.

"I wasn't disbarred for not knowing the law," Holloway said.

"Really," Aubrey said. "What were you disbarred for, then?"

"It's not actually important at the moment," Holloway said.

"You know I can find out," Aubrey said.

"Then find out," Holloway said, and nodded toward Aubrey's assistant. "Have Landon here search it out on the network. It's a public record; it's not hard to find. But in the meantime, I want to talk about our situation here, now."

Aubrey nodded, and started walking again. "Come on, Holloway," he said. "I want to show you something."

In a few moments, the three of them were looking at a massive rockfall. It was the part of the cliff Holloway had dropped to the riverbed. Workers and machines were crawling over it. "Look familiar?" Aubrey said to Holloway.

"It's in a slightly different configuration than I'm used to seeing it in," Holloway said.

"I'll bet," Aubrey said. "It's going to cost us a couple million credits to clean this up, you know. CEPA regulations require us to return this rockfall area to a pristine state before we can exercise exploit rights. It's stupid, but that's Colonial Authority regulation for you."

"I thought you'd made an ecological exception request," Holloway said. He noted with a bit of satisfaction that both Aubrey and Landon were surprised he knew this. *Good,* Holloway thought. *Let them wonder what else I know.*

"We have," Landon said, after a second. "But they're granted rarely, if at all."

"And in the meantime, we're on the hook for this expense," Aubrey said.

Holloway nodded toward the rockpile. "After this fell, I pulled sunstones the size of chicken eggs out of the seam, almost with my bare hands. You'll probably find enough sunstones in this pile alone to pay for the cost of cleaning this up, and make a profit besides."

"No doubt we will," Aubrey said. "But you're missing the point."

"Being in the black for cleaning up an ecological mishap is not the point?" Holloway said.

"The point is that you caused this 'ecological mishap,' as you call it," Aubrey said. "Whether we make a profit off it or not, it's still a black eye for ZaraCorp that you caused to happen."

"It wasn't intentional," Holloway said.

"It doesn't matter," Aubrey said. "ZaraCorp has to appear to be attuned to ecological sensitivities, especially since we *are* requesting an ecological exception for this seam. We have to convince some bureaucrat in a CEPA office a hundred eighty light-years away that we're going to be careful about the messes we're going to make, and that we're going to clean them up after we're done. What is going to make that argument less than convincing is the fact that the principal surveyor of the seam is someone who rather cavalierly caused an ecological disaster right at the start."

"The environmental lobbies already know your name, Mr. Holloway," Landon said. "Their discussion forums are full of outrage that you've trained your dog to detonate explosives."

"There's no proof of that," Holloway said.

"Proof is not something that is of great concern to these people, Mr. Holloway," Landon said.

"Where are the two of you going with this?" Holloway asked. "Because if you don't mind, I'd rather we just cut to the chase."

"Fine," Aubrey said. "Here it is. I think you'll be a public relations disaster that ZaraCorp doesn't need. I think it'd be better for all of us, including you, if you just went away. So I want to buy you out."

"Really," Holloway said. "And I suppose it would be too much to assume you want to buy me out for what my percentage of this sunstone seam is actually worth."

"We don't know what it's worth," Aubrey said.

"Your Director of Exploitation estimated eight hundred billion to one-point-two trillion credits," Holloway said. "I remember those sums quite clearly. I'm sure you do, too."

"Be that as it may, there are any number of variables," Landon said. "Sunstone density. Environmental challenges to exploiting the seam. Market forces."

"ZaraCorp has spent decades building up sunstones as the rarest gem in the universe," Holloway said. "I think we can assume it's done its job, marketwise."

"The sheer size of this find could create a glut," Aubrey said.

Holloway looked over at Aubrey. "Let's you and I pretend that we both know what the phrase *monopoly on distribution* means in this context," he said. "So. What are you offering?"

Aubrey looked over at Landon. "Three hundred fifty million credits," Landon said.

"All at once?" Holloway said.

"Over ten years," Landon said.

"You've got to be joking," Holloway said. "You want me to sell out for less than ten percent of what my claim is worth, and you won't even give it to me all at once?"

"Thirty-five million a year is not an insignificant amount of money," Landon observed. "Especially for someone like you, who has grossed twenty-one thousand credits in the last year."

"I agree," Holloway said. "But a hundred million a year or so is an even *less* insignificant amount of money, isn't it."

"We'd also offer you warrants on ZaraCorp stock," Landon said.

"Voting stock?" Holloway asked.

"Of course not," Landon said, annoyed. Only Aubrey family members received voting stock. "Class B."

"With my hundred million a year, I could buy as much Class B ZaraCorp stock as I want," Holloway said. "And maybe some BlueSky stock, too. To diversify my E and E sector portfolio."

"Christ," Aubrey said. The mention of BlueSky appeared to have pinked him a bit. "Let's get this over with. Five hundred million credits, Holloway, in your account, right now. Take it, jump the next ship off Zara Twenty-three with your dog, and be the single richest contractor in the history of ZaraCorp."

"What's the catch?" Holloway said.

"No catch," Aubrey said. "Landon here can call up the amount and we can do it right here on this rockpile. But you have to give up all rights and claims. And then you have to leave."

"How much time do I have to think about this?" Holloway asked.

"Until I get bored with you and walk away," Aubrey said.

"Well, in that case, I'll give you my answer now," Holloway said. "Which is that you can take your offer and jam it sideways. I don't like being pressured into making deals, and I don't give a damn whether you're going to run the company one day or not. I have legal rights to this claim. I'm going to exercise them, and profit from them, and I'm not going to be bought off for less than what I'm rightfully owed, simply because it'll be convenient for you." He jerked his thumb at Landon. "And though it clearly pains Landon here when someone speaks to you in less than a groveling tone, I'll tell you this right now, and this *is* a promise: Try to cut me out or shut me down one more time, and you'll see just how big a public relations nightmare I can be. Fact is, right now you need my cooperation more than I need your money. You need to remember that."

Aubrey looked over at Landon. "Told you," he said.

"Yes, quite," Landon said, looking at Holloway. Then he pulled out his infopanel and pressed it. "And since we were in fact prepared for the quite dramatic pissing all over our offer, Mr. Holloway, I've just sent you our surveying requests, which you'll find waiting for you when you get back to your skimmer. There seems to be a large tributary branch running off the main sunstone seam. We could have had some of our other surveyors map it, of course, but we were aware you might have concerns vis-à-vis *Teppo,* and we wouldn't want you to think you were intentionally being left with nothing to do. As a warning, it requires jungle floor mapping, so do watch out for predators."

"And try to avoid any other major ecological disasters, if you can manage that," Aubrey said.

"I think I can manage," Holloway said.

"We'll see," Aubrey said. Holloway turned to go.

"One other thing, Holloway," Aubrey said.

Holloway turned. "Yes?"

"You have rights to this seam and you can be sure you'll get every last thing that's coming to you, while you're here and after you're gone," Aubrey said. "But your contract runs out in five months. When that happens, your time really is up. You're getting a ride home and after that, no amount of money will ever get you another contract with this company. Hell, once you get home, you won't even be able to book passage on another ZaraCorp ship. Every subsidiary we own will automatically bounce you back. That's *my* promise to you. Just so you know."

"Seems a bit drastic," Holloway said.

"It probably is," Aubrey said.

"Do you do this with everyone who annoys you?" Holloway asked.

"No," Aubrey said. "Just you. You inspire that reaction in people, Holloway."

"It's a gift," Holloway said. "But as long as we're talking promises, now that you've had your strong-arm attempt, are you going to release the compensation you've been illegally withholding from me? The cost of the initial exploration of the seam came out of my own pocket. Now that you're exploiting it, you're obliged to pay me back. And my dog is out of explosives."

"Lovely," Aubrey said. He nodded to Landon. Landon fiddled with his infopanel.

"Done," Landon said. "Enjoy your eight thousand two hundred sixteen credits, Mr. Holloway. Don't spend it all in one place."

Holloway smiled in spite of himself as he walked away.

Joe DeLise was waiting at Holloway's skimmer. "You didn't steal anything, did you?" Holloway asked.

DeLise smiled. "I'm sure going to miss you, Jack," he said.

"Don't get mushy, Joe," Holloway said. "I'm not going anywhere just yet."

sabel came up to the skimmer as soon as it landed. "We need to talk," she said.

"Yeah, we do," Holloway said, exiting the vehicle. "You think you could stop telling people that I let Carl detonate explosives?"

"What?" Isabel said.

"Stop telling people I let Carl set off explosives," Holloway said.

"You *do* let Carl set off explosives," Isabel said.

"Yes, but you don't have to *tell* people about it," Holloway said. By this time the topic of conversation had come over, tail wagging. Holloway petted him. "I'm apparently becoming famous galaxy-wide for it. I'd rather not be."

"When you train your dog to blow things up, it tends to be noted," Isabel said. "And for the record, I *don't* talk about it. The only time I *did* talk about it was at that inquest, which I will remind you, Jack, was caused by your own procedural shortcuts."

"You didn't have to talk about it *then,* either," Holloway said.

"Really?" Isabel said, thinning her lips. "Because I was under the impression that when one is forced to testify at a company inquest and continuing one's job is contingent on telling the truth, when one is asked 'What other unusual surveying practices have you personally witnessed Jack Holloway engage in?' it might be prudent to describe what they are."

"It didn't make my problems any easier," Holloway said.

"Well, I'm sorry my telling the truth about the stupid things you do is inconvenient for you," Isabel said, in the clipped, quiet voice she used when she was truly pissed off. "Although now that you mention it, your calling me a liar about that and other things at your inquest didn't do wonders for *me,* either. When the inquest gave you the 'not proven' judgment, *I* got a markdown in my employment record. It says that my 'judgment might be impaired due to close or romantic relationships.' I suppose that may be true enough, because I *was* with you, which was a clear case of impaired judgment. But it wasn't impaired in the way they thought it was, and I certainly don't deserve a mark against me because *you lied,* Jack."

Holloway watched Isabel, remembering the cold fury she'd shown him after the inquest, which this outburst was a pale echo of. "I told you I was sorry," Holloway said.

"Right, when you tried to give me that rock," Isabel said. "And I told you then that I'd be happy to hear you were sorry when you meant it. But you're still angry with me about something *you* did. So I guess I'm still waiting for you to actually be sorry."

By this time, Baby Fuzzy had come up to Isabel and tugged on her pant leg. Isabel looked down. Baby Fuzzy held out her arms. Isabel picked her up, sat her in the crook of her arm, and scratched her head. Baby Fuzzy seemed to enjoy this.

"She really is like a cat," Holloway said. The conversation he was having with Isabel had gone bad quickly. Holloway was ready to dump it and start a new one.

"She's really not," Isabel said. "That's what I had *wanted* to talk to you about, before you started hammering on me about Carl and we got sidelined."

"Sorry about that," Holloway said. "That's a small, immediate apology. I had a meeting with Wheaton Aubrey the Seventh, and it was brought up."

"I take it the meeting didn't go well, then," Isabel said.

"No," Holloway said. "He condescended to me, I was antagonistic to him, he made a dismissive offer couched in contempt, I threw it back in his face and promised legal action if he tried to cross me again."

"So, the usual with you," Isabel said.

"I suppose," Holloway said.

"The more I know you, the more I realize why you live hundreds of kilometers from anyone else," Isabel said.

"Let's get back to the thing you wanted to talk about," Holloway said. He started walking toward the cabin; he wanted a beer.

"All right," Isabel said. "These fuzzys. These animals you've discovered. I'm starting to wonder if they *are* animals."

"I think you'll be laughed out of the biologist club if you suggest they're plants," Holloway said.

"That's not what I'm saying, obviously," Isabel said. "When I say I don't think they're animals, I mean I don't think they're *just* animals. I think they're something more."

Holloway stopped walking and turned to face Isabel. "Tell me you're not about to say what I think you're about to say," he said. "Because I *know* I don't want to hear it."

"I think they're sapient," Isabel said. "I think these creatures are intelligent on a level beyond just animals. These things are *people,* Jack."

Holloway turned, irritated, and threw up his hands. He resumed his walk to the cabin. "You could have told me that before I turned down half a billion credits, Isabel," he said.

Isabel followed, confused. "What does that have to do with anything?" she said.

"Zara Twenty-three is a Class Three planet," Holloway said. He paused at the cabin door and pointed to Baby Fuzzy, who now appeared to be dozing lightly. "If *that* is a person, then this becomes a Class Three—a planet—a planet with native sapient life—and ZaraCorp's E and E charter is suspended. That means everything stops here, Isabel. No more mining, no more drilling, no more harvesting. It means I don't get paid for the sunstone seam."

"Well, I'm sorry you might possibly be out a bit of money, Jack," Isabel said.

"Jesus, Isabel," Holloway said. He opened the door. "A *bit* of money? Try at least a couple billion credits. That's *billion,* with a *b.* Saying that's a *bit* of money is like saying a forest fire is a nice way to roast some marshmallows." He went into the cabin. Isabel followed.

Inside the cabin, the other fuzzys lounged about; it had gotten hot and humid outside and Holloway's cabin had climate controls. As Holloway glanced over, he saw Mama Fuzzy had taken a book down from the bookcase and she and Papa were examining it carefully. Closer examination showed Mama Fuzzy was holding it upside down.

"Maybe they're not as smart as you think," Holloway said, pointing out the upside down book to Isabel. He reached into his kitchen cooler to retrieve a beer.

Isabel looked at him, and then set Baby Fuzzy down. She padded off toward the rest of her family; Isabel headed to the kitchen. "Papa," she said. The fuzzy looked up from his book, curious, then headed toward the kitchen.

"Excuse me," Isabel said to Jack. She pushed him aside to get at the cooler. From the cooler she retrieved smoked turkey, cheese, mayonnaise, and mustard. She set them on the small kitchen table. She closed the cooler, and then reached over to the counter to take the last two bread slices and placed them on the table. Finally, she opened the utensil drawer and put a butter knife next to all the food. She looked down at the fuzzy.

"Papa," Isabel said. "Sandwich."

The fuzzy squeaked in joy.

Four minutes later all the fuzzys were enjoying their share of the sandwich Papa Fuzzy had made, up to and including clumsily wielding the butter knife to make six mostly equal sections, the last of which had been presented to Carl with great gravity.

"You could have taught him to do that," Holloway said. "I once taught a dog to detonate explosives."

"Not to take anything away from Carl, whom I love," Isabel said, "but it's one thing to teach an animal to step on a detonator panel to get a treat. It's another thing to teach it how to make a *sandwich*. Much less then divide it equally among five other animals."

"A monkey could do it," Holloway said.

"Name one," Isabel said.

"*I'm* not the biologist," Holloway said.

"Really," Isabel said, mildly. "There's also the small matter that even if I could have trained Papa to make a sandwich, *I* didn't. I came in here not long after you left for your meeting and found Papa making one. Either he saw you making one or he's even more clever than I thought. Which would go to my point."

"He saw me make one," Holloway said. He started putting away the sandwich fixings.

"So what we're saying is that this animal, having observed you make a sandwich once, managed to remember where the ingredients were, retrieved them, organized them, and re-created a sandwich recipe from memory, not once, not twice, but three times," Isabel said.

"Three times?" Holloway said.

"After I caught him doing it, I made him do it again, just to be sure," Isabel said.

"You're going to make them fat," Holloway said, closing the cooler.

"He gave the second one to me," Isabel said.

"How sweet," Holloway said, dryly. He took another swig of his beer.

"Which in *itself* shows higher-order cognitive function," Isabel said. "It's called theory of mind. Papa assumed that when I asked him to make another sandwich, that I was asking him to make it for me, because I was hungry. He was attributing intent and reason to me."

"I know what theory of mind is," Holloway said. "You know who else has theory of mind? Monkeys. And some species of squid. Even Carl here tries to figure out what I'm thinking." From the floor, Carl, hearing his name, thumped his tail on the floor a couple of times.

"Squids don't make sandwiches," Isabel said.

"I doubt there's been a scientific study on that matter," Holloway said. "The bread gets soggy."

"Stop that," Isabel said. "Neither do monkeys, and neither does Carl. And certainly none of them could do it from seeing you do it once. These aren't just animals, Jack." She bent down again to get a beer for herself.

"But it doesn't mean they're *sapient,*" Holloway said. "I know these things are smart, Isabel. That's why I recorded Papa in the first place and gave you the recording. These little guys are a big find. I knew you'd want to see them. But it's a hell of a leap from 'smart little monkey' to 'sapient people.' Have you ever heard them speak?"

"They definitely communicate," Isabel began. Holloway held up his hand.

"Not in contention," Holloway said. "They squeak and squeal with the best of them, and they definitely have animal-level communication down pat. Given. But is there evidence they have speech? Language? Some manner of communication that goes beyond what we would see in other very smart animals?"

Isabel was quiet for a moment. "No," she said, finally. She took a drink of her beer.

"You know that matters," Holloway said. "I was required to take a class in xenosapient law at Duke. I don't remember that much of it, because it wasn't going to be my specialty anyway. But I remember *Cheng versus BlueSky Incorporated*. It's the one where a company biologist maintained the Nimbus Floaters of BlueSky Six were sapient and went to court in their behalf to stop the exploitation of the planet. The court ended up having to develop a checklist of criteria to judge the sapience of a creature, and speech—or 'meaningful communication that conveys more than the immediate and presently imminent'—was part of that checklist. It's canon law."

"It's not the only thing on the list," Isabel said.

"No, but it's a big one," Holloway said. "It's what tripped up Cheng. He couldn't prove the floaters spoke."

"You're not exactly an impartial party on this," Isabel said.

"No, I'm not," Holloway said. He motioned out toward the Fuzzys, who had finished their meals and retired to the floor once more, to look at the book or to nap on Carl. "If our little friends here are just really smart animals, then I get to be a billionaire. If they're people, then I'm just another schmuck out of a job, and I have a very good reason to believe that I'd have trouble getting another prospector gig. So yes, I'd say I'm a pretty interested party."

"Glad you know it," Isabel said.

"I do," Holloway said. "But even if I weren't, I'd still be telling you to be absolutely sure that what you've got is what you think it is. Because the minute you file a Suspected Sapience Report, ZaraCorp is required by law to suspend all activity on this planet. Everything comes to a screeching halt while a court decides on our fuzzy friends' sapience. It won't just be me you'll cost billions. And if the ruling goes against the fuzzys, you're going to spend the rest of your life as a grocery clerk. So before you say anything about sapience to anyone, you need to be absolutely sure. Are you absolutely sure, Isabel?"

Another moment of silence from Isabel. Then, "No. No, I'm not *absolutely* sure. I'm not saying I am. I need to study them more."

"All right, then," Holloway said. "So study them some more. Take your video and make your observations and do whatever it is you need to do. There's no need for you to rush any of this. Take your time. Take lots of time."

Isabel snorted. "Enough time for you to become a billionaire, you mean," she said.

"That would be nice," Holloway said. "I could very happily live with that."

"I know *you* could," Isabel said, and then motioned to the Fuzzys. "But could they?"

"I don't follow you," Holloway said.

"This is their planet, Jack," Isabel said. "If they are sapient, everything we take out of this world is a little less for them to use for themselves. Maybe you're not aware of how efficient Zara-Corp is at stripping a planet of its easily accessible resources—or maybe you don't *want* to be aware—but I know. I read the biological impact reports on all the planets ZaraCorp exploits. Some of the first planets ZaraCorp received its E and E charters for are already at depletion levels approaching Earth's, when it comes to rare metals and minerals. Even common ores are being pulled out of the ground at hugely accelerated rates. That's just a few decades of work. And ZaraCorp is much better now at doing this than it was even a decade ago."

Holloway thought of how quickly the camp was springing up at the sunstone seam. He took another swig of his beer and finished it.

"So if they are sapient, even if we waited just a year or two, think of how much less they would have to work with," Isabel said. "Taken before they can use it for themselves."

"They're at the level where they've just discovered sandwiches," Holloway said. "Working a sunstone seam is not high on their agenda."

"You're missing the point," Isabel said. She set down her beer. "The point is *when* they are ready, it won't be there. That sunstone seam you found is the result of millions of years of heat and pressure. ZaraCorp is going to pull it all out of the ground in a decade, if it takes even that long. And that's it for the sunstones; the creatures whose bodies made them are extinct. And then there are the other ores and minerals. It'll take millions of years for the planet to replenish these minerals. Some might not ever replenish at all. What does it leave for them?"

"I get what you're saying," Holloway said. "And you're probably right. I still think you should be sure before you try to claim sapience. Not saying you shouldn't make the claim. Just saying you should be sure. This is me trying to talk to you as a friend, here."

"Thanks," Isabel said. "I know. I'm just thinking, is all. Do you ever stop to think how lucky we are that, in this part of space at least, humans were the sentient creatures who got smart first?"

"It's crossed my mind," Holloway said.

Isabel nodded. "Now," she said, "imagine what would have happened if half a million years ago, some alien creature landed on *our* planet, looked at our ancestors, decided that they weren't actually people, and just took all the planet's ores and oil. How far would we have ever gotten?"

Isabel motioned to the Fuzzys, who were now all asleep on the cabin floor. "Seriously now, Jack," she said. "How far do you think *they're* going to get once we're through here?"

Chapter Eleven

Holloway had two thoughts when the front rotors of his skimmer failed. The first thought was *What the hell?* This was because while having a single rotor crap out was not all that unusual, having two die simultaneously was.

The second thought was *Oh, shit.* This was because Holloway was by himself in the middle of nowhere, and he was about to crash-land on the jungle floor, where something large would almost certainly try to eat him.

Holloway smacked the manual override on the autopilot and jerked up the yoke on the skimmer. He'd worry about getting eaten later. Right now he needed to avoid the crash landing. If he could get the skimmer on the ground without cracking it up, he might be able to get it fixed and get out of there. If he crashed and broke the skimmer, his odds of ending the day partially digested rose astronomically.

Holloway reached along the dash of the skimmer for the pull-cords for the emergency rotor engines. All the rotors were driven by the same power plant mid-skimmer, underneath the passenger

cabin, and controlled by computer rather than by direct manipu-
lation. But drive shafts wore down and computer hardware and
programs degrade over time, two facts that presented real problems when one's conveyance traveled up to a thousand meters
above the ground. In the event of emergency, small motors built
directly into the rotors themselves could be engaged. The motors were too small for movement, and their power lasted only a
matter of minutes. Their only purpose was to stabilize the craft
and allow for an immediate landing.

Holloway grabbed the pullcords for the front rotors and
yanked viciously. The pullcords tensed and snapped as the taut-
ened cords yanked the activation pins out of the EREs. If Holloway survived, he'd have to have the EREs recharged and the
cables and pins reset. It was one of those things that by manufac-
turer design was impossible to do by oneself and required a
trained and licensed professional. Who would insist on recharg-
ing and resetting all the EREs, not just the ones that got used.
Holloway would have to spend a thousand credits to have it done,
cursing as he did so.

None of which concerned Holloway in the least at the moment. At the moment, he was praying the EREs had held their
charge since the last time he had gotten them replaced, more than
a year earlier.

They had. The front rotors clicked into default position and
sputtered to life. A timer flashed onto Holloway's info panel; he
had two minutes and thirteen seconds to land. Holloway mini-
mized the timer and clicked on his undercarriage cameras, looking for a place to park.

The area, which Holloway had been surveying over the last
three days per orders, was heavily forested. He'd been having a
difficult enough time getting the skimmer through the forest
canopy that he'd been relying on small remote-controlled robots

to set the acoustical charges and the data collectors. They had gotten the job done, but took far more time than getting the skimmer down and using the digger/driller built into the vehicle.

But now he didn't have a choice. He was going to have to go in. Holloway nudged the skimmer forward, using its rear rotors, to a patch of the canopy that looked less impenetrable than every other part of the local canopy. He double-checked his seat restraints and then hit the EMERGENCY LANDING button on the dash.

The seat restraints tightened to a breath-shortening degree, and Holloway heard the *pop* as the head restraint inflated and then formfit around his skull, obscuring his vision. Other restraints did the same for his legs and arms. The chair, which generally swiveled, locked in a forward position. Holloway was immobilized; he was now in the hands, so to speak, of the skimmer's automated systems. Holloway was briefly grateful that he left Carl behind with Isabel and the Fuzzys. It promised to be a rough ride down.

It was. The skimmer lurched sickeningly as it began its rapid but hopefully computer-controlled descent, dropping faster than under gravity alone, using the skimmer's mass and build strength to snap tree branches when they couldn't be gotten out of the way of. The jolting of the cabin and the thunderous cracking sound told Holloway there was going to be a pile of lumber when he landed.

Seven meters from the ground, twelve short-burst rockets on the skimmer's undercarriage blasted on, the thrust of each precisely calculated using the skimmer's current position to arrest the descent, level the skimmer, and land it more or less gently on the jungle floor. As the thrusters kicked in, Holloway felt the painful tug of his internal organs falling the millimeter or so internally at descent speed before being slowed by the rest of his body. The nerve-rattling thump of the landing informed him that this landing was on the "less" side of gentle rather than "more."

The seat restraints slackened and the inflatable restraints hissed as they released; the skimmer's rotor drive shut off. Holloway pulled himself out of his seat and grabbed the infopanel for a status update. The skimmer had registered denting, and the left rear rotor's maneuvering apparatus was knocked off beam during the landing. If Holloway ever got the skimmer running again, it would be able to provide lift but not forward motion. But overall the skimmer survived. Holloway had landed without crashing.

Holloway registered the fact and then ignored it. Now that he'd landed, he had other things to worry about. He moved through his cabin to one of the large cargo holds, pulled it open, and yanked out the bundle marked EMERGENCY PERIMETER FENCE.

"Here we go," Holloway said to himself. He lowered the top off the skimmer and legged himself over the side.

When one lands on the jungle floor with a skimmer, via crash or otherwise, it makes a terrific racket. Most of the nearby creatures, evolutionarily designed to equate loud noise with predatory action and other dangers, will bolt to get out of the way. But eventually they come back. The ones that are actual predators come back sooner, intuiting in their predatory way that a big loud noise might, when finished, result in some small helpless creature being wounded or slowed down enough for it to be picked off without too much struggle.

What this meant to Holloway was that he likely had two minutes, give or take ninety seconds, to set up the emergency perimeter fence. After that, something large and hungry would definitely be on its way to see what might be for lunch.

Holloway wasted none of that time. He moved quickly, firmly

setting six stake poles in a perimeter around the skimmer, extending them to their full two-meter length. That finished, he unrolled the magnetized fence material, feeling it snap into place at each stake. The perimeter was tight around Holloway's skimmer. The vehicle was large, and the fence not so much.

Holloway clicked the final bit of fence to the first stake, which held the fence's power source at its base. Once activated, the power source would do two things. It would strengthen the fence by making it one large electromagnet; as long as the stake poles were reasonably secure it would be difficult for anything to pull down the fence. It would also course twenty-five thousand volts of electricity through the fence whenever it registered a contact, frying whatever touched it.

The power source was rated for twelve hours when fully charged. After what happened to Sam Hamilton (and his monkey), Holloway made sure the power source on his emergency perimeter fence was always charged.

Holloway double-checked to make sure the fence was secure, and then pressed the green button to prime the power source. He stood back to wait for the five-second power-up and the hum of the electromagnetic current.

There was nothing.

Holloway glanced down at the power source. An LED was blinking next to the primer button. Holloway didn't have to read the lettering next to the light to know that it meant the power source was uncharged.

"Oh, bullshit," Holloway said, out loud. Holloway knew the power source was charged. He'd checked it during his monthly loadout of inventory.

A bit of movement beyond the fence caught Holloway's eye. He looked up. Thirty yards away a pair of zararaptors were eyeing him back, with a look that signified curiosity, hunger, or both.

Holloway, very casually to all outward appearances, walked back from the tight perimeter of his fence, got himself into his skimmer, and then closed it up good and tight. Then he went looking for his shotgun.

A zararaptor was called such not because the creatures reminded anyone of raptor birds, but because they reminded them of those *other* raptors, the smart and predatory dinosaurs that had roamed the earth, thankfully millions of years before humans could be on the menu. Like those raptors, these were reptilian, were obviously carnivorous, and walked bipedaly on powerful legs, which ate up distances on the jungle floor yet were agile enough to leap over and avoid the various obstacles that humans would stumble over. Unlike those raptors, these raptors had blunt, almost feline heads and strong arms that ended with hands featuring opposable digits. Zararaptors could grab at and hold their prey, gripping their limbs so they could not escape fangs.

Upon arrival on Zara XXIII, Holloway and every other new surveyor was made to watch footage of zararaptors attacking and killing unwary humans, in video caught by surveillance cameras, security feeds, and in one case, by a tragically overconfident surveyor himself. That one was the most difficult to watch, in no small part because the surveyor's blood had spattered up on the lens, obscuring the view. But it brought home the point that human brains, fine though they might be, were no match for the zararaptor's speed, grip, and teeth.

In the now-covered skimmer, Holloway pretended he wasn't on the verge of panic and knelt next to the small storage area by his seat. He opened it and fished out his shotgun. It was a small, blunt thing with a short barrel; it'd be useless at anything other than a very short distance. Holloway suspected at the moment it'd be perfect for his situation. He'd purchased it when he arrived on Zara XXIII but had never had to use it. It looked like there was a first time for everything.

He opened the barrel to load in shells and looked into the storage area for the box of ammunition that always lay nestled next to the shotgun.

It wasn't there. Holloway felt a chill.

There was a metallic rattle outside the skimmer. Holloway looked up at the noise. The zararaptors were at the fence, pulling at it.

The fence.

Holloway suddenly had a crazy and desperate idea, because crazy and desperate ideas were the only things left to him at the moment. He grabbed for his infopanel as one of the zararaptors separated the fence material from the stake posts.

In most ways Holloway's skimmer was basic. He'd purchased it from another surveyor who had gone bust and was looking to make any sort of money he could before dragging his ass back to planet Earth. The skimmer was built for purpose rather than for beauty, with a large cargo area and a spartan interior covered by a standard retractable roof/window combination. Four large rotors, cowled so as not to julienne unwary flying creatures or surveyors, were stationed at the corners of the vehicle, providing lift and maneuvering capability.

Holloway had done almost nothing to improve the skimmer after he purchased it. He liked a flashy conveyance as much as the next guy—he had been a lawyer, after all—but part of the point of a flashy conveyance was showing it off, and on Zara XXIII, there was no one to show off to. People there were obsessed with the getting of money, not the exhibition of it. So there was nothing to prove in the direction of ostentation. In a way it was freeing.

Nevertheless, Holloway had splurged on one thing. The

skimmer's previous owner had equipped it with a single utilitarian speaker, for likewise utilitarian use—announcements from the skimmer and the infopanel, communication with his contractor rep, and so on. Holloway had blanched at this. If he was going to be spending most of his time in the skimmer, he was going to want to listen to music and audiobooks and other things that would keep his brain entertained while his eyes and hands and everything else were busy. Holloway wanted a sound system.

The sound system he got was ridiculously expensive, not because he wanted that particular system, but because it was the only one the ZaraCorp general store carried. Most surveyors, he was told, listened to their music on earbuds and went for the utilitarian speakers for their skimmers. The shopkeep offered Holloway what he assured him was a nice deal on a pair of formfitting earbuds. Holloway, who disliked the idea of sticking anything smaller than an elbow into his ear, bit the bullet and paid for the ridiculously expensive sound system.

The zararaptors had torn down the emergency fence and were now circling the skimmer, trying to make some sort of sense of it, and determining how to get past its hard outer shell to the soft chewy treat inside. Holloway focused on not wetting himself and on calling up his sound system's diagnostic software.

One of the things that made the sound system so expensive, or so the general store shopkeep explained to Holloway, was that the system put out sounds above and below the human range of hearing—the range of the system was in fact 2 kilohertz to 44.1 kilohertz. The point of this range was that even if humans couldn't hear in those ranges, there were psychoacoustic effects that propagated above and beyond human hearing range, effects that were lost in conventional sound systems whose speakers reproduced less than the human hearing range. This sound system reproduced everything, the shopkeep said, allowing for the best sound performance short of real life.

At the time, Holloway told the shopkeep that he suspected that was all just a bunch of sales bullshit. The shopkeep agreed that it probably was, but that Holloway was paying for it anyway, so he might as well know the excuse for it.

The zararaptors began pounding on the skimmer windows with their hands, first in open palm smacks and then with fists. The windows rattled but held; they were composite windows built to survive bird impacts at nearly 200 kilometers per hour. They could handle an animal fist.

One of the zararaptors broke away from the skimmer. Holloway, despite himself, watched the thing go. Its gaze was fixed on the ground, as if looking for something. Suddenly it paused and bent down and came up with an impressively large rock. It looked back at the skimmer and then swung its arm back in a frighteningly accurate simulation of a cricket bowler.

Huh, tool user, some part of Holloway's brain said. *I'll have to tell Isabel about that.* Then Holloway ducked involuntarily as the very large rock sailed through the air at a viciously flat trajectory. It smacked full into the front side window, leaving a small but distinct crack. The zararaptor rushed toward the skimmer to try again.

Holloway tore his attention away, back to his infopanel, and to the sound system's diagnostic software, which had now loaded.

When Holloway purchased his sound system, he had looked at the horribly complex sound system software for half an hour, with its various frequency tests and acoustical settings and options. Then he decided that life was too short to geek out on speakers, went back to the front screen of the software, and checked the box for AUTOMATIC MAINTENANCE. This meant the software would take care of itself, and Holloway could just listen to his music and books. Holloway was on that screen now, jabbing the button for MANUAL MAINTENANCE instead.

The zararaptor was now directly outside the window. It was reaching down to pick up the rock.

The infopanel screen changed, and a page of menu items displayed, in no apparent particular order. *Goddamn lousy user interface,* Holloway thought, and found the FREQUENCY TESTING option just as the zararaptor rammed the rock into the window with force, expanding the crack about a millimeter.

Holloway pressed the FREQUENCY TESTING option on the screen and was then treated to a soothing splash page graphic while a man's voice explained, in warm, rich tones, how calibrating the Newton-Barndom XGK sound system across all frequency ranges would assure the listeners of total sonic enjoyment.

Holloway screamed in frustration and fear and searched desperately for the SKIP INTRO option. He found it at the same time the second zararaptor had picked up its own rock and started beating it against the same window as the first raptor. They were taking turns breaking the window. The window shattered as Holloway loaded up what he was looking for.

Holloway launched himself away from the window and reached over to the one manual control on the dash associated with the sound system: the volume knob. He gripped the knob as the first zararaptor punched the glass in the window, popping it out in a single sheet, and then drew its head into the skimmer cabin, hissing. It was clearly planning to jam its way into the skimmer. The other zararaptor stayed outside, waiting for Holloway to be flushed out.

Holloway managed not to crap himself while he waited for the zararaptor to get about halfway into the skimmer. When it had, he jabbed a button in the infoscreen. The sound system kicked on as it ran the frequency test for the 22.5- to 28.0-kilohertz range. Holloway cranked the volume knob, turning it over hard and fast.

The zararaptor in the window screamed and thrashed and beat its toothy head against the side of the skimmer in a frantic attempt to pull its head out of the vehicle. After several terrifying seconds, the creature managed to reverse out of the skimmer, scrambling away from the broken window. The other raptor was retreating with it. Holloway was so relieved he almost cried.

But the zararaptors, while clearly annoyed, did not flee. After a moment they began to circle the skimmer. Holloway was briefly confused about this. Then he started the frequency test again, cranked up the volume even higher, and opened the skimmer roof and windows.

The zararaptors, confronted with an omnidirectional blast of painful high-frequency sound, screeched angrily and ran into the trees.

Holloway watched them go, disbelieving. Then he fired up the infopanel's sound recorder, made sure it could record inaudibly high frequencies, and recorded the frequency test. He set it to play on a repeating loop.

Five minutes later the jungle was silent, save for the wind through the trees. Apparently it wasn't only the zararaptors who hated high-frequency blasts of noise.

Holloway felt himself developing a headache from it, like Aubrey said he would, a few days ago. But there was nothing for it at the moment: The alternative to a headache was having one's brain gnawed upon. Holloway would stick with the headache for now.

He reached for the infopanel again and did another diagnostic test, this time for his front rotors. The diagnostic found nothing physically wrong with the rotors. They were operating within normal parameters.

Holloway looked around him to make sure his sound barrier was still working and then did a software diagnostic, targeting the subsystems relating to the rotors. They seemed fine, too. A diagnostic for general drive systems also turned up no errors or file corruption.

If there was nothing wrong with the hardware and nothing wrong with the software, could it really have been just a fluke—just a momentary glitch in the system? Holloway had to admit that it could have been, but he didn't like it. It would mean that his missing ammunition was just a fluke, too, as well as his drained fence power plant.

Holloway was willing to accept the combination of any two of those things as just bad luck or bad karma or whatever. But all three things together and at once smacked of intention to him. It sounded bad paranoid, and he wasn't generally the bad paranoid type, but what else could it be? Someone had just tried to kill him.

Who had access to the skimmer? Holloway did, obviously, but unless he was sleepwalking in an overtly suicidal sort of way, he was not a suspect.

Isabel had been at his treetop compound for a week now, so she would've had plenty of opportunity. But while Holloway had certainly given Isabel good reason to be angry with him over the time he had known her, the idea that she would try to kill him was inconceivable. That wasn't how she was built. And even if it *were,* Holloway thought wryly, Isabel wouldn't be sneaky about it. She'd come at him head-on.

But that didn't leave anyone else. Holloway's life really was without a great deal of physical human contact. The only people he'd seen in the last week were Isabel and Aubrey and his lackey, Landon. But neither of them had been near the skimmer. Well, Landon had, but—

Holloway's brain froze for a moment as he finally remembered the other person he'd seen in the last week.

Holloway flicked on his infopanel and did a search diagnostic on his skimmer's operational programs, looking for any programs that had been loaded or modified in the last week. He found two. One was the rotor power management program, which had been modified. The second was a program that had been added four days previous. It had no descriptor, but Holloway could guess what it did, and to which other program, and who had put it there to make sure that Holloway's defenses were compromised.

"Son of a bitch," Holloway said. He directed the infopanel to begin a system wipe and total reinstallation from factory settings. It would take time Holloway didn't want to spend on the jungle floor, but he had no intention of trying to fly anywhere in his skimmer until he'd reverted its operating system to system defaults and vaporized whatever the hell that new program was.

The reinstall took two hours, during which time Holloway's headache became a blinding migraine and his nose developed an incessant bleed. Holloway spent the last half hour on the ground chewing on aspirin, first aid kit gauze shoved into his nostrils.

By the time Holloway was back in the air, the sun was setting. He pinged Isabel. She didn't answer. This didn't entirely surprise Holloway; she was probably busy watching the Fuzzys do calculus or teaching them metaphysics. Holloway waited for the voice mail signal.

"Isabel, it's Jack," he said. "Listen, I need to go to Aubreytown to handle a thing. It shouldn't take too long, but I need you to do me a favor. If I don't call you back by about midnight, I want you to call your new friend and have him come looking for me. Because if you don't hear from me by midnight, I think that one way or another, there's a real good chance I'm going to need a lawyer."

olloway walked into Warren's Warren and found Joe DeLise right where he expected him to be: at the bar, third stool from the right. It was the Joe DeLise Memorial Drinking Stool; DeLise sat there enough that the stool padding conformed to the contours of his ass. If someone else was sitting on it when DeLise came in, they weren't sitting there for long. DeLise would just stand next to them, glaring, until they got the hint. One time a contract surveyor didn't get the hint. DeLise sat elsewhere and waited for the surveyor to head out of the bar. The surveyor was found the next morning in the alley, not dead, but with an impressive crease in his forehead. DeLise didn't have to do too much glaring after that.

Holloway walked up to DeLise, waited to see the man's stunned look, and then slugged him right in his big fat face. DeLise tumbled off the stool, beer bottle clattering to the floor. The bar, moderately crowded, went silent.

"Hi, Joe," Holloway said. "I know you're surprised to see me."

From the floor, DeLise gawked at Holloway, disbelieving. "You just hit a cop, you dipshit," he said.

"Yes I did," Holloway said. "I hit a cop, in front of witnesses, in a bar that's got a security camera whose feed is piped directly into the Security offices. So that way, if you have a mind to make me disappear *this* time, everyone's going to know it was you, you fat gelatinous turd. You're not going to get a chance to try to kill me twice."

"I don't know what the hell you're talking about," DeLise said.

"Of course not," Holloway said. "But I am curious about why you tried to kill me, Joe. We've never liked each other, but I didn't think you had that much of a problem with me. So how about it? Was this just because I pissed you off out there at the camp? You couldn't take a few mean words? Or was this something you've been planning for a while? You can tell me."

DeLise pulled himself off the floor. "You're under arrest, Holloway. For assaulting a security officer."

"Excellent," Holloway said, and held out his hands, close together. "Arrest me, you glutinous tub of lard. Then when you and I go to the Security offices, I'm going to call a lawyer, and then I'm going to tell him a story about you and my skimmer, and all the things that happened to it when it was left alone with you a few days ago. It's a really good story, and it's going to end with your flabby ass doing time. So go ahead and arrest me. I really want you to, Joe. Let's do this." Holloway pushed out his hands in the direction of DeLise.

DeLise stood there, furious, but didn't move.

"That's what I thought," Holloway said. "It looks like you're just going to have to take that punch and like it. But look at it this way: I nearly got eaten by a pair of zararaptors today, and all you had to pay for that was my fist in your stupid face. I think you're getting off pretty easy, don't you? But a word of warning,

Joe. Try it again, and you better hope you succeed. Because there's not going to be much left after I'm done with you. It's a promise."

Holloway turned and started toward the door, trying not to let a grin ruin the completely artificial badass act he'd been trying to pull off since he'd entered the bar. Assaulting a security officer was not something one could usually get away with. Holloway had weighed the odds and figured as long as he had witnesses watching and a secure video feed recording, he could make it stick. DeLise had too much to lose by retaliating now. Even if he saved it up for later, the video of Holloway accusing him of attempted murder would always be in the ZaraCorp security files, unerasable.

It was actually better than officially accusing DeLise of trying to kill him. This way Holloway didn't have to prove anything. This was as close as Holloway was going to come to having an insurance policy against future murder attempts. It was smartly done. Very smartly done. Holloway glanced up in the direction of the security camera with the intention of saluting jauntily as he left the bar.

The socket for the camera was empty.

Holloway stopped and turned to the bartender.

"Damn thing broke a week ago," the bartender said. "Haven't had time to replace it."

Any other thoughts Holloway might have had on the matter were disrupted by the pool cue DeLise applied to the back of his head. Holloway dropped and was out before he hit the floor.

* * *

"I don't see why you didn't cave in his head in the alley," Holloway heard a voice say.

"Too many witnesses," said another voice, this one belonging to Joe DeLise. "The asshole got that part right. So I had to drag him here."

"You're still going to cave in his head," said the other voice.

"Yes, but now it'll be for resisting," DeLise said. "You'll back me up on that, right?"

The other voice laughed.

Holloway risked opening his eyes and immediately regretted it. The light stabbed at his retinas. He forced himself to keep them open and to focus on his surroundings. Eventually they came clear: He was in the ZaraCorp security holding cell. He'd been there before, on a drunk and disorderly, a couple nights after Isabel left him.

"Your friend is up," a form said, in the distance. Another form walked over to the holding cell and resolved itself into DeLise. DeLise, still in his civilian clothes, smiled at Holloway.

"Hello, Jack," DeLise said. "How are you feeling?"

"Like some jackass hit me when I wasn't looking," Holloway said.

"That happens to you a lot, doesn't it?" DeLise said. "You know, for someone who thinks they're smart, you do some very stupid things. Like not looking up to see if a security camera is actually there."

Holloway closed his eyes. "I'm going to have to give you that one, Joe."

"It's a classic," DeLise said. "I'll be telling my friends about it for years."

"You're not really still planning to cave in my head, are you," Holloway said. "After tonight, too many people know you have motive."

DeLise snorted. "Christ," he said. "People in that bar are so scared of me, they don't even sit on my stool when I'm not there.

Warren tells me that while I was out working at the camp, the place would fill up and my stool would still be open. Shit, Jack. No one there is going to remember anything but that you hit me and I arrested you. Everything else is going to get fuzzy, real fast."

"So why did you do it, Joe?" Holloway asked. He cracked open his eyes again to look at DeLise. "Screw with my skimmer, I mean. You didn't answer that question in the bar. I didn't know you hated me that much."

"Not a lot of people like you, Jack," DeLise said. "Even the people who like you don't like you. And I never liked you."

"That sounds like an admission to me," Holloway said.

"I keep telling you, I have no idea what you're talking about," DeLise said, mildly. "All I know is that you assaulted me, and then I brought you here, and then you got out of hand and I had to put you down. It's not that complicated a story."

"Good," Holloway said. "It means you might be able to keep it straight."

DeLise smiled. "I'm sure going to miss you, Jack," he said.

"You've said that to me before," Holloway said.

"I meant it both times," DeLise said. "Now, you get your rest. We have to make it look good when you resist and I have to drop you."

"Of course," Holloway said.

"Don't worry, Jack," DeLise. "I won't make it hurt too much."

"I appreciate that, Joe," Holloway said. "I really do."

DeLise smiled and walked off. Holloway tried to focus on the fact that he likely had only a few hours of life left, but eventually decided his head hurt too much to think and slipped back into unconsciousness.

Some indefinite time later, Holloway was nudged awake. "Holloway," said a voice he didn't recognize. "Time to get up."

"So I can get beat to death?" Holloway mumbled. "Call me unmotivated."

"You have a concussion, Holloway," the voice said. "It's a bad idea to sleep with one of those."

Holloway lifted an eyelid. The voice he didn't recognize was attached to a man he didn't recognize either. "Who are you?" he asked.

"Well, if everything goes well, I'm the guy who's going to keep you from getting beat to death in a holding cell," the man said. "Now get up, please."

Holloway grimaced and attempted to lift himself off the floor. The man reached down to help him up. "Steady," he said.

"Easy for you to say," Holloway said.

The man smiled, and then turned to the trio of security officers outside the holding cell, one of whom was Joe DeLise, now in uniform.

"I'm taking Mr. Holloway with me," he said. His voice had shifted from friendly to something else entirely. "He needs medical attention."

"He's not going anywhere, Mark," one of the security guards said. Holloway recognized him as Luther Milner, who ran the graveyard shift. "This asshole assaulted a security officer. We have witnesses."

"Uh-huh," the man now known as Mark said. "These would be witnesses at the same bar where the allegedly assaulted officer beats the shit out of anyone who sits on his favorite stool, right? Because anyone in that bar is going to make a credible witness."

"Hey, he hit *me,* Counselor," DeLise said. "Don't be trying to make it the other way around. That's not the way it played out."

"Of course not," Mark the now apparently a lawyer said. "Just like if I hadn't managed to get here in time, Mr. Holloway's neck would have been broken because he was resisting. Isn't that right? Isn't that how this was going to play out?"

"I don't like your tone, Sullivan," DeLise said.

"And *I* don't like that you think it's jolly good fun to beat someone to death in a ZaraCorp holding cell, Mr. DeLise," Mark Sullivan the lawyer said. "I have a problem with it personally, but more to the point I have a problem with it as ZaraCorp's lawyer. I realize you're under the impression you don't have to answer to anyone here, but Zara Twenty-three is still technically Colonial Authority land, and murder is murder. And if a Zara-Corp employee murders someone on ZaraCorp property, well, that doesn't look very good for the company, now, does it? Are you stupid, Mr. DeLise?"

"What?" DeLise said.

"I said, 'Are you stupid?'" Sullivan said. "It's a simple question. But if you like I can make it simpler. Are you dumb? There."

"Watch it," DeLise said.

"Or what, DeLise?" Sullivan asked, dropping the honorific. He let go of Holloway and got right into DeLise's face. "You thinking of beating me to death, too? Because no one would miss the associate general counsel for an entire goddamned planet, would they? Threaten me ever again, DeLise, and I'll make sure the rest of your life is spent guarding bat shit in a ZaraCorp guano mine. If you don't think I can do it, piss in my direction *one more time.* Do it."

DeLise said nothing. Sullivan stepped back to Holloway.

"I really like you," Holloway said, to Sullivan.

"Shut up," Sullivan said back. Holloway smiled.

Sullivan returned his attention to DeLise. "Now, Mr. DeLise," he said. "I asked you a question: Are you stupid?"

"No," DeLise growled.

"Really," Sullivan said. "Because you could have fooled me.

Because, as I'm sure you know, Mr. Holloway here has recently discovered the single largest sunstone find in the history of the known universe. Possibly worth more than a trillion credits, of which his cut is going to be several billion credits. You know this?"

"Yes," DeLise said.

"Good. Now tell me, Mr. DeLise, what do you think will happen when Mr. Holloway suddenly shows up dead *in a ZaraCorp security holding cell*? Is anyone anywhere in the known universe going to believe an idiot security guard's story that he was *resisting*? Or is the Colonial Authority going to open up a full investigation, prying into all of ZaraCorp's businesses here, looking for other examples of corporate intimidation and assassination? Are the Colonials going to halt exploitation of the sunstone seam while it conducts its investigation, costing millions to the corporation?

"Are Mr. Holloway's heirs and assigns going to blithely stand by during all of this, or are they going to sue for wrongful death, adding millions to the billions they already stand to inherit? And are *you*, Mr. DeLise, going to end up doing anything other than spending the rest of your life in a two-and-a-half-by-three-meter prison cell once ZaraCorp decides the easiest way to make this all go away is to pin it all on you? Tell me *again* you're not stupid, Mr. DeLise. I would really like to hear it."

DeLise, entirely cowed now, turned his gaze away.

Sullivan glared at all three security officers. "I need to make this crystal clear. You need to understand this and you need to make sure every other security officer understands this as well. There is one person on Zara Twenty-three *you cannot touch,* and it is Mr. Holloway. He is worth too goddamn much. If *anything* happens to him, the Colonial Authority will be here, and it will shove microscopes as far into our collective asses as they will go.

Your job from this moment on is to make sure he stays alive and happy. And, Mr. DeLise, if that means *you* spend the rest of your time here being punched in the face by Mr. Holloway every time he sees you, then what you'll do is smile and ask if you can have another. Do you understand me?"

"Yes, sir," DeLise said in a tone that Holloway suspected he hadn't used since he was eight years old. The other two officers nodded.

"Good," Sullivan said, and looked back to DeLise. "Now tell Mr. Holloway you're sorry."

"What?" DeLise said, genuinely shocked.

"You tried to stave in the back of his head with a pool cue, as I understand it," Sullivan said. "That needs an apology. Do it. Now."

Holloway watched DeLise's face and wondered if it really was possible to induce a stroke. As amusing as that was, Holloway suspected Sullivan might have taken things one step too far for DeLise's little cow brain. "It's all right," Holloway said. "In fact, I should be the one apologizing to Joe. Let's just say I went out celebrating at another bar and had a little too much fight in me and Joe had to bring me back down to earth. No harm, no foul. Let's forget it."

Sullivan looked at Holloway, figuring out what he was doing and why. "Fine with me," he said, after a minute. "Fine with you, Mr. DeLise?"

"Fine," DeLise said, looking squarely at Holloway with a look that suggested the two of them should never ever be alone in a room together. That was all right with Holloway.

"Fine," Sullivan said again. "Then I think we're done here. I'm taking Mr. Holloway with me. Unless there are any additional objections?"

There were none.

"You are damn good," Holloway said, when they were outside the security offices. "I can see why Isabel likes you."

"Glad you think so," Sullivan said. "Because we're never doing that again. Our mutual friend just burned through a lot of her personal credit getting me to save your ass back there. I was happy to do it, because I think you know how I feel about her."

"I do," Holloway said.

"If you have a problem with that, I need you to tell me now," Sullivan said. "I don't like surprises."

Holloway shrugged. "I screwed up with Isabel," he said. "She's not the sort who lets you screw up with her twice. You're good."

"Good," Sullivan said. "Like I said, happy to help her, and to help you. But that's a onetime event. You assaulted a security officer. And not just any security officer. One that gets his kicks being an asshole with a badge. That's just dumb. You screw up again like that, Holloway, and you're on your own. I hope I'm making myself clear."

"You are," Holloway said. "You're right. I was dumb. I won't do it again. Or at least I won't expect you or Isabel to bail me out if I do."

"Fair enough," Sullivan said. He looked Holloway up and down. "How do you feel?"

"Like I got my head bashed in," Holloway said.

"There's a reason for that," Sullivan said. "Right, then. First, hospital, to get that concussion checked. Then you can borrow my couch for the rest of the night. Where's your skimmer?"

"With Louis Ng," Holloway said, naming Aubreytown's mechanic. "He's banging out some dents and restringing my EREs. It'll be ready tomorrow around noon."

"You have an accident?" Sullivan asked.

"I'll tell you about it later," Holloway said. "Hey, did you really mean it that if anything happened to me that the Colonial Authority would look into it?"

"If you died in ZaraCorp security custody?" Sullivan said. "That's a given. If you wrapped your skimmer around a tree, probably not. But there's no reason for *them* to know that." Sullivan motioned back toward the security office. "They certainly seem to have it in for you."

"Not all of them," Holloway said.

"DeLise for sure," Sullivan said.

"Yeah," Holloway said. "Thanks for saving my ass. I owe you. You're going to have to wait until they start mining those sunstones for me to repay you, though. I'm spending most of my money on fixing my skimmer."

"You can repay me by giving me a lift," Sullivan said. "When Isabel got me out looking for you, she said to have you bring me back with you. She says there's something she wants to talk to me about in my capacity as ZaraCorp's counsel. I have no idea what that's about. Do you?"

"I might," Holloway said. He rubbed his head and felt a new headache coming on.

Chapter Thirteen

D o you mind if I ask you a personal question?" Sullivan asked Holloway.

Holloway glanced back at Sullivan, who was sitting on a side bench in the skimmer. It was not well designed for extra passengers; the side bench sat two, and not terribly comfortably. Sullivan didn't complain.

"You kept me from being beaten to death," Holloway said, turning forward again to watch the endless jungle pass under the skimmer, on its way back to his treetop compound. "That rates a couple of honest answers."

"How did you get disbarred?" Sullivan asked.

Holloway snorted in surprise. "Okay, I wasn't expecting that," he said. "I thought you were going to ask me what happened with Isabel and me."

"I heard that story from her already," Sullivan said. "Her version of it, anyway. But she says you wouldn't talk about the disbarment."

"It's not hard to find the details," Holloway said. "It got written up in the newsfeeds. I don't talk about it because it was a case of me being stupid."

"When you sell it like that, I definitely want to hear about it," Sullivan said.

Holloway sighed and hit the autopilot, then swiveled around to face Sullivan. "Clearly, you know I was lawyer," he said.

"Clearly," Sullivan said.

"Actually I was a lawyer like you," Holloway said. "I worked for a corporation. Alestria."

Sullivan furrowed his brow, searching his brain for the company data. "Pharmaceutical company," he said, finally.

"Right. Founded by a bunch of crunchy types committed to saving the Amazonian rain forest by using botanicals to create medicines," Holloway said. "But that never panned out, so they went back to the old-fashioned way, synthesizing drugs in a lab. So, about twelve years ago, they get approval for their drug Thantose."

Sullivan's eyes widened. "I remember that," he said.

Holloway nodded; very few people wouldn't remember Thantose. It had been marketed as a safe sleeping and anxiety aid for children, specifically tailored to compensate for the neurochemical differences between children's brains and those of adults. It had sold well until an Alestria executive farmed out the production of the drug to a Tajik vendor, in the guise of slashing costs and helping a developing economy but in point of fact because the executive received a quite sizable kickback from the vendor.

The Tajik vendor then cut costs of its own, cutting two of the three active chemicals in the drug with cheaper but pharmacologically inert isomers, which changed the relative strengths of the chemicals, and thus the effects of the drug. Two hundred children died; another six hundred went to sleep and their brains never woke up.

"Did you work on the class action suit?" Sullivan asked.

Holloway shook his head. "I worked on the criminal cases against the executive. Jonas Stern. He was up for criminally negligent homicide and Alestria for corporate manslaughter. Stern had his own lawyer for the homicide counts, but I was attached for the corporate manslaughter charges. The cases were combined and being heard by the same jury."

"So what did you do on the case to get disbarred?" Sullivan asked. "Did you tamper with the jury? Bribe the judge?"

"I punched Stern," Holloway said.

"Where?" Sullivan asked.

"In the face," Holloway said.

"No," Sullivan said. "I mean, did you punch him while the two of you were in court?"

"Yup," Holloway said. "In front of judge, jury, cocounsel, and a couple dozen reporters."

Sullivan looked at Holloway, uncomprehending. "Can I ask why?" he asked finally.

"Well, if you ask the North Carolina Bar, it was because the case was going badly for the defense and I was trying to force a mistrial by attacking Stern, thus intolerably prejudicing the jury," Holloway said.

"Did you get a mistrial?" Sullivan asked.

"There *was* a mistrial," Holloway said. "Of course. But I didn't *get* the mistrial, because that's not why I punched him."

"Then why did you do it?" Sullivan asked.

"Because he was a smug, heartless asshole," Holloway said. "We were in court listening to testimony from parents who had given their kids our product, which killed them because Stern was too busy lining his pockets to worry about what our production line was doing. These parents were in the dock bawling their eyes out, and I'm sitting next to Stern, and he's grinning and chuckling about it all, like the parents are trying out for roles in a soap opera, and he's judging whether or not they get the part. I finally couldn't take it anymore. So I tapped him on the shoulder and then I broke his nose."

"That was dumb," Sullivan said.

"It was dumb," Holloway agreed. "But it felt really good."

"Just like punching DeLise was dumb, too," Sullivan said.

"That also felt great at the time," Holloway said.

"I would suggest to you that punching people is no way to go through life, however," Sullivan said. "Since the first incident led to you being disbarred and the second led to you almost getting killed. It has a poor record of long-term success for you."

"Point taken," Holloway said. "In any event, there was a mistrial, I was fired and then disbarred, and then I was told by the North Carolina AG that I had a choice between being arraigned for jury tampering or leaving the planet. And here I am."

"Whatever happened to Stern?" Sullivan asked.

"He was shot on the steps of the courthouse during the retrial," Holloway said. "A grandfather of one of the dead kids. He got told earlier in the day by his doctor that he had Stage Four lung cancer. He went home, got his gun, shot Stern between the eyes, and then surrendered to the cops right there on the steps. Local community took up a collection for his bail, and the DA dragged her feet long enough for Grandpa to die at home."

Sullivan shook his head. "Doesn't make it right. Any more than what you did," he said.

"I suppose not," Holloway said. He turned back to the skimmer controls to make sure they hadn't wandered off course; they hadn't. "But sometimes it feels good to do the wrong thing."

"Would that include telling that inquiry that Isabel was lying when she told them about you teaching your dog to blow things up?" Sullivan asked.

"Oh, that," Holloway said. "*Now* you're going to bring up what happened between me and Isabel."

"I'm just trying to get it all clear in my head," Sullivan said.

"I don't claim any high-minded purpose for that," Holloway said. "It was something that would have gotten my surveying contract canceled, and I couldn't have that. You'll recall I'm not really allowed to go back to North Carolina. It's not like I had any place else to go. I knew when I did it that it was the end of me and Isabel. She's not the sort of person to forget something like that. But I didn't feel I had much of an alternative."

"She still likes you," Sullivan said.

"She likes me as much as she thinks I deserve," Holloway said. "She likes my dog more."

"The dog didn't lie about her during an inquiry," Sullivan said.

"They never called the dog to testify," Holloway said.

"You're an interesting person, Jack," Sullivan said. "I wish I could figure out what you were thinking when you punched Stern and when you turned on Isabel."

"Well, I think that's the thing," Holloway said. "I think it's clear that sometimes I just don't think."

"I think you do," Sullivan said. "It's just you think about you first. The 'not thinking' part comes right after that. When it's time to deal with the consequences."

Holloway glanced back again. "You know what, Mark," he said. "If it's all the same to you, I'd really like you to come up with another topic of conversation now."

∙ ∙ ∙ ∙

Holloway introduced Sullivan to Carl and the Fuzzy Family when they landed; he had briefed the lawyer as they flew in so he wouldn't be too surprised. Sullivan acquitted himself well with the introduction to the creatures and then turned to Isabel. Holloway politely looked the other way as Sullivan and Isabel kissed their welcomes but noticed that the Fuzzy Family did not. They gawked openly at this previously unknown form of human interaction.

Sullivan noticed as well. "I haven't had that big an audience for a kiss since I was king of the prom," he said. He bent down to get a better look at the creatures. They crowded around him, equally curious. Carl, who had seen rather more humans than the Fuzzys, went to greet his master.

Isabel looked over at Holloway. "You survived," she said.

"Thanks to Mark here," Holloway said, petting his dog. "Thank you for passing along the message."

"You didn't think I wouldn't," Isabel said.

"No," Holloway said. "It's been long enough since we broke up."

Isabel laughed at that.

By this time Baby Fuzzy had managed to cuddle up to Sullivan. "They are awfully cute, aren't they?" he said, petting Baby. "This one in particular. She reminds me of a cat I had."

"Actually she's not a 'she,' " Isabel said.

"Really?" Sullivan said.

"Really?" Holloway said.

"Yes, really," Isabel said. "That's what you get for assuming patriarchy."

"You were calling Baby 'she' the last time I checked," Holloway said.

"That's what I get for assuming *you* checked these things, Jack," Isabel said. "But I should have known better."

"Thanks," Holloway said.

"You're welcome, but I didn't mean it like that," Isabel said. "Other advanced animal life on this planet reproduces sexually, but there's only one sex. The creatures produce haploid sex cells that can fertilize other cells but also have cloacal cavities where young can grow, either as eggs or live young, depending on the species."

"So they're hermaphrodites," Sullivan said.

"No," Isabel said, and then caught Sullivan's confused look. "If this were Earth, you would say that, because there are two sexes there. But animals on this planet never developed male–female differentiation. There has always been only one sex. Life here is unisexual." She turned her gaze back to Holloway. "And I *knew* that, which is why I say I should have known better, Jack."

"So you're sure our fuzzy friends are all 'its,' then," Jack said.

"Pretty sure," Isabel said. "Their sexual organs are similar to those of other large creatures."

"How do you know?" Holloway said.

"Quite obviously because I checked," Isabel said.

"Oh, *ick*," Holloway said.

"You would have made a shit biologist, Jack," Isabel said.

"I have to side with Jack here," Sullivan said. "That *is* pretty disturbing."

"Thank you, Mark," Holloway said.

Isabel looked at the two of them sourly. "Are you two done?" she said.

"So are these all clones, then?" Sullivan asked, setting Baby down and looking at the rest of the Fuzzys. "Because they don't look alike."

"They're not clones," Isabel said. "If they're like other creatures here, their haploid cells have a protein coat that is different for each individual. The haploid cells won't fuse with other cells that feature the same protein coat. The only way you get clones is in situations of environmental stress, when the body chemistry changes to create haploid cells without the protein coat. But that's very rare."

"Now you're just showing off," Holloway said.

Isabel stuck her tongue out. "I wrote a paper on it," she said. "If I recall, Jack, you once said you read it."

"I probably did," Holloway said. "It doesn't mean I *understood* it."

Isabel snorted and then motioned to the Fuzzys, who by this time had gotten bored and had walked off to do their own things. "It does settle one thing: The fuzzys are definitely of this planet. They have the same gross morphology as other vertebrate animals here, and they seem well adapted to their environment. I wasn't really doubting whether they were native, but it's good to have some biological evidence. I have genetic samples, which I'll need to check back in the lab to confirm. Once I have that, I'm ready to move forward."

"Oh, boy," Holloway said. "Here we go again."

"Move forward on what?" Sullivan said, looking at Isabel and then at Holloway.

"Your girlfriend has it in her head that our little fuzzy friends are people," Holloway said.

"People?" Sullivan said. He turned back to Isabel.

"Yes," Isabel said.

"As in *people* people, not just 'I think of my pets as people' people," Sullivan said.

"Is it that hard to believe?" Isabel asked.

"A bit," Sullivan said. "They're cute and friendly and seem pretty smart, and I already want to get one for my niece back in Arizona. But that doesn't make them people."

"Thank you again, Mark," Holloway said.

"Clearly this is a bone of contention between you two," Sullivan said, looking at Isabel but nodding in the direction of Holloway.

"It is," Isabel said, to Sullivan. "But unlike Jack here, I have something more to go on than the desire not to have the fuzzys get in the way of his payday. While he's been off doing whatever he's been doing—"

"Almost getting eaten by zararaptors," Holloway interrupted.

"—I have been spending time with the fuzzys and watching how they live their lives, recording them and taking notes," Isabel said. "I've been here a week now. It's not a huge amount of time, but it's long enough to know there is no way these creatures are not sentient." She turned to Holloway. "You almost got eaten by zararaptors?"

"Yeah," Holloway said.

"Why didn't you say something?" Isabel said.

"By the time I called you, I was no longer in danger of being consumed," Holloway said. "And I needed you to be worried about what I was going to do instead of what I had done."

"You still should have told me," Isabel said.

"You're not my girlfriend anymore," Holloway said.

"As a *friend*," Isabel said.

"Is this going to go somewhere?" Sullivan said. "Because as fascinating as the interpersonal relationship between the two of you is, I'd like to get back to this thing about these creatures maybe being people. I mean, that *is* why you had me come out here, Isabel, right?"

"Sorry," Isabel said. "Jack brings that out in me."

"I've noticed he brings that out in a lot of people," Sullivan said. "Noted. Let's table it for now."

"All right, fine," Isabel said, and shot one more glance at Holloway.

In spite of himself, Holloway had to admire how Sullivan was able to get Isabel back on track. It was one thing Holloway had never been able to do. Whenever he inevitably pissed her off, he ended up making it worse by trying to make it better. The two of them had been at loggerheads enough at the end that there was a constant state of irritation between them. Holloway should have been smart enough to navigate the arguments— he'd been a trial lawyer, and a damn fine one, until he popped Stern in the snout—but there was something about Isabel that just made him want to argue. It was not a great way to have a relationship.

"Wait," Holloway said. Isabel and Sullivan glanced back over to him. "Isabel, you're right," he said. "I should have told you. As a friend. I'm sorry."

Holloway could see the various sarcastic responses of amazement that he had actually apologized for something and *meant* it bubble up behind Isabel's eyes—and then stop there.

"Thank you, Jack," is what she actually said. He nodded.

"The fuzzys?" Sullivan asked, prompting.

"Why don't we go into the cabin," Isabel said. "We'll all sit down and have a beer and I'll run you some of my recordings and notes, and you can both decide for yourself whether what I have to show you is convincing enough."

"Drinks and a show," Holloway said. "I'm all for that. Hell, I'll even buy."

• • •

Isabel spent two hours showing Holloway and Sullivan excerpts of her recordings, showing them the various activities that, she was convinced, showed sentient intelligence, above and beyond mere animal intelligence. From time to time, while they were watching, one fuzzy or another would climb up and watch the recordings as well, only to leave a few minutes later. The creatures had gotten jaded about seeing themselves on the infopanel.

The video portion of the presentation done, Isabel called up her notes, cross-referencing the behavior of the fuzzys with behavior of human, Urai, and Negad sentients. Isabel was a good and careful scientist, and her work was checked, double-checked, footnoted, and referenced. By the end of the presentation, and despite himself, Holloway was almost convinced his little fuzzys were people, too.

"It seems thin," Sullivan said, after Isabel was done.

"What?" Isabel said, disbelieving.

"I think you heard me, Isabel," Sullivan said, not unkindly. "It seems thin to me."

"You have a strange definition of *thin,* then," Isabel said.

"Actually, my definition of *thin* is very precise in this case," Sullivan said. "The reason I think it's thin is because these things don't speak. If they're not speaking to each other—and to us—then you've got a hard sell to make."

"Jesus, you sound like Jack," Isabel said. Holloway smiled wryly at this. "Speech is only one criterion for sentience. *Cheng versus BlueSky* listed several others as well."

"I know that," Sullivan said. "But while I'm a general counsel and not an expert on xenosapient law, I do know this: In the mind of the layman—which will include any judge this case would go in front of—the ability to speak is a prohibitive indicator of sentience. It's not only prohibitive, it's very nearly prejudicial."

Isabel looked at Sullivan sourly. "You're telling me that if the fuzzys meet every single other criterion for sentience under *Cheng,* that it won't matter simply because they don't speak."

"What I'm saying," Sullivan said, "is that to date, we have not discovered a confirmed sentient species that doesn't speak. There are things humans do that Urai don't. There are things Urai do that Negad don't. Things Negad do humans don't. And so on. What we *all* do, Isabel, is speak."

"It doesn't mean it's not possible," Isabel said.

"No," Sullivan said. "It's possible. But your problem here, Isabel, and no offense, is that you're thinking like a biologist, and not a lawyer."

Isabel smirked. "I don't really see it as a problem."

"Normally it's not," Sullivan said. "But this is going to be decided in court, not in a lab. And you have to remember this: If your friends here are sentient, then ZaraCorp loses its charter here. That's trillions of credits in mineral losses, including the sunstone seam Jack just found. ZaraCorp's revenues, profits, and stock price will take a huge hit. None of this matters to you, but it matters to ZaraCorp. So if you go and file a Suspected Sapience Report without having evidence that these little guys can speak, the one thing all other sentient species do, I guarantee you that ZaraCorp's lawyers will zero in on the fact and ride it all the way home."

"I would," Holloway said.

"And so would I," Sullivan said.

"But you won't," Isabel said.

"Wouldn't I?" Sullivan said. "I represent ZaraCorp, Isabel. Not you or these fuzzys here. If Janice Meyer tells me to argue the case, I'm required to do it."

"Lovely," Isabel said, turning away from her boyfriend.

"Not that it would happen," Sullivan said. "Because, come on, Isabel. A sentience case is the sort of thing lawyers live to argue, on either side. I know Janice sure as hell doesn't want to be general counsel on Zara Twenty-three forever. She'd hit me with a skimmer if I were in her way to try this one. But the reason you asked me out here was to get my perspective on this, right? This is my perspective: If you file an SSR now, you're going to get crushed."

"So you think I should just keep quiet about the fuzzys," Isabel said. "Like Jack."

"I never said keep quiet," Holloway said. "I said be absolutely sure."

"I *am* absolutely sure," Isabel shot back. "But what I'm hearing is that being absolutely sure isn't good enough. And by the time I have enough evidence to convince anyone else, ZaraCorp will have this planet entirely mined out. So I might as well just shut up."

"Actually, you can't do that now," Sullivan said.

"What?" Holloway got that out before Isabel did.

"Colonial Authority law requires that any evidence of sentience must be reported by its chartered E and E corporations as soon as it's discovered," Sullivan said. "And now that you've spoken to me, a duly recognized legal representative of ZaraCorp, I'm obliged by law and by company regulation to report it to my superiors."

"You never said anything about that before," Isabel said.

"You didn't tell me what you wanted me to come out here for," Sullivan pointed out. "And besides that, think a minute, Isabel. You asked me to come out in my capacity as a lawyer. I haven't stopped being ZaraCorp's lawyer, any more than you've stopped being ZaraCorp's biologist."

"But you just said that if I file an SSR, I'm going to lose," Isabel said. "The fuzzys will lose."

"Not to mention every bit of work here will shut right down," Holloway said.

Sullivan smiled and held up his hand. "Everyone take a deep breath," he said. "Isabel, there's still a way for the fuzzys' sentience to get a hearing without them or you getting squashed. And Jack, there's a way to make it happen without initially putting your royalties at risk."

Isabel and Holloway looked at each other. "Well?" Holloway said, to Sullivan. "Are you going to tell us?"

"I was actually enjoying the dramatic pause," Sullivan said.

"Don't be a jackass, Mark," Isabel said.

"Fine," Sullivan said. He put down his hand. "You'll note I said that the E and E corporation is obliged to report any evidence of sentience. That means that the report comes from ZaraCorp, not from you or me."

"Okay," Isabel said. "So what?"

"So what it means is that this allows ZaraCorp to have a process for making the report," Sullivan said. "You could file an SSR directly, but as Jack so eagerly points out, it's hugely disruptive. So what we do instead is ask for an inquiry on evidence of sapience instead. The inquiry is essentially the company asking for a ruling to decide if the evidence it has supports filing an SSR. The ruling can decide for filing, against filing, or for further study."

"What does that last one mean?" Holloway asked.

"It means that the judge orders the evidence examined by Colonial Authority experts on xenosapience, and while they study the issue, the E and E corporation is allowed to do business as usual," Sullivan said. "It's the 'everybody wins' scenario."

"Everybody does *not* win," Isabel said. "Anything the company takes out of the planet isn't there for the fuzzys to use later."

"The Colonial Authority requires the company to put a certain amount of the revenue of the planet in escrow pending resolution of the study," Sullivan said. "Just in case."

"How much?" Isabel asked.

"Ten percent," Sullivan said.

"Ten percent!" Isabel exclaimed. "That's ridiculous."

"It's better than nothing, which is what they'll get if you go straight for an SSR right now," Sullivan said.

"Not that I really want to raise objections to this, but Zara-Corp running an inquiry on whether or not ZaraCorp should stop exploiting a planet seems chock-full of conflict of interest," Holloway said.

"The inquiry is presided over by a Colonial Authority judge for that very reason," Sullivan said. "Which means the ruling has the force of law. So if the judge decides ZaraCorp has to file an SSR, the company has two weeks to file, and two weeks after that to bring all exploitation to a halt pending a ruling."

"So what we're aiming for here is a 'needs more study' ruling," Holloway said.

"*We're* not aiming for anything," Sullivan said. "That's up to the judge. But like I said, I think a 'needs more study' ruling is the one where everyone here wins. Isabel, you win because not having evidence of the fuzzys speaking isn't as problematic as it would be with a full SSR court case. At least xenosapient experts would come to make a determination one way or another. Jack, you win because one way or another, you'll get paid. Maybe you won't get billions out of the sunstone seam, but you'll get millions, and I think you can live with that."

"Probably," Holloway said.

"ZaraCorp wins because it does everything by the book, so no one anywhere can object," Sullivan said. "Even if it does have to abandon Zara Twenty-three, the company has time to build the news into its stock price. No huge fluctuations, no major panics, and no surprises, which corporations hate most of all. And as for the fuzzys—"

All three humans looked over at the fuzzys. Four of them were napping on the floor. The fifth, Pinto, had climbed up on the work desk and was leaning over the edge. Suddenly the fuzzy squeaked and flung itself off the desk, landing directly on Grandpa Fuzzy's head. Grandpa Fuzzy (who Holloway realized was not actually a grandpa at all, but it really was too late to change names now) let out a surprised grunt and then went after Pinto, smacking the younger fuzzy in the head as they ran about. Carl, thrilled that something was going on, gave chase as well. Three seconds later all the fuzzys were running about like idiots, slapping each other like it was a scene out of a fur-bearing slapstick.

"—at least they'll get a chance to prove they're people," Sullivan finished. He waved in the direction of the Fuzzys. "Although I've got to tell you, Isabel, this is not exactly convincing me you've got a bunch of geniuses here."

"Well," Isabel said, mildly, "I think you're underestimating the crack comedy timing involved."

"I don't think so," Sullivan said.

"I have to agree with Isabel," Holloway said. "This is better than the Three Stooges."

"Fair point," Sullivan said.

"The three who?" Isabel asked.

The men looked at her with a mixture of horror and pity.

On the floor of the cabin, the Fuzzys and Carl collapsed in exhaustion.

sabel and Sullivan returned to Aubreytown later that evening, Sullivan jammed uncomfortably into the skimmer's small passenger seat, which he shared with Isabel's samples, notes, and remaining supplies. Holloway saw them off and noticed the Fuzzy Family did not seem horribly put out at their leaving. Either the creatures were not terribly sentimental or they simply were of the "out of sight, out of mind" variety. Carl seemed depressed Isabel was gone, however, and moped about. Not even Pinto tugging on his ears or Baby snuggling up to him cheered him up.

Three days later Holloway received a secure, confirmation-required notice that he was expected to appear at an inquiry in Aubreytown in eight days, to give testimony concerning the "fuzzys." Holloway smiled. Isabel had indeed wasted no time getting the ball rolling.

A few minutes after he had received his summons, Chad Bourne was on the line. "You're trying to get me fired, aren't you," he said, without preamble, when Holloway slapped open the voice-only circuit.

"Hello to you, too," Holloway said. He was having his morning coffee. Papa Fuzzy, who Holloway knew was not in fact a papa, was sniffing curiously at the stuff in his cup.

"Cut the crap, Holloway," Bourne said. "Why didn't you tell me about these things?"

"You're referring to the fuzzys," Holloway said.

"Yes," Bourne said.

"Why would I tell you about them?" Holloway said. "Do you want detailed reports on every animal I encounter? I live in a jungle, you know."

"I don't want reports on every single animal, no," Bourne said. "However, a report on animals that might get all of us kicked off the planet because they're this world's equivalent of cavemen might be nice."

"They're not cavemen," Holloway said. "They live in trees. Or did, until they colonized my house." Holloway pushed the cup toward Papa, to let the fuzzy try the beverage.

"Jack Holloway, master of the absolutely irrelevant objection," Bourne said.

"And anyway, they're not people, which is why I didn't bother telling you about them," Holloway said. "They're just very clever little animals."

"Our staff biologist thinks otherwise," Bourne said. "And no offense, Jack, but it's possible she knows more about the subject than you."

"Your staff biologist is very excited about a major discovery," Holloway said, watching Papa sniff the coffee in greater detail. "And while she's a biologist, she's not actually an expert in xenosapience. Her having an opinion about whether the fuzzys are people is like a podiatrist having an opinion on whether you need your liver replaced."

"Wheaton Aubrey doesn't seem to have the same opinion,"

Bourne said. "And you didn't just have the future chairman of ZaraCorp stalking into your cubicle and screaming at you for ten minutes because one of your surveyors didn't bother to tell you about discovering sentient life. I was already on his shit list for giving you point-four percent. Now I think I'm on his list of people to have assassinated."

"Trust me, Chad," Holloway said. "They're not sentient." Papa ducked its head and took a hesitant sip of the coffee.

"Are you sure about that?" Bourne asked.

Papa spit out the coffee and fixed Holloway with a look that said, *There's something wrong with you.*

"Yeah," Holloway said. "I'm pretty sure about that." He picked up his coffee and took another sip.

"I want to come out and see these things for myself," Bourne said.

"What?" Holloway said. "No way."

"Why not?" Bourne asked.

"Well, for one thing, Chad, unless you've been holding out on me, you're not an expert in either biology or xenosapience," Holloway said. "Which means you're just coming out to stare at the things. I'm not running a zoo here. For another thing, I don't really want to spend that much time with you."

"I can certainly appreciate that, Jack, but you don't have much choice in the matter," Bourne said. "Per your contract, as your ZaraCorp contractor rep I am allowed and in some circumstances even *required* to perform an on-site inspection to make sure your equipment and practices conform to ZaraCorp regulations. So, guess what, I'm coming out. I'll be there in about six hours."

"Lovely," Holloway said.

"I'm as excited as you are," Bourne said. "Trust me." He broke the connection.

Holloway gazed down at Papa Fuzzy. "If I knew you were

going to be this much trouble, I would have let Carl eat you that day."

Papa Fuzzy stared back up at Holloway, unimpressed.

• • •

Bourne didn't come alone.

"If he steps out of that skimmer I'm throwing him over the side," Holloway said, pointing at Joe DeLise, who sat in the front passenger seat of the four-seat skimmer that had just landed at Holloway's compound.

Wheaton Aubrey VII, stepping out of the back passenger compartment with Brad Landon, was taken aback. "Is there a problem?" he asked.

"Yes," Holloway said. "I hate his guts."

"I don't think you like anyone in this skimmer, Holloway," Aubrey said. "It's not in itself a good enough reason to keep Mr. DeLise in his seat. I brought him because by company regulation I'm supposed to have a security detail when I leave Aubreytown. The board is touchy about me going into the wilds alone."

"I don't give a shit," Holloway said.

"It's very hot to be sitting inside a closed skimmer," Landon said.

"So crack a window and give him a bowl of water," Holloway said. "If he puts a foot on my property, I'm parting his hair with a shotgun."

"You're adding murder to your résumé, Mr. Holloway?" Landon asked.

"It's not murder if he's a trespasser on private property and he refuses to leave when told to," Holloway said.

"He's a ZaraCorp security officer, on a planet administrated by the company," Aubrey said.

"Then he can show me his search warrant," Holloway said.

"If he doesn't have one, he's trespassing. And so are you and Landon, now I think about it. The only one with an actual invitation to be here is Chad."

"So you're going to shoot all of us, then," Aubrey said.

"Tempting, but no," Holloway said. "Just him. If you don't think I won't, by all means have him get out of the skimmer."

Aubrey looked over to Bourne, who had stepped out of the front driver's side of the skimmer. "I have no idea what this is about," Bourne said.

DeLise did nothing but glare through all of this.

"Leave him your key fob," Aubrey said, finally, to Bourne. "That way he can run the air conditioner." Aubrey turned to Holloway. "All right? Or do you have any other unreasonable demands?"

"Is there a reason you're here, Aubrey?" Holloway asked. He pointed at Bourne. "I know why he's here; he wants a day at the petting zoo. What do you want?"

"Perhaps I'm curious about the creatures myself," Aubrey said. "I might lose a fortune to them. I think I should at least get a chance to see them."

"Sorry," Holloway said. "They're not here right now."

"You didn't keep them here?" Bourne said. "You knew we were coming."

"I knew *you* were coming," Holloway said. "I wasn't expecting an entourage. And no, I didn't keep them here, Chad. They're not my pets, they're wild animals. They come and go when they please. After the first couple of days they started going back out into the trees. I imagine they're doing whatever it is they did before I met them. Just like I come and go when I please, doing what I did before *I* met them."

"When will they be back?" Bourne asked.

"Let me reiterate the part about them being wild animals,"

Holloway said. "It's not like they leave me their day planner when they go."

"Then maybe we can talk about something else," Aubrey said.

"What else is there to talk about?" Holloway asked.

"Do you mind if we go inside to discuss it?" Aubrey said. "Because at this point I find it ironic that the only person sitting in air-conditioning is the guy you apparently want to kill."

Holloway glanced at DeLise, who was still glowering. "Fine," he said. "Come on."

Inside the cabin, Carl greeted Bourne, whom he knew and liked, while Holloway discreetly repositioned his desktop security camera so it had a better angle on the outside world and Bourne's skimmer, and tilted the hat so the camera could see outside.

"So this is the famous explosives-detonating dog," Aubrey said, petting Carl.

"Alleged," Holloway said. "Not proven." He turned back to his guests and sat down at his desk.

"Of course," Aubrey said.

"What do you want to talk about," Holloway said.

Aubrey glanced over to Landon. "We have concerns about this upcoming inquiry into the sapience of these animals you've found," Landon said.

"I would imagine," Holloway said.

"We understand you've been called to testify at the inquiry," Landon said.

"That's right," Holloway said.

"We're wondering what you're planning to say," Landon said.

"I have no idea," Holloway said. "I don't know what the judge is going to ask me."

"I would imagine that the judge would ask you to corroborate the report that Miss Wangai has submitted," Landon said.

"That's possible," Holloway said.

"And will you?" Landon asked.

Holloway looked at the three men in his cabin. "I think we can skip the preliminaries here," he said. "If they ask if I saw the things Isabel saw, then I'm going to say yes. Because I did. It doesn't mean I agree with her that the fuzzys are people. If you're thinking of trying to convince me not to agree with Isabel's conclusions, you don't have to worry about that. I don't. What's more, Isabel knows I don't. So you don't have to bribe me to say it."

"That's not good enough," Aubrey said.

"It's pretty damn good," Holloway said.

"Not really," Aubrey said. "She's a biologist. You're a surveyor. Her opinion counts for more than yours."

"So what?" Holloway said. "I live with the damn things. Her opinion might be worth more than mine, but mine will be good enough to keep the judge from ordering ZaraCorp to submit an SSR right off. The worst-case scenario here is that the judge orders more study. If you play that right, that gets you two or three years right there before there's any final decision on the fuzzys' sapience. More than enough time to exploit that sunstone seam."

"I understand you're focused on the sunstone seam, Holloway," Aubrey said. "But there's more at stake than your half a percent. This planet is unusually heavy with metals and minerals, even beyond sunstones. It's why there are sunstones in the first place. It's the richest planet in ZaraCorp's E and E territories. If we lose this planet, it puts ZaraCorp in a vulnerable position."

"Why are you telling me this?" Holloway said. "There's no reason I need to know any of that. It's not *my* problem, outside the very limited issue of the sunstone seam."

"I'm telling you so you *understand,* Holloway," Aubrey said. "Because it could *become* your problem, if you want."

Holloway looked over to Landon. "I'm guessing that's your cue to speak."

Landon smiled. He opened the folder he was carrying and walked the few steps to Holloway to hand him a paper document from inside it. Holloway examined the document. "It's a map," he said.

"Do you know what it's a map of?" Landon asked.

"Yes," Holloway said. "It's a map of the northeast continent."

"It's a map of the one continent on Zara Twenty-three that ZaraCorp has not begun exploiting," Landon said. "We only this last month received the go-ahead from the Colonial Authority to work the continent."

"Okay," Holloway said. "So?"

"So it's yours," Aubrey said.

"Excuse me?" Holloway said.

"Zarathustra Corporation is initiating a pilot program in which a single surveyor will be responsible for the exploration and exploitation of a continent," Landon said. "This surveyor can handle the job however he wants, probably by operating exactly how ZaraCorp currently does in dealing with its surveyors. The difference is that the head surveyor will receive five percent of the exploitation revenues for his administration of the continent."

"Minus operating costs and whatever percentage he allows his own contractors, of course," Aubrey said.

"Yes," Landon said. "So call it four-point-seven-five percent."

Holloway grinned. "I suppose this means you're not kicking me off the planet at the end of my contract," he said.

"It would appear not," Landon allowed. "If you agree."

"And you're keeping this from looking like a completely transparent bribe to me how?" Holloway asked.

"Because it reduces the amount of staffing ZaraCorp has to

have on planet, which saves us money," Landon said. "And also because the five percent contracting fee is tax-deductible."

"ZaraCorp already pays almost nothing in taxes," Holloway said.

"Call it insurance," Aubrey said.

Holloway hooked a thumb at Bourne. "So I become a multibillionaire by doing *his* job," he said.

"On a somewhat larger scale," Landon said. "But, yes. Best of all, you can staff out the whole job. You don't even need to be on planet. You can be back home on Earth, watching the revenues by the pool."

"What do I have to do for all of this?" Holloway asked.

"Destroy Miss Wangai's credibility," Aubrey said.

"That's not going to be easy," Holloway said, after a minute. "Not to mention it will look really bad for you to give me a continent after this."

"Give us credit for subtlety, Mr. Holloway," Landon said. "We will wait an appropriate amount of time before we make the announcement. And Miss Wangai will not be punished in the slightest for asking for the inquiry, which by law she was required to ask for. Indeed, she will be promoted to head up one of our labs back on Earth."

"Which is to say, kicked upstairs, far away from here and the fuzzys," Holloway said.

"You'll do something good for her career for once," Aubrey said. "She'll get kicked upstairs, you'll get kicked upstairs, even Bourne here will get kicked upstairs."

Holloway looked at Bourne. "Really," he said.

"Well, sort of," Aubrey said. "We told him he could work for you. Figured you'd be motivated to take care of him."

"I suppose I would be," Holloway said. Bourne, for his part, looked thoroughly miserable, as he had through the entire conversation. He knew he was being used as cover for Aubrey's trip out to Holloway's compound, and knew what happened to little people caught in the middle of big people's plans. Holloway almost pitied him. "So that takes cares of the humans," he said. "What about the fuzzys?"

Aubrey shrugged. "If they're important to you, take them with you to the continent," he said. "Give them their own reservation. Whatever. ZaraCorp will even chip in for a 'save the fuzzys' fund. Make us look good to the folks back home. Just as long as no one gets the idea these things are people."

"Isabel has video of the fuzzys," Holloway said. "Secure and unmodifiable video, showing them doing things she believes indicate sentience."

"You taught your dog to blow up things, Mr. Holloway," Landon said.

"It's not the same thing," Holloway said, seeing where Landon was going and echoing Isabel's arguments to him. "And if you're suggesting I say Isabel taught the fuzzys tricks to perpetrate a hoax, I'm curious how you think you're then going to be able to turn around and promote her."

"She didn't train the fuzzys, you did," Landon said. "Admit to the judge that you trained the animals to do these things before Miss Wangai arrived. We're not disputing the animals are smart. You could easily have taught them how to do these things. Say that you perpetrated an innocent hoax. As a prank. She was taken in and filed a request for an inquiry before you could come clean. That way she's completely blameless, and you just look like you were playing a mean but innocent joke."

"It'll make me look like an asshole," Holloway said.

"Everyone thinks you're an asshole anyway, Holloway," Aubrey said. "No offense."

"None taken," Holloway said.

"Besides, for the amount of money we're talking about, you can afford to be an asshole," Aubrey said.

"Well, when you put it that way," Holloway said.

"Mr. Holloway, this is a very serious offer," Landon said. "There's too much at stake here. This inquiry has to end with the judge ruling against our filing an SSR. Every other option is failure. You have the power to get the right ruling here for everyone."

"Sure," Holloway said. "And all I have to do is make Isabel look like a fool."

"Not to put too fine a point on it, Holloway, but you've done that before, haven't you?" Landon said, nodding at Bourne. "Mr. Bourne here tells us that you sold her out before during an inquiry. She said you taught your dog to blow things up. You called her a liar. You didn't have a problem with it then, when the only thing at stake was your surveyor contract. Now that you have the potential to become one of the richest men in the universe, you might have some extra motivation."

"I suppose I might," Holloway said.

"Good," Aubrey said. "Then we have a deal."

"I have to emphasize, Mr. Holloway, that we were never here," Landon said.

"Of course not," Holloway said. "Only your cover man Bourne was here, and he just came out to see the animals."

"We understand each other fully," Landon said.

"Oh, we do," Holloway said. "We really do."

Chapter Fifteen

When his guests had left, Holloway reached over for his infopanel and punched up the feed from the security camera. If any of the three men who had been in the house had seen the camera, they didn't note it, which was just as well since Holloway planned it that way. There was a reason he kept the hat on the camera stand.

For the first several minutes the video showed nothing but the skimmer with Joe DeLise in it, fiddling with the dash buttons and the key fob and generally looking bored. Holloway fast-forwarded through this and then slowed down the feed when something popped up on the hood of the skimmer. Holloway zoomed in; it was Pinto, the rambunctious fuzzy.

Pinto walked over to the windshield of the skimmer, clearly curious about the human inside. The human inside appeared to view the fuzzy sourly. Pinto pressed its little face against the glass to get a better look at DeLise. DeLise smacked the inside of the glass with his hand.

Pinto drew back, startled, but then seemed to realize that the human smacking the glass was not any sort of trouble for it.

Pinto smooshed its face up to the glass again. DeLise smacked the glass again. This time Pinto didn't move. DeLise smacked the glass a third time, and again. Holloway zoomed in on DeLise's face; he was yelling. The skimmer was too far away to pick up the words, and the microphone had been muted in any event.

Holloway frowned at this. He'd had the security camera on DeLise, but having an audio record of what was said in the cabin would have been useful insurance. He must have accidentally hit the microphone's mute button when he moved it to get a better angle on the outside. Nothing for it now.

Holloway zoomed out again to see Pinto, back away from the glass now, watching the yelling DeLise with interest, perhaps wondering why the human didn't get out of the skimmer and try to catch it or hurt it. After a few minutes, after DeLise calmed down, the fuzzy moved up to the glass again. DeLise was resolutely ignoring the little creature.

Pinto turned around, squatted, and very deliberately rubbed its ass on the glass, right in front of DeLise's face.

DeLise exploded into rage, leaning back into his seat to kick up at the windshield. Apparently only DeLise's absolute certainty that Holloway would blow his head off with a shotgun kept him in the skimmer. Otherwise Pinto would have been dead meat at this point.

Holloway tracked back the video to watch this part again, a huge grin on his face.

Moving forward again, Pinto looked up, as if calling to someone or something. Sure enough, a minute later another fuzzy showed up on the hood of the skimmer: Grandpa. The two of them stood on the hood as if they were holding a conference on something, and then Pinto rubbed its butt on the windshield again, prompting another kick against the glass from DeLise.

Grandpa Fuzzy, clearly not impressed, whacked Pinto across

the head and pulled the smaller fuzzy off the glass, then pushed it off the hood. Pinto took off for the nearest spikewood. Grandpa then turned and looked back at DeLise, walking up to the glass to do so. DeLise spat and fumed.

After several moments of this the fuzzy appeared to reach a decision, squatted, and rubbed its own ass against the glass. Then it slowly walked off the hood of the skimmer as if it were taking a Sunday stroll. Holloway laughed out loud, alarming Carl.

Holloway fast-forwarded past several minutes of DeLise doing nothing, then stopped again when the security guard's three fellow travelers returned to the skimmer. At the sight of them, DeLise opened the front passenger door and risked taking a step out of the skimmer to stand up and start yelling at them as they approached. This was followed by a minute or two of DeLise gesticulating and pointing toward the spikewood Pinto and then Grandpa had climbed up when they departed. Aubrey and Landon briefly walked over to glance up at the spikewood, as if to look for the creatures. Then they returned to the skimmer and the vehicle lifted off, going out of frame several meters above Holloway's platform.

Note to self: Give Pinto and Grandpa a beer the next time you see them, Holloway thought. He wouldn't actually give them a beer; he tried giving a little to Papa and Mama Fuzzy once, just to see how they liked it, and they had both spit it out. Fuzzys liked water, preferably from the running faucet, which still fascinated them, and fruit juice. Every other liquid they gave a pass. But in this case, it would be the thought that counted. Anyone who didn't like DeLise was all right by Holloway at this point, regardless of species.

Anyone, said a voice in his head that sounded suspiciously like Isabel.

Holloway shook it off. Yes, *anyone,* but that didn't mean the fuzzys were sentient. Carl was someone, too, but that didn't make him the equivalent of a human. It was entirely possible to think of an animal as a someone—as a person—without attributing to them the sort of brainpower that accompanies actual sentience.

Holloway glanced down at his dog, splayed out on the floor. "Hey, Carl," he said. Carl's eyebrows perked up; well, one of them did, anyway, giving the animal a rather unintentionally sardonic look.

"Carl, speak!" Holloway said. Carl did nothing but look at Holloway. Holloway never taught him the "speak" trick. The idea of having a dog intentionally bark its head off for no particular reason never appealed to him.

"Good dog, Carl," he said. "Way to not speak." Carl snuffled noncommittally and then closed his eyes to get back to sleep.

Carl was a good dog and good company and not a sentient creature in any standard that would matter to the Colonial Authority. Neither were chimpanzees or dolphins or squids or floaters or blue dawgs or wetsels or punchfish or any other number of creatures who were clearly more clever than the average animal species and yet still not quite there. In over two hundred worlds explored, only two creatures matched up to human sentience: the Urai and Negad, both of whom shared enough common examples of big-brained activities that it would have been impossible not to ascribe them the sentience humans had.

Well, no, not impossible, some pedantic part of his brain reminded him. In both cases, there was a substantial minority of the exploration and exploitation industry community who argued against their sentience. Both Uraill and Nega (formerly Zara III and BlueSky VI) were rich enough in resources that it was worth their time to take a stab at it, particularly in the case of the Negad, whose civilization at time of contact was roughly equivalent to the hunter-gatherer tribes of the North American continent around 10,000 B.C. Pointing out to E & E lawyers that by their standards they would deny sentience to some of their direct ancestors didn't seem to bother them any. Lawyers are trained to disregard such irrelevancies. The Negad didn't read, didn't have cities, and only arguably had agriculture. Three strikes and they were out, as far as the E & Es and their lawyers were concerned.

Holloway picked up his infopanel again and backed up the video feed once more to watch Pinto and Grandpa. If the E & Es would argue against the Negad, they would have a field day with the fuzzys. No cities, literacy, or agriculture here, either, as well as no language, no tools, no clothing, and apparently no social structure beyond the family unit—or something close enough to it given their weird unisexual biology that it was a distinction without difference.

It would be better for them not to be sentient, Holloway thought. Just because they were sentient wouldn't be a guarantee they'd be recognized as such. Not when so many people had such a vested interest in them not being so. Better to be a monkey and not be able to understand what's been taken from you, than to be a man and be able to understand all too well—and be helpless to stop it.

Carl scrambled up from the floor and headed to the cabin door, tail wagging. He poked his snout at the dog door, swinging it out slightly. It was caught by something, which held it open, and Carl backed away.

A second later the Fuzzy Family made its way through, back from whatever small, furry adventure they had been having with their day. Each of them greeted Carl with a pat or a rub, with the exception of Baby, who wrapped itself around Carl's neck for a hug. Carl tolerated this well, and gave Baby a lick when it disentangled itself from him.

Papa Fuzzy walked over to Holloway and stared up at him in that way Holloway knew was the fuzzy telling him it required his assistance. Holloway, thus reminded of his role as fuzzy butler, grinned and followed the creature into the kitchen area, where Papa stopped at the cooler. Holloway, who knew the fuzzy was capable of opening the cooler if it chose, appreciated that it was asking permission. He opened the cooler.

"Well, go on," Holloway said, motioning. The fuzzy dived in and a few seconds later hauled out the very last of the smoked turkey.

"I don't think you want that," Holloway said. "It's on the verge of going bad." He took the turkey from the fuzzy, fished out the last two remaining turkey pieces, and held them up for Carl, who was passionately interested. "Sit," he said to Carl, who sat with an altogether enthusiastic thump. Holloway tossed the turkey to Carl, who snapped it out of the air and swallowed it in about a third of a second.

Papa watched this and then turned to Holloway and squeaked. Holloway assumed the squeak to mean *I'm sorry, but I must kill you now.*

Holloway held up his hand. "Wait," he said, and went into the cooler, pulling out a second package. "My friend," he said, holding out the package to the fuzzy, "I think it's time to introduce you to a little something we humans call 'bacon.'"

Papa looked at the package doubtfully.

"Trust me," Holloway said. He closed the cooler and went looking for a frying pan.

Five minutes later, the smell of bacon had attracted all the Fuzzys and Carl, who stared up at the cabin's tiny stove with rapt attention. At one point Pinto attempted to climb up to snatch some semi-cooked bacon out of the pan; it was pulled down by

Mama and handed over to Grandpa, who smacked the younger fuzzy across the head. Head-smacking was apparently Grandpa's major mode of communication with Pinto.

Soon enough, six strips of bacon were cooked and sufficiently cooled for consumption. Holloway handed each excited fuzzy a bacon strip and kept the last one for himself. Carl, sensing the abject injustice of a situation in which everyone had bacon but him, whined piteously.

"Next batch, buddy," Holloway promised. He peeled off the next batch of strips and turned to place them into the pan. He turned around again to see how the Fuzzys were enjoying their cured, nitrated treat, and saw Papa Fuzzy holding out a piece of its bacon to a very attentive Carl. Papa squeaked. Carl sat. Holloway smiled at the fact that Papa Fuzzy was trying to copy what he'd done with the turkey.

Papa opened its mouth again. Carl instantly lay down. Papa opened its mouth a third time and Carl rolled onto his back, tongue lolling out. Papa tossed the bacon piece to Carl, who gobbled it up greedily. Then it continued to enjoy the rest of its treat.

A spatter of bacon grease on Holloway's arm brought his attention back to the fact that he was still actually cooking food. He finished up the second round of bacon, distributing it equally among the Fuzzys and Carl, each of whom was delighted at the second serving; bacon had now clearly replaced smoked turkey as the king of all meats, at least for the Fuzzys. Holloway put the rest of the uncooked bacon into the cooler, cleaned and stowed the pan, and then walked back over to his desk and picked up his infopanel.

When Isabel departed, she had left Holloway a set of her videos and notes concerning the fuzzys, partly as a courtesy and partly for archival purposes. If anything happened to her set of data, his set would probably still be fine. Holloway accessed the data now, calling up video files in particular. He fiddled with them, changing some of the presentation parameters.

He did this for the next several hours.

Chapter Sixteen

This is how the inquiry works," Sullivan said to Holloway. The two of them were standing outside Aubreytown's single, and cramped, courtroom. "The judge enters and makes a few prefatory statements. Then there's a presentation of the materials. Isabel is handling that. It's mostly pro forma because the judge already has all of Isabel's records and recordings, but if she wants to ask Isabel questions about any of it, this is when she'll do it. Then a representative from ZaraCorp will question the experts, which in this case are Isabel and you. The judge can also ask questions during this period. At the end of it, the judge will issue a ruling."

Holloway frowned. "So ZaraCorp gets to question me and Isabel. Who's representing us?"

"No one's representing you. It's an inquiry, not a trial," Sullivan said.

"There's an official legal ruling issued at the end of it," Holloway said. "Sounds like a trial to me."

"But you're not accused of a crime, Jack," Sullivan said. "You and Isabel are like witnesses, not defendants."

"Right," Holloway said. "It's the fuzzys who are the defendants."

"In a manner of speaking," Sullivan said.

"So who's representing *them*?" Holloway asked.

Sullivan sighed. "Just promise me you won't antagonize the judge," he said.

"I swear to you that I am not here to antagonize the judge," Holloway said.

"Good," Sullivan said.

"So what is your role in this inquiry?" Holloway asked.

"I have no role," Sullivan said. "I recused myself because it involves Isabel, and my boss was fine with that. I told you she was hot for this inquiry. She thinks it's her ticket off this rock. And look, here she comes now." Sullivan nodded down the hallway of the Aubreytown administrative building, where Janice Meyer was striding toward the two of them and the courtroom. Behind her, a young assistant was carrying her case files.

"What's she like?" Holloway asked.

"What do you mean?" Sullivan said.

"As a human being," Holloway said.

"I haven't the slightest idea," Sullivan said, murmuring now that his boss had gotten close up.

She stopped in front of the two men. "Mark," she said, by way of greeting, and then looked at Holloway. "And Mr. Holloway. Good to see you again." She held out her hand; Holloway took it and shook.

"Interesting new species you've found," Meyer said.

"They are full of surprises," Holloway said.

"Has Mark here explained to you how today's inquiry is going to work?" Meyer asked.

"He has," Holloway said.

"It's not a trial," Meyer said. "So remember that there's no need to feel hesitant about answering the questions I'm going to ask you."

"I promise to tell the whole truth," Holloway said. Meyer smiled at this, which made Holloway wonder if she knew anything about Aubrey's secret trip out to his compound. She turned to Sullivan, nodded, and entered the courtroom, assistant trailing behind.

"As a boss, she's ambitious," Sullivan concluded.

"It's not bad for you," Holloway said. "Ambitious bosses leave vacant jobs behind them."

"True enough," Sullivan said, and then smiled broadly as he saw another person down the hall: Isabel. She smiled in return and when she came up to Sullivan, gave him a warm but publicly decorous kiss on the cheek. She turned to Holloway.

He held out his hand. "Jack Holloway," he said. "I'm your fellow expert witness."

"Very cute, Jack," Isabel said, and gave him a peck on the cheek. "Are you nervous about this?"

"No," Holloway said. "Are you?"

"I'm terrified," Isabel said. "What I tell the judge here could mean the fuzzys are recognized as people. I don't want to screw it up. I don't think I've been this nervous since my doctoral defense."

"Well, that turned out all right, didn't it?" Holloway said. "So you have a track record."

"When did you get in?" Isabel asked.

"Carl and I landed about an hour ago," Holloway said.

"Where's Carl?" Isabel asked.

"He's in the skimmer," Holloway said. "Relax," he added, catching Isabel's expression. "The skimmer has autonomous climate control. He's cool as a cucumber. You can see him after the inquiry just to be sure."

"Speaking of which," Sullivan said, "it's time for the two of you to get in there. This thing starts in a few minutes, and Judge Soltan isn't the sort to be kept waiting."

• • •

Judge Nedra Soltan came in and took her seat without preamble; there was no bailiff to announce her arrival or to tell everyone to stand. By the time everyone had stood up, Soltan had already sat down.

"Let's get through this as quickly as possible," Soltan said, and then looked at her inquiry timetable. "Dr. Wangai?"

"Yes, Your Honor?" Isabel stood. Holloway sat next to her, at the table generally reserved for the defense. Janice Meyer and her assistant sat at the table usually reserved for the prosecution. *Not a trial my ass,* Holloway thought. The audience portion of the courtroom was empty save for Brad Landon, in the back row, whose expression was one of polite boredom, and Sullivan, who sat directly behind Isabel.

"Our schedule calls for you to give an overview of the research materials," Soltan said.

"Yes, Your Honor," Isabel said.

"Is there anything new that you're going to add to the materials that wasn't in the package you sent to me?" Soltan asked. "Because if there's not, I'd just as soon skip it."

Isabel blinked at this. "Skip it?" she said. She glanced over at the large monitor that had been brought in for her presentation.

"Yes," Soltan said. "Your report was comprehensive to the point of exhausting, Dr. Wangai. If all we're going to do here is get a recap, I'd rather not."

"The point of the presentation was to give you time to ask any questions you might have on the material," Isabel said. "I'm sure you have questions."

"Not really, no," Soltan said, blandly. "So, shall we move forward?"

Isabel glanced over at Holloway, who arched his eyebrows an infinitesimally small amount, and then back at Sullivan, who was utterly blank. "I suppose," she said finally, turning back to Soltan.

"Good," Soltan said. She looked over at Meyer. "That's fine with you as well, Ms. Meyer?"

"Not a problem, Your Honor," Meyer said.

"Excellent," Soltan said. "Two hours off the schedule already. We may be out of here before lunch. You may sit, Dr. Wangai."

Isabel sat, looking a little numb.

"Now—" Soltan picked up her schedule again. "—Ms. Meyer, I believe it's time for you to question the experts. Which would you like to question first?"

"I believe Dr. Wangai is the first on the schedule," Meyer said.

"Very well," Soltan said. "Dr. Wangai, go ahead and sit in the witness stand." Isabel got up from the table, walked over to the witness stand, and sat down. "Normally I'd place you under oath, but this is an inquiry and thus more informal," Soltan said. "You are however still required to tell the truth and to answer questions as fully as possible. Do you understand?"

"I do," Isabel said.

"You're on," Soltan said to Meyer.

Meyer stood. "Dr. Wangai, please state your full name and occupation."

"I am Dr. Isabel Njeru Wangai, and I am the Zarathustra Corporation's chief biologist for Zara Twenty-three," Isabel said.

"And where did you receive your doctorate, Dr. Wangai?" Meyer asked.

"The University of Oxford," Isabel said.

"I hear that's a good school," Meyer said.

Isabel smiled. "It's all right," she said.

"And so you studied xenosapience there," Meyer said.

"No," Isabel said. "My research there focused on the sarco-monad Cercozoa."

"You've lost me," Meyer said.

"They're protists," Isabel said. "Very small one-celled organ-isms."

"What planet are these protists from?" Meyer asked.

"They're from Earth," Isabel said.

"So your training in biology, while from a very good school indeed, is grounded in terrestrial biology—creatures from Earth. Is that accurate?" Meyer asked.

"It is," Isabel said. "But I have been chief biologist here on Zara Twenty-three for close to five years now. I have a substantial amount of practical experience working with and studying extra-terrestrial biology."

"Any of it relating specifically to xenosapience?" Meyer asked.

"Not until recently, no," Isabel said.

"So you're new to the field," Meyer said. "Very new."

"Yes," Isabel said. "However, the evaluation I performed on the fuzzys was done using criteria well established in the xenosa-pience field. The criteria are designed to be useful without re-gard to experience."

"Do you really believe that?" Meyer asked. "As a scientist, do you really believe that people who are not trained in a particular field are as able to make assessments as experts in that field? Especially when all they are armed with is a checklist?"

"I am however not anyone," Isabel said. "I am a trained biol-ogist with years of practical experience in xenobiological study."

"So experience does matter," Meyer said. "Even so, Dr. Wangai. I don't doubt your experience and knowledge in your particular field is considerable, but I have to wonder if your assessing these creatures for xenosapience isn't like a podiatrist advising a patient on whether his liver needs to be replaced."

Holloway shifted in his chair suddenly; he recognized the analogy as his own. When Chad Bourne showed up with Aubrey and the others in tow, Holloway assumed as a matter of course that his conversation with Bourne had been listened in on. Having his own words used to smack Isabel around, however, was a signal to Holloway that this inquiry had been choreographed top to bottom; it was the very essence of a show trial. The only person who didn't know it was Isabel.

"I don't think your analogy is as accurate as you think it is," Isabel said.

Meyer smiled. "Perhaps not," she said. "Let's move on from that, then. Dr. Wangai, please tell us how you came to learn of the fuzzys."

"Jack Holloway told me about them and gave me a video recording he'd made of one of them," Isabel said. "The video was interesting, but it wasn't secure, so I wanted to be able to see them for myself and to get them on secure video, so there would be no concern of tampering or altering of the data."

"After Mr. Holloway gave you that first recording, how long was it until you went to see the creatures?" Meyer asked.

"Five days in total, I think," Isabel said.

"You said that when Mr. Holloway gave you the first recording, you had concerns about the data being tampered with or altered," Meyer said. "Was there a reason you were concerned about that?"

"That's not an accurate representation of my statement," Isabel said.

"We could have the court reporter play back your statement if you like," Meyer said.

"That's not necessary," Isabel said, the tiniest bit of frustration creeping into her voice. Holloway wondered if anyone but he would notice it there. Sullivan might, he decided. He glanced over to the other man, but his expression was unreadable. "What I meant was that Jack's video was not recorded on a secure device," Isabel continued. "Even if it was genuine—which I did not doubt it was—it would not be something I could use as evidence in, for example, an inquiry like this."

"You called Mr. Holloway 'Jack' just now," Meyer said. "Are you familiar with him?"

"We're friends, yes," Isabel said.

"Have you ever been more than friends?" Meyer asked.

Isabel paused. "I'm not entirely sure that's relevant," she said.

"I'm not entirely sure it is, either," said Soltan.

"I assure you, Your Honor, I'm going somewhere with this," Meyer said.

Soltan pursed her lips for a second, considering. "Fine," she said. "But get where you're going quickly, Ms. Meyer."

Meyer turned back to Isabel. "Dr. Wangai," she prompted.

Isabel looked at Meyer coolly. "We were in a relationship," she said. Her words had become decidedly more clipped, as they did when she was exceptionally pissed off.

"But no longer," Meyer said.

"No," Isabel said. "We broke it off some time ago."

"Any particular reason?" Meyer asked.

"We had different memories of a certain event," Isabel said.

"Would this be a reference to a previous Zarathustra Corporation inquiry, in which you claimed Mr. Holloway had taught his dog to set off explosives, among other things, and Mr. Holloway claimed that you were lying about the account?" Meyer asked.

"Yes," Isabel said.

"Who was lying during that inquiry, Dr. Wangai?" Meyer asked.

"The inquiry's ruling regarding the allegations was 'not proven,'" Isabel said.

"That's not what I'm asking," Meyer said. "I know what the ruling was. I'm asking for your opinion here, and for the record, your answer here will in no way have an effect on your current or future employment with ZaraCorp. So, Dr. Wangai, who was lying in that inquiry?"

"It wasn't me," Isabel said, looking directly at Holloway.

"So, Mr. Holloway lied," Meyer said.

Isabel looked back over at Meyer. "I believe my answer was sufficiently clear," she said.

"Yes," Meyer said. "Yes it was. And it's also true that as a result of this ruling, you received a note in your employment record, correct?"

"You said you were going somewhere with this," Soltan said, interrupting Meyer.

"I'm there," Meyer said. "Dr. Wangai is an excellent scientist who has made a major discovery with these fuzzys, as she calls them. There is no doubt either in her competence in her particular field or in the valuable service she's done for the science of biology in recording and describing these creatures.

"But it's also true she is not trained in xenosapience," Meyer continued. She pointed at Holloway. "It's true that the person from whom she learned about the creatures, Jack Holloway, is a former romantic partner with whom she had a bad breakup. It's true that she believes that Mr. Holloway has lied about her before, in a situation where there was actual professional damage to her career. And finally it's true that we know Mr. Holloway is at least alleged to be able to teach animals how to do relatively complex tricks.

"So: Mr. Holloway discovers these very clever little animals and decides to share the discovery with his former girlfriend. When she gets excited about them, Mr. Holloway decides to have a little fun and teaches them a few tricks which *to the untrained observer* look like evidence of sapience. It takes Dr. Wangai several days to get to Mr. Holloway's home; he has time to train these creatures. She arrives and she gets gulled. Simple as that."

Soltan frowned at this. "You're suggesting this entire thing is nothing more than Mr. Holloway's malicious attempt to damage an ex-girlfriend's professional reputation, Ms. Meyer."

"I don't think you have to ascribe actual maliciousness to Mr. Holloway," Meyer said. "Dr. Wangai calls him a friend now. It's possible that Mr. Holloway was simply trying to have a little bit of fun with someone he knew would already be excited by the discovery of a major new species."

Soltan gazed over at Holloway; this made him uncomfortable. "It doesn't strike me as a particularly amusing joke," the judge said.

"Perhaps not," Meyer said. "But it's a better theory than professional sabotage. Or at least a nicer one."

Soltan turned to Isabel. "Dr. Wangai," she said. "Is it possible that Mr. Holloway tricked you?"

"No," Isabel said.

"Why is that?" Soltan asked. "Because you're too competent to be fooled or because Mr. Holloway wouldn't do such a thing?"

"Both," Isabel said.

"It's been established that your training isn't in xenosapience," Soltan said. "It's also been established that you believe that not only has Mr. Holloway lied to you, he's lied *about* you during an official inquiry."

Isabel said nothing to this, and stared again at Holloway.

"If I may," Meyer said, after it became clear Isabel wasn't going to answer. "The note added to Dr. Wangai's file is of some relevance."

"Go on," Soltan said, to Meyer.

"Dr. Wangai," Meyer said, gently. "Do you remember what the note that was added to your employment record states?"

"Yes," Isabel said. Her voice had a note of resignation Holloway hadn't ever heard in it before.

"What does it say, Dr. Wangai?" Meyer asked.

"It says that my judgment might be impaired due to close or romantic relationships," Isabel said.

Meyer nodded and looked over to Soltan. "I have no other questions for this expert," she said. Soltan nodded and told Isabel that she could step down.

Holloway found it hard to look at Isabel as she walked back to the table. Meyer's line of questioning was nothing at all about the fuzzys and everything about her: her competence, her professional ability, her personal judgment, and her relationships with others. She had been made to look like a fool in all of them.

Isabel sat in her chair and looked straight ahead, pointedly not looking at Holloway. Sullivan reached over and put his hand on her shoulder, to comfort her. Isabel took it and held it, but didn't look back at him. She kept staring forward, with a look on her face. Holloway knew what the look meant. It meant that Isabel, finally, understood what all the other players knew: that this inquiry didn't really matter. The decision about the fuzzys had already been made, and these were just the motions they had to go through to get there.

Isabel knew that she had been demolished up there on the stand. Holloway knew that his role in the play was to deliver the coup de grâce.

Chapter Seventeen

When Judge Soltan called his name, Holloway got up from the defense table and installed himself at the witness stand. The judge reminded him that he would have to speak the truth. Holloway looked into the courtroom at Brad Landon, and said he would. Landon gave him an almost imperceptible nod.

Isabel followed Holloway's gaze and saw Landon. She turned back to Holloway, her expression unreadable.

"Mr. Holloway, please state your full name and occupation," Janice Meyer said to Holloway.

"I'm Jack Holloway, and I've been a contract surveyor and prospector here on Zara Twenty-three for over eight years," he said.

"How long have you known Dr. Wangai?" Meyer asked.

"I met her briefly when she arrived on Zara Twenty-three," Holloway said. "I made better acquaintance of her a year later, when she and I were guests at Chad Bourne's annual holiday party for the surveyors he represents. We started a relationship several months after that, which lasted for about two years, at which point we broke up for reasons already noted today."

"What is your current relationship with Dr. Wangai?" Meyer asked.

Holloway looked at Isabel, whose expression now was blank. "We're friends, but I have things to apologize for," he said.

Meyer nodded. "Now, you discovered these creatures that you and Dr. Wangai call 'fuzzys' recently, is that correct?"

"About a month ago now, yes," Holloway said. "One of them got into my cabin."

"And Dr. Wangai has spent how much time with them during this period?" Meyer asked.

"She spent about a week studying them at my compound," Holloway said.

"It doesn't seem like a very large amount of time," Meyer observed. "Especially to make a determination that these creatures are sapient."

"Isabel's a scientist and believes she knows what to look for," Holloway said. "I suspect she believes she observed enough to know, otherwise she wouldn't make the claim."

"Do you support her claim?" Meyer asked.

"Isabel is aware that she and I have had differing opinions on the matter," Holloway said, "and the last time we spoke about it, I repeated that I did not believe the fuzzys were sentient."

"Why do you think you two have such a difference of opinion?" Meyer asked.

"You mean, aside from the fact that I discovered a sunstone seam that will be worth billions of credits to me so long as the fuzzys are determined not to be sentient," Holloway said.

Meyer blinked at this. "I think we're all aware you're a Zara-Corp contractor," she said.

"Well, besides that, I had observed the fuzzys longer than Isabel had," Holloway said. "And while I am not a scientist and can speak only as a self-interested layman, the fuzzys initially struck me as nothing more than clever animals, like monkeys or perhaps the universe's smartest cats."

"Are they smart enough to be trained?" Meyer asked.

"I don't think there's any doubt about that," Holloway said. "I've trained my dog to do all sorts of tricks, and each of the fuzzys is smarter than my dog."

"Smart enough to learn enough tricks that could fool a biologist?" Meyer asked.

"If the biologist in this case was not an expert on xenosapience, and if her own excitement about the discovery kept her from observing certain obvious things, sure," Holloway said.

"You're suggesting Dr. Wangai was not observant," Meyer prompted.

"She was observant, but I know there were some lapses," Holloway said.

"That's not an accusation to be made lightly against Zara Twenty-three's chief biologist," Meyer said.

"I'll give you an example," Holloway said. "After I met the fuzzys, I assigned them gender roles, based on certain assumptions I made: Males would be aggressive and boisterous, females nurturing and sweet. So I called them Papa Fuzzy and Mama Fuzzy and so on. For several days, Isabel assumed that the fuzzys were actually male and female, even though as the planet's biologist, she knew that most animals on the planet didn't have genders like they do back on Earth. She admitted to me that she initially assumed the fuzzys were male and female because I had told her so, and she assumed I had checked."

"That's a pretty substantial lapse in observation," Meyer said.

"I don't suppose you have any evidence of this aside from your word on it."

Holloway pointed past Isabel. "Mr. Sullivan over there heard her say it," he said. "To be clear, Isabel did figure it out eventually. It just took a few days."

"Because you told her otherwise," Meyer said.

"Yes," Holloway said. "I didn't intend to mislead Isabel; it was just my own assumption. It was innocent. But I did end up misleading her."

"No one's blaming you for intentionally causing damage to Dr. Wangai's professional standing," Meyer assured him. "But, Mr. Holloway, is there possibly another way you misled Dr. Wangai? Not by what you told her, but by what you *didn't* tell her?"

Holloway looked uncomfortable. "Yes," he said, finally. "I suppose I did. And up here now, I'm quite embarrassed about it. I wish I didn't have to admit to it."

"You *do* have to admit to it, Mr. Holloway," said Judge Soltan.

"I know," Holloway said. "Of course. I think it would be easier to explain, however, if I could use the monitor Isabel set up to give you her briefing. Would that be all right?"

"How long will this take?" Soltan asked.

"I will be as brief as I possibly can," Holloway said. "Trust me, I want to get this over as quickly as you do."

"All right," Soltan said.

Holloway pointed to the defense table. "There's data that I need on the infopanel."

"You may leave the witness stand, but you are still providing testimony and must tell the truth," Soltan said.

"I understand," Holloway said. He stood up, exited the stand, and walked over to the defense table, where his infopanel lay. He ignored it and went to Isabel, who couldn't stand to look at him.

"Isabel," he said.

"Please don't talk to the other expert at this time, Mr. Holloway," Soltan said.

"I'm sorry, Your Honor," Holloway said. "But I don't need the data on my infopanel. I need the data on hers."

"I don't understand," Soltan said.

"Nor do I," Meyer said.

"The data in Isabel's infopanel is secure video, taken with cameras and recorders designed for scientific and legal verifiability," Holloway said. "I am well aware that my own truth on the stand has been challenged, not the least by Isabel here. I want to be sure everyone can believe what I'm going to say, and that I haven't tampered with the evidence I'm going to show you."

Soltan nodded. "Dr. Wangai, please give Mr. Holloway your infopanel," she said.

Isabel handed over the machine.

"Thank you," Holloway said. "Are all your video records accessible?"

"I'm signed in," Isabel said, tightly. She was avoiding saying any more to Holloway than she absolutely needed to.

"Did you change the file names of the videos?" Holloway asked.

"No," Isabel said.

"Okay," Holloway said. "Thanks." Isabel didn't respond. Holloway glanced over to Sullivan, whose own expression didn't appear to be particularly friendly. He too had figured out the show trial nature of the inquiry.

Holloway tapped the infopanel and opened a pipe between it and the monitor. The monitor flicked on and awaited input.

"We've already established that Dr. Wangai, despite her considerable competence and talent as a scientist, does sometimes allow her assumptions to overrule her skills as an observer and her knowledge of this planet's faunasphere," Holloway said. His voice had become animated and precise; it was the voice Holloway used as a trial lawyer. Both Soltan and Meyer jumped a little at the change in tone. Holloway noted that but didn't let the notation show on his face. "Taking my word for the fuzzys being gendered is the obvious example. But there's another one that she missed."

Holloway tapped the panel again, and a video played out on it: an image of Papa, Mama, and Grandpa Fuzzy sitting together in a semicircle, eating bindi fruit.

"As we all know, one of the major signifiers for sapience is the capacity for speech. Per the *Cheng* ruling, this means 'meaningful communication that conveys more than the immediate and presently imminent.' To date, three species are known to communicate at a level that satisfies *Cheng*: humans, Urai, and Negad. It is what each of these species have in common.

"But there is another thing that humans, Urai, and Negad also share in common: Their speech is vocalized, and the vocalization for each falls within a range that is perceivable by the human ear. In fact, it's the humans who have the greatest range of frequencies in their speech, while the Negad have the least. The point is, we can *hear* when humans, Urai, and Negad are speaking."

Holloway paused the video. "A couple of weeks ago I was visiting the new camp ZaraCorp is building to exploit the sunstone seam I discovered. While I was there, I was shown these large speakers posted around the fence line. They were blasting sound at an incredibly high decibel level in order to scare away the zararaptors and other large predators of the jungle—but while I could *feel* the speakers pounding away, I couldn't hear them, because they were emitting their sound at twenty-five kilohertz. That's higher than human hearing can register."

"I'm waiting to hear relevance, Mr. Holloway," Soltan said.

"Exactly," Holloway said. "You're waiting to hear relevance, but you can't, because you're listening too low. We all have been. The loudspeakers on the fence line work because the predators of Zara Twenty-three hear higher frequencies than we do. And they hear higher frequencies not for some random reason, but because it makes evolutionary sense for them to do so. Say, because their prey and other small animals make sounds in that range."

Holloway reset the video and popped up a settings overlay on top of it. "One of the nice things about the research-level camera Dr. Wangai used to record the fuzzys is that unlike most commercial cameras, it records data humans don't perceive on their own," he said. "For example, in addition to recording the visible color spectrum, it records into the infrared and ultraviolet frequencies. You have to use filters to see these data, of course, but the data are there. It also records sounds above and below human hearing. You have to use filters for them, too."

Holloway flipped through the overlay's menus and reset the video's audio filters to bring sounds above human hearing range into audibility. He started the video again.

It was the same image of Papa, Mama, and Grandpa Fuzzy sitting in a semicircle. Only now it sounded as if they were talking to each other.

"Look," Holloway said, quietly, and pointed. "Look how they wait their turn to speak. Look how they respond to whatever the other is saying." He turned up the volume of the monitor; the chittering between the fuzzys got louder. "You can hear the structure of the language."

After a few more moments Holloway paused the video, closed it, and pulled up another one, this one of Grandpa Fuzzy and Pinto. Now beside the head-smacking was a constant stream of noise from Grandpa, interrupted occasionally by a squeak from Pinto. The squeak sounded, of all things, petulant.

Pause, close, open another video. In this one Mama Fuzzy was grooming Baby Fuzzy. The noises coming from Mama Fuzzy in this one were different from the noises in the other videos: softer, more sibilant.

"My god," Isabel said. "Mama's *singing*."

In the video Baby Fuzzy added its voice to Mama Fuzzy's, the two creatures joined in harmony. Everyone watched and listened to the video for a moment.

Then Holloway paused the video and looked over to Isabel. "I'm sorry, Dr. Wangai," he said, walking to her. "But this is yet another case of your observational skills failing you. You knew, I presume, that Zara Twenty-three creatures could hear above the human hearing range, which implies quite strongly that they or other creatures make noises above that range as well. Yet, just as you let my assertion of the fuzzys' genders get past you, so you also worked from the implicit assumption that speech for the fuzzys would be like speech for any other sentient species—something you could hear. And thus, the most important part of your argument for the fuzzys' sentience—their ability to speak—went unheard and unobserved."

Holloway held out Isabel's infopanel to her. She took it, shaking.

Holloway turned to Meyer, who was looking at him with the same expression she might have if he had stripped naked right there in the courtroom. "And this is how I misled Isabel, Ms. Meyer, Your Honor," he said, turning briefly to nod in the direction of the similarly shocked-looking Judge Soltan. "I mentioned that the last time I spoke to her I told her I didn't believe the fuzzys were sentient, because I didn't. But then I saw one of the fuzzys make my dog sit and lie down and roll over—vocal commands. I couldn't hear them, but I remembered that other animals here heard higher frequencies, just like my dog could. So I went back through the data and found the fuzzys had been speaking all along.

"I misled Isabel by not telling her this," Holloway said. "And thus by making her think that I disagreed with her about the sentience of the fuzzys, when in fact over the last few days I have become completely convinced of it. They speak, Ms. Meyer, Your Honor. They speak and discuss and argue and sing. That's not a trick you can fake, no matter how clever an animal you are, or how clever you, as a human, might be with training animals. These aren't just animals. These are people.

"And Dr. Wangai," Holloway said, turning to Isabel again, "I was wrong. I was wrong to keep this information from you, and for allowing you to enter into this inquiry without all the facts you needed to defend your assertion, and for allowing anyone to cast doubt on your reputation. It was wrong. I was wrong for ever doing it or for ever allowing it. I am sorry."

Holloway turned away from Isabel and sat back down in the witness stand.

"I'm done with my presentation," he said, to the judge.

Chapter Eighteen

This proves nothing," Meyer said, once she had gained enough composure to begin again.

"It proves that we can't immediately discount the idea that the fuzzys have speech," Holloway said. "That's something. It's something fairly big."

"You could very well have taught them to make these sounds," Meyer said.

"Are you suggesting that I created a hoax so byzantine that it includes teaching animals to speak something no one could hear?" Holloway said. "To what end, Ms. Meyer? If it was a trick to fool Isabel, then it failed, because she didn't know of it until just a couple minutes ago."

"It's a hoax to put the Zarathustra Company in an uncomfortable financial position," Meyer said.

"Then it's a hoax that also puts me in an uncomfortable financial position, because I stand to lose billions if the fuzzys are deemed sentient," Holloway said. "I have a very distinct and obvious reason to hope the fuzzys are simply animals."

Meyer opened her mouth; Holloway held up his hand. "I

know where you're going next," he said. "The only possible way this does me any good is if I've somehow set things up to short ZaraCorp stock on the market, in the hope of reaping the benefit when the stock price falls. But to forestall such an argument, I'm willing to give Judge Soltan complete access to all my financial and communication data for the last couple of years. She's more than welcome to have forensics experts go through the data to look for evidence that I'm trying to manipulate ZaraCorp stock. But I can tell you right now that she won't find it. My only financial holdings at this point are the royalties ZaraCorp automatically puts into my account at the Zarathustra Corporate Bank. I think I earn half a percent on that annually."

"But we have no way of knowing if these sounds are speech!" Meyer said. "You're a surveyor, not an expert on xenosapience. And we've already established that Dr. Wangai has no formal training in xenosapience. Neither of you can even knowledgably guess at what those sounds mean."

Holloway saw Isabel's eyes widen; she knew the hole Meyer had just fallen into. Holloway smiled. "You are quite correct, Ms. Meyer," he said. "So I suggest we let someone who *can* knowledgably guess give an expert opinion. I suggest we call Arnold Chen."

"Who?" Meyer said.

"Arnold Chen," Holloway repeated. "He received his doctorate in xenolinguistics. University of Chicago, I believe. He works in the same office as Dr. Wangai. Just down the street from here. I understand he was mistakenly assigned to Zara Twenty-three. Lucky for us he's here."

"Is this correct?" Soltan said to Meyer.

"I don't know," Meyer said. She was thoroughly confused by the course of events.

"Excuse me, Your Honor," Isabel said. "Jack's correct. Dr.

Chen is a xenolinguist. He's also likely to be in his office right now."

"Doing what, exactly?" Soltan said.

"That's a good question, Your Honor," Isabel said. "I'm sure Dr. Chen would like to know what he's supposed to be doing as well."

"Let's bring him in," Soltan said.

"If I may make a suggestion, Your Honor, have one of your clerks bring him in, rather than one of ZaraCorp's people," Holloway said.

"What is that supposed to mean?" Meyer asked.

"I think given the circumstances there is a reasonable chance someone might attempt to coach the expert," Holloway said. "I can think of some examples in my own experience where such a thing was attempted."

Meyer kept quiet after that one, lips thinned.

"Fine," Soltan said.

"I'd also suggest not telling Dr. Chen why he's been called," Holloway said. "Let him experience the video clean."

"Yes, all right," Soltan said, irritated. "Any more suggestions on how I should do my job, Mr. Holloway? Or are you done now?"

"Apologies, Your Honor," Holloway said.

Soltan eyed Holloway sourly and then turned to Meyer. "Are you finished with this expert?" Soltan asked.

"I have nothing more to say to Mr. Holloway," Meyer said. She eyed Holloway like he was a bug.

"Mr. Holloway, you are excused," Soltan said. "We'll take a fifteen-minute break while my clerks retrieve Dr. Chen." She got up and went to her chambers. Meyer packed up her notes, flung them at her assistant, and stormed out of the court, assistant scrambling to catch up. Holloway noted that Landon had disappeared as well, no doubt to catch up his boss on the events of the day.

Holloway got out of the stand and was surprised to find Isabel in front of him. "Hello," he said.

Isabel very suddenly gave him a large hug. Holloway stood there and took it, surprised; it had been a while since he had more physical contact with her than a polite peck on the cheek. Indeed, when Isabel stopped hugging him, she planted a kiss on his cheek that was more than polite. It was actually friendly.

"Apology accepted," she said, stepping back. Sullivan by now had come up behind her.

"Well, good," Holloway said. "Because if you didn't accept that one, I would have given up."

"Thank you, Jack," Isabel said. "In all honesty and sincerity, thank you."

"Don't thank me yet," Holloway said. "If it turns out the fuzzys are actually people, I'm going to be broke and out of a job, and then me and Carl are showing up on your doorstep."

"I'll be sure to give Carl a good home," Isabel said.

"Oh, nice," Holloway said, and looked over to Sullivan. "You see how far good deeds get you in this life," he said to him. Sullivan smiled but said nothing. He looked distracted. Isabel gave Holloway another quick peck and then did the same to Sullivan before leaving the courtroom.

Holloway turned his attention to Sullivan. "I'm out of the doghouse," he said.

"If only you had managed it while the two of you were still dating," Sullivan said.

"Yes, well," Holloway said. "Let my misfortune be your example, Mark."

"Jack, you and I need to talk," Sullivan said.

"Is this about Isabel?" Holloway asked.

"No, not about Isabel," Sullivan said. "It's about everything else."

"That's a lot," Holloway said. "I don't think we have time to cover everything else besides Isabel in the next five to ten minutes."

"No, we don't," Sullivan said. "Let's you and I go have a talk at the end of this little farce."

"Farce?" Holloway said, mock shocked. "This is a sober application of judicial wisdom."

Sullivan cracked a smile at this. "I don't mind admitting to you that this is going differently than I expected," he said.

"I don't think you're the only one thinking that at the moment," Holloway said.

* * *

Dr. Chen was ushered into the courtroom by one of Soltan's clerks. The xenolinguist looked confused, and depending on one's observational inclinations, either freshly awoken from a nap or slightly drunk.

"Dr. Arnold Chen?" Judge Soltan asked.

"Yes?" Chen said.

"We are calling you to give testimony on a video that concerns a subject you are knowledgeable about," Soltan said.

"This is about the other night, isn't it?" Chen said. "I admit I drank too much, but I didn't have anything to do with the rest of what went on."

"Dr. Chen, what are you talking about?" Judge Soltan said, after a minute.

"Oh, nothing," Chen said, hastily.

Soltan peered at Chen. "Have you been drinking today, Dr. Chen?"

"No," Chen said. He looked embarrassed. "I was, um."

Soltan looked over at her clerk. "He was asleep at his desk when I found him," said the clerk.

"Late night, Dr. Chen?" Soltan said.

"A bit, yes," Chen admitted.

"But you are able to *think* right now?" Soltan asked. "Your brain processes are not currently compromised by alcohol or any other drug, recreational or pharmaceutical?"

"No, ma'am," Chen said. "Your Honor. Um."

"Have a seat at the witness stand, Dr. Chen," Soltan said. Chen took a seat. Soltan glanced over at Holloway. "You're up, Mr. Holloway," she said.

Holloway stood and borrowed Isabel's infopanel once more, and opened a pipe between it and the monitor. "Dr. Chen, I'm going to show you a video," Holloway said. "Don't worry, the events of the other night aren't on it."

Chen looked at Holloway blankly.

"Just watch the video and give us your impressions of it as it goes along," Holloway said. He queued up the video of Papa, Mama, and Grandpa Fuzzy eating the bindi.

"What are those?" Chen asked, looking at the still image. "Are those monkeys? Cats?"

"You'll see," Holloway said, and started the video.

Chen watched for a minute, thoroughly confused. Then it was like a 50,000-watt light went on in his head.

Chen looked up at Holloway. "Can I?" he asked, motioning to the infopanel. Holloway glanced at Soltan, who nodded. He handed the infopanel to Chen. The xenolinguist grabbed it and reversed the video and played the first parts again. He turned up the volume to hear better. He moved the video back and forth for several minutes.

Finally he looked up at Holloway. "You know what they're doing," Chen said.

"You tell me, Dr. Chen," Holloway said.

"They're talking!" Chen said. "My god. They're really talking." He looked back at the monitor. "What are these things? Where did you find them?"

"Are you sure they're talking?" Meyer asked from her table.

"Well, no, I'm not *one hundred percent* sure," Chen said. "I'm just going from what you're showing me here. I'd need to see much more to be certain. But, look—" He paused the video and backed it up slightly, and ran it again. "Listen to what they're doing here. It's phonologically varied but it's not random."

"What does that mean?" Holloway asked.

"Well, look," Chen said. Whatever sleepiness he'd had in him was well and truly shaken off now. "Take birdsongs. They repeat with very little variation. Phonologically they're very consistent. They're not what we typically consider language. Language uses a limited number of phonological forms—phonemes—but then it uses them in an almost infinite number of combinations, according to the morphology of the language. So, varied but not random."

Chen pointed to the conversing fuzzys. "What these little guys are doing is like that. If you listen, you can hear certain forms used over and again. Here—" Chen moved the video to another portion, where Papa Fuzzy was speaking. "—that *tche-* sound. It comes up a lot, but it's joined to other sounds as well. Just like we use particular phonemes over and again, particularly ones that represent vowel forms in our language."

"So this is a vowel?" Holloway asked.

"Maybe," Chen said. "Or maybe a prefix, since just listening here it always seems to precede other sounds. I couldn't tell you what it means or represents."

"So it could just be noises they make," Meyer said. "Like a cat's meow. Or a birdsong."

"Well, neither cats nor birds vocalize just to vocalize," Chen said, sounding slightly snotty. Holloway grinned. After years of having not a goddamn thing to do, Dr. Chen's brain was back with a vengeance. "And no, I don't think so. Your cat has a different sound for 'I'm hungry' and 'I want out of the house' but its vocabulary is not what you would call complex nor does the sound in itself convey complex meaning. Same with birdsongs. What these creatures are doing—the variation but apparently within a system—suggests that the sounds are words in themselves." Chen looked up. "Is there more video?"

"Lots more," Holloway said.

Chen looked like a kid getting a puppy for Christmas. "Excellent," he said.

"Dr. Chen," Soltan said. "Is this language? Is this speech?"

"Are you asking for a determination?" Chen said. "Because I don't have enough data."

"Guess, then," Soltan said.

"If I had to guess, then, yes, sure," Chen said. "And not just because of phonology and apparently morphology. Look at how the creatures react and respond to each other in this video. They're clearly listening attentively and responding, not with rote or instinctual sounds, but with new patterns of sound. If it's not language—if it's not speech—then it's something very close to it."

"Does it warrant further study, in your opinion?" Soltan asked.

Chen looked up at the judge like she was stupid. "Are you kidding?" he asked.

"You're in my courtroom, Dr. Chen," Soltan growled.

"I apologize," Chen said. "It's just that this is tremendously exciting. This is the sort of thing that you pray for as a xenolinguist. What are these things? Where are they from?"

"They're from here," Holloway said.

"Really?" Chen said. Then it hit him. "Oh," he said, looking around the room. "*Oh*. Wow."

"Yes," Holloway said. "Oh, wow."

Soltan looked over to Meyer. "Any other questions for Dr. Chen?"

Meyer shook her head. She could see where this was going. Soltan excused Chen; Holloway just about had to tear the info-panel from his grip.

"Based on the information provided today, I've decided there is not sufficient cause to order the Zarathustra Corporation to file a Suspected Sapience Report," Soltan said, after Holloway and Chen had sat down. "However, these creatures are from all evidence clearly something more than just animals. Whether they rise to the level of true sapient beings is a determination that no one here, with all due respect to Drs. Wangai and Chen, is able to state definitively. If there was ever a case in need of additional study, this would be it.

"I will be filing a request with the Colonial Environmental Protection Agency, under whose auspices sentience determination is administered, to dispatch the appropriate experts here for additional study and to make a decision regarding the sentience of the 'fuzzys.' Until that time, the Zarathustra Corporation will continue its normal operations, with the understanding that it will now conform to CEPA guidelines regarding exploitation of disputed worlds. I'll be posting the inquiry ruling later today. Any objections, Ms. Meyer?"

"None, Your Honor," Meyer said.

"Then this inquiry is adjourned," Soltan said. She rose and disappeared into her chambers.

Chapter Nineteen

Holloway was walking Carl, finding a good place for the dog to take care of his business, when Wheaton Aubrey VII appeared in front of him as if by magic.

Holloway peered around Aubrey. "Where's your shadow?" he asked. "I wasn't aware you were allowed to go anywhere but the bathroom without your body man."

Aubrey ignored this. "I want to know why you pulled that stunt in the courtroom," he said.

"I'm wondering what part of it constitutes the stunt for you," Holloway said. "The 'telling the truth' part, or the 'not telling you I was going to tell the truth' part."

"Cut the shit, Holloway," Aubrey said. "We had a deal."

"No, we didn't," Holloway said. "*You* said we had a deal. I don't recall agreeing that we did. You assumed we did and I didn't bother to correct your misapprehension."

"Jesus," Aubrey said. "You can't be serious."

"Jesus I am," Holloway said. "And if you want to take it to court, you'll find there's quite a lot of case law that supports my point of view. Oral contracts are shaky enough as it is, but oral contracts in which one of the parties does not audibly and explicitly give consent to the agreement are not worth the sound waves they are spoken through. Not that you'll be wanting to take this to court, of course. Encouraging perjury is not looked upon very kindly by any court I can think of. And while I don't know if encouraging someone to perjure themselves at one of these quasi-legal inquiries constitutes a prison worthy offense, at the very least I would guess that it's a slam-dunk that the supposed deal wouldn't have legal standing in the first place."

"Let's assume for a moment that you and I both know that none of anything you just driveled on about matters one bit," Aubrey said. "And let's also pretend that both of us know what's actually true here, which is that the last time you and I spoke, you had every intention of doing exactly what we had planned. All right?"

"If you say so," Holloway said.

"Well, then," Aubrey said. "I repeat: I want to know why you pulled that stunt in the courtroom."

"Because they're *people,* Aubrey," Holloway said.

"Oh, bullshit, Holloway," Aubrey spat. "We both know you don't give a damn about whether they're *people* or not, especially when you're looking at billions of credits. You're not built that way."

"You haven't the slightest idea how I'm built," Holloway said.

"Apparently not," Aubrey agreed, "because I assumed that despite all evidence to the contrary, you were capable of logical thought, and of working for your own advantage when necessary. Doing this doesn't help you at all. The only thing it does is let you make nice with that biologist. I hope the pity sex you get out of that is worth the billions you just pissed away, Holloway."

Holloway counted to five before replying. "Aubrey, you talk like someone who's never gotten the shit beat out of him for being an asshole," he said.

Aubrey opened his arms, wide. "Take your shot, Holloway," he said. "I'd really like to see you try."

"I already took my shot at you, Aubrey," Holloway said. "You might recall. It's why we're having this little conversation right now."

Aubrey put his arms back down. "This wasn't about me," he said.

"No," Holloway agreed. "That was just one of the side benefits."

"You know those fuzzy creatures of yours are never going to be found sentient," Aubrey said.

"I'm well aware you're going to throw a lot of resources into making the case against them," Holloway said. "Which is not the same thing."

"We're going to make that case," Aubrey said.

"Then you're out the relatively minimal cost of the legal proceedings and your paid experts and what have you," Holloway said. "For ZaraCorp, that's next to nothing. You, Aubrey, probably make more in interest off your share of the company each day. So what. But if you *don't* make the case, then the fuzzys have the right to their own planet, in which case all of this is immaterial, and you should consider what you have stripped off the planet a gift, rather than your right. You really can't complain."

"I still don't understand why you did it," Aubrey said.

"I already told you why," Holloway said.

"I don't believe you," Aubrey said.

"As if I *care* about that," Holloway said. "Look, Aubrey. It could take the experts years to make a determination. If you have your way with your own lawyers and experts, that will certainly be true. In which case you still have years to exploit the planet. More than enough time to prepare your company and your stockholders."

"Or they might make a determination within months," Aubrey said. "In which case the company is screwed."

Holloway nodded. "Then I suggest you prioritize your efforts," he said. "You've said yourself that sunstone seam I found is worth decades of revenues for ZaraCorp. If I were you, I'd be putting just about everything I could into it."

"It's already our top priority," Aubrey said.

"Now it'll be your top priority with a special sense of urgency, won't it," Holloway said.

Aubrey suddenly grinned, grimly. "*Now* I understand why you did it, Holloway," he said. "Having us exploit the sunstone seam in our usual way wouldn't get you rich enough fast enough. You wanted as much as you could get as quickly as you could get it. So you show Judge Soltan just enough of your little talking monkeys to force her to rule for more study—but not enough so that she requires us to file an SSR. Zarathustra Corporation is put into the position of having to focus on the single most profitable project on the planet, which you just *happen* to have discovered."

Holloway said nothing to this.

"This proves you don't actually give a shit about those little fuzzys of yours," Aubrey said. "You'll still get your percentage of the sunstone seam whether the experts decide the fuzzys are sentient or not. You've played your biologist friend, and you played ZaraCorp at the same time. Very nicely done. I can almost admire it. Almost."

"It's not as if ZaraCorp won't see the benefit of it," Holloway said. "If you exploit that seam quickly, you're creating an endowment for your company. You hold the monopoly on sunstones. You can store those sunstones and dribble them out over decades, whenever you need an extra boost to the bottom line. That I get my bit up front is neither here nor there."

"We have a monopoly only if the fuzzys are found not to be sentient," Aubrey said.

"You have a monopoly either way," Holloway said. "As I mentioned to someone else recently, the fuzzys only recently discovered sandwiches. Sentient or not, there's no way they're going to be ready to handle the world of interplanetary business. It's unlikely the Colonial Authority will allow them to for decades. It was only a decade ago the CA decided the Negad were competent enough to enter into resource deals on their own planet. The fuzzys are far behind where the Negad were when they were declared sentient. ZaraCorp's monopoly isn't going anywhere anytime soon."

"It will still cost us hundreds of millions of credits to refocus all our planetary resources on that seam," Aubrey said.

Holloway shrugged, and the message was clear enough: *Like I care.*

"And we might decide not to," Aubrey said.

"I understand the Aubrey family doesn't see fit to give ZaraCorp voting stock to the plebian masses," Holloway said. "But the folks who own class B stock in the company can still sell it when they see the corporate governance doing something stupid. Like, say, not exploiting a sunstone seam that's arguably worth the rest of the entire planet combined, when there's an excellent chance the entire planet will soon be placed off-limits to future exploitation. The only real question in that case is how low the stock will go. I'd guess not *quite* low enough for Zarathustra Corporation to get delisted. But one never does know, does one."

Aubrey smiled another mirthless smile. "You know, Holloway, I'm delighted that the two of us have had this little chat," he said. "It has put so many things into perspective."

"I'm glad it has," Holloway said.

"I don't suppose you have any other surprises you want to share with me," Aubrey said.

"Not really," Holloway said.

"Of course not," Aubrey said. "They wouldn't be surprises then, would they."

"The man has a learning curve," Holloway said.

"One other thing," Aubrey said. "I've decided that when your contract runs out, I'm going to have ZaraCorp renew it. All things considered, I think you'll do us less damage here than anywhere else. And I want you where I can keep track of you."

"I appreciate the vote of confidence," Holloway said. "I don't suppose you still plan on giving me that continent, though."

Aubrey walked off.

"Didn't think so," Holloway said. He turned to Carl. "There goes a real piece of work," he said to his dog.

Carl returned the comment with a look that said, *That's nice, but now I really do have to pee.* Holloway continued their walk.

*   *   *

"You're late," Sullivan said, as he answered his door.

"I got waylaid by a very pissed-off future Chairman and CEO of Zarathustra Corporation," Holloway said.

"That's an acceptable excuse," Sullivan said, and then glanced down at Carl, who was lolling his tongue at the lawyer.

"I promised Isabel I'd bring Carl around," Holloway said. "I assumed she'd be here."

"She'll be around a bit later," Sullivan said. "Why don't you both come in." He stood aside from the door.

Sullivan's apartment was the standard-issue Zarathustra Corporation off-planet living space: twenty-eight square meters of floor plan divided into living room, bedroom, kitchen, and bath. "I think it's disturbing my cabin is larger than your apartment," Holloway said, entering.

"Not that much larger," Sullivan said.

"Higher ceiling, in any event," Holloway said, looking up. He could place his palm flat on the ceiling if he wanted to.

"I'll give you that," Sullivan said, walking through the front room to the kitchen. "You also don't have an intern living above you playing noise until the dead hours of the morning. I swear I'm going to make sure that kid never gets another job with the company. Beer?"

"Please." Holloway sat, followed by Carl.

"So what did Aubrey waylay you about?" Sullivan asked. "If you don't mind me asking."

"He asked me what I was thinking in the courtroom today," Holloway said.

"Funny," Sullivan said, coming back into the living room and handing Holloway his beer. "I was thinking of asking you the same thing."

"Probably not for the same reasons, however," Holloway said.

"Probably not," Sullivan said. He twisted the cap off his own beer and sat. "Jack, I'm about to tell you something I shouldn't," he said. "The other day Brad Landon came into my office and told me to draft up an interesting sort of contract. It was a contract ceding operational authority for the entire northwest continent of the planet to a single contractor, who in return for handling substantial operational and organizational tasks for ZaraCorp, would receive five percent of all gross revenues."

"That's a nice gig for someone," Holloway said.

"Yes it is," Sullivan said. "Now, I was instructed to design the contract so that unless certain stringent production quotas were met, the contractor got very little, but you'll understand that 'very little' in this case is a distinctly relative term. Whoever got this gig would be rich beyond just about any one person's ability to measure wealth."

"Right," Holloway said.

"So I'm wondering why you just threw that away today," Sullivan said.

"You don't know that contract was meant for me," Holloway said.

"Come on, Jack," Sullivan said. "I think you've figured out by now that I'm not stupid."

"Are you asking me this question as ZaraCorp's lawyer or Isabel's boyfriend?" Holloway asked.

"Neither," Sullivan said. "I'm asking you as me. Because I'm curious. And because on the stand today you did something I didn't expect."

"You thought I was going to sell Isabel out," Holloway said.

"Not to put too fine a point on it, but yes, I did," Sullivan said. "You stood to make billions and you let it slip past you. Given your past history, you don't strike me as the overly sentimental type. And, no offense, you've sold out Isabel before."

"None taken," Holloway said. "It wasn't about Isabel."

"Then what was it about?" Sullivan asked.

Holloway took a slug of his beer. Sullivan waited patiently.

"You remember why I was disbarred," Holloway said.

"For punching that executive in the courtroom," Sullivan said.

"Because he was laughing at those parents in pain," Holloway said. "All those families were torn up to hell, and Stern felt comfortable enough to laugh. Because he knew at the end of the day our lawyers were good enough to get him and us out of trouble. He knew he'd never see the inside of a prison cell. I felt someone needed to send him a message, and I was in the right position to do just that."

"And this relates to our current situation how?" Sullivan asked.

"ZaraCorp was planning to steamroll over the fuzzys," Holloway said. "It was planning to deny the fuzzys their potential right to personhood on no more basis than because it could, and because the fuzzys were in the way of expanding their profit margins. And you're right, Mark. I stood to profit quite handsomely myself from the whole business. It was in my interest to go along."

"Very much in your interest," Sullivan said.

"Yes," Holloway agreed. "But at the end of it I have to live with myself. It was wrong of me to punch Stern in the courtroom, but I didn't regret it then and I don't now. ZaraCorp might eventually show that the fuzzys aren't sentient, but if they do, at least they'll do it honestly, and not just because I went along with them and made it easy for them. Maybe what I did today wasn't the smart thing to do, but if nothing else, ZaraCorp isn't laughing at the fuzzys anymore."

Sullivan nodded and took a drink of his own beer. "That's very admirable," he said.

"Thanks," Holloway said.

"Don't thank me yet," Sullivan said. "It's admirable, but I also wonder if you're not completely full of shit, Jack."

"You don't believe me," Holloway said.

"I'd like to," Sullivan said. "You talk a good game, and it's clear your lawyer brain has never completely turned off. You're good at presenting a scenario in which you always end up, if not the good guy, at least the guy with understandable motives. You're persuasive. But I'm a lawyer too, Jack. I'm immune to your charms. And I think underneath your rationalizations there are other things going on. For example, your story about why you punched Stern in that courtroom."

"What about it?" Holloway asked.

"Maybe you did do it because you couldn't stand the sight of him, or the idea of him laughing at those parents," Sullivan said. "But on a whim, I also checked the financial records of your former law firm. Turns out that two weeks before you punched Stern, you received a performance bonus of five million credits. That's more than eight times your previous highest performance bonus."

"It was my share of a patent infringement settlement," Holloway said. *"Alestria versus PharmCorp Holdings.* And others got bigger bonuses out of that than I did."

"I know, I read up on the bonuses," Sullivan said. "But I also know most of the big bonuses were paid out a couple months before yours was. Yours is interestingly timed. And it's enough for a corporate staff lawyer to contemplate disbarment and the loss of his livelihood with a certain cavalier lack of concern."

"You're just speculating now," Holloway said.

"It's not just speculation," Sullivan said. "I also know the North Carolina attorney general's office looked into it. Contrary to what you just said, Jack, the general consensus was that Stern and Alestria were on the way to losing that case. And you've said yourself that the reason you were disbarred is because everyone believed you intended to precipitate a mistrial. In this case, everyone may be right."

"The AG's office couldn't prove anything about that bonus," Holloway said, irritated now.

"I'm aware of that too," Sullivan said. "You wouldn't be here if they could have. But as you well know, 'not proven' is not the same as 'disproven.'"

"The difference being that I don't have anything to gain by revealing the sentience of the fuzzys," Holloway said. "I didn't have to do it, but I did."

"Yes, you did," Sullivan said. "And in doing so you forced the judge to order more study—which will force ZaraCorp into an immediate strategic review of its resource allocation here on Zara Twenty-three. I wouldn't be entirely surprised if sometime very soon it's announced that nearly all exploitation resources on the planet are going to be focused on that sunstone seam of yours, Jack. Which will make you rich, fast, no matter what happens with the fuzzys. And that's a fact I'm very ambivalent about."

"You have a problem with me getting rich?" Holloway asked.

"Getting rich? No," Sullivan said. "But maneuvering to become super-rich? Yes. I do have a problem with it. Because I feel responsible for it. I'm the one who mentioned the 'more study' option to you and Isabel. It didn't occur to me when I mentioned to you that you could still make millions under that option that you might find that amount insufficient, and find a way to maneuver yourself into more."

"It's an interesting theory," Holloway said.

"I thought you might like it," Sullivan said. "Don't misunderstand me, Jack. In one sense I'm pleased you did what you did, for whatever reason you did it. No matter what they told you, Isabel's professional reputation wouldn't have survived the accusation that she was taken in by a prank. You would have killed her career. Unlike your previous situation, she has no multimillion-credit bonus cushion for when her career craters. So whether for your own selfish reasons or not, you did the right thing. Isabel is never going to hear me suggest you did it for any other reason than vindicating her. Fair enough?"

Holloway nodded.

"Good," Sullivan said. "But there's something else going on here that I think you need to be aware of. Something I know you didn't think about. And that's the future of the fuzzys themselves."

"What about it?" Holloway asked.

"How do you feel about the fuzzys, Jack?" Sullivan said.

"I just showed evidence of their sentience," Holloway said. "I think that's an indicator."

"Not with you, it isn't," Sullivan said. "I just spent a lot of time pointing out that you have a funny way of being amazingly self-interested. It serves your purpose to suggest the fuzzys are sapient. You don't get any credit for it if it's just another tool in the box for your long con game against ZaraCorp."

"It's not," Holloway said.

Sullivan held his hand up. "Don't," he said. "Just turn off the bullshit for the moment, Jack. Turn off that lawyer brain of yours and the thinking three steps ahead and the self-absorption and that overriding love of money you have, and answer me seriously and honestly. Do you actually *care* what happens to these fuzzys, or don't you?"

Holloway took a drink from his beer, reconsidered, and finished all of it. "Leaving aside everything else?" he asked Sullivan. "Leaving aside all your theories and rationales and possible explanations for my actions?"

"Yes," Sullivan said. "Leaving aside all that for now."

"Between you and me," Holloway said.

"Between you and me," Sullivan said.

"Then yes," Holloway said. "Yes, I care what happens to the fuzzys. I *like* them. I don't want anything bad to happen to them."

"Do you think they're sentient?" Sullivan asked.

"Does it really matter?" Holloway asked.

"You said you were going to stop with the bullshit," Sullivan said.

"I am," Holloway said. "The no bullshit answer is that right now I don't particularly care if they are proved sentient or not. Maybe Isabel is right, that they're people, and that as people they have their rights. Maybe it's not right for me to hope to make some money off this planet before that's determined, but that's my own issue to deal with. In the end, though, whether or not they're judged to be people, the fact is, if finding them sentient works to their advantage in the long run, that will make me happy."

Sullivan stared at Holloway for a moment, then finished his own beer. "That's good to know," he said. "Because now I'm going to tell you something else I probably shouldn't tell you. Which is that I was hoping that when you got up on that witness stand today, Jack, that you *would* have lied your ass off about pulling a prank on Isabel."

"What?" Holloway said. Of all the possible things Sullivan could have said to Holloway, this was not even close to being one he would have expected.

"You heard me," Sullivan said. "I wish you had lied and that the judge ruled that the fuzzys weren't sentient."

"You're going to have to explain that one to me," Holloway said. "You were just explaining how that would have destroyed Isabel's credibility. I'm confused."

"It would have destroyed her credibility, but it might have saved the fuzzys," Sullivan said.

"You have not made yourself any clearer," Holloway said.

"Have you actually ever read *Cheng versus BlueSky Corporation*?" Sullivan asked. "The ruling that established the criteria for proving sentience?"

"Back in law school," Holloway said.

"I read through it again because of all of this," Sullivan said. "Read *Cheng* and its aftereffects. Do you remember why the court ruled against Cheng?" Sullivan asked.

"Because he couldn't prove that the Nimbus Floaters were sentient," Holloway said. "He couldn't prove that they had speech."

"That's correct," Sullivan said. "People remember that he

couldn't prove it; what they don't remember is *why* he couldn't prove it. The reason why he couldn't prove it was because they were all dead. In the time between when Cheng filed his case and the time it reached the high court, the Nimbus Floaters went extinct."

"They died off," Holloway said.

"No," Sullivan said. "They were *killed* off, Jack. Their numbers were never large, and once Cheng filed his suit, they started dropping fast."

"They would have been given protected status as soon as the case was filed," Holloway said.

Sullivan gave Holloway a lopsided grin. "Yes, on a planet with no oversight, and a resident population of surveyors and workers whose livelihoods would disappear if the floaters were recognized as sentient," he said. "You tell me how well the words 'protected status' would work in a situation like that."

"Point," Holloway said.

"No one was ever caught killing the floaters, of course," Sullivan said. "But a population doesn't just decline that quickly for no reason. There was no climate event, no bug the resident animals caught from humans, nothing like that. The only explanation that fits the data was intentional human predation."

"I'm sure you weren't the only one who noticed this," Holloway said.

"No," Sullivan said. "In the wake of *Cheng,* the Colonial Authority changed procedures to keep it from happening again. Now when there's suspicion of predation the CA is supposed to appoint a Special Master to bring it to a halt. But Special Masters can be appointed only after an SSR is filed or ordered. That hasn't happened here. Right now, the fuzzys have no sort of legal protection at all."

"So you think people will hunt them," Holloway said.

"I think it's inevitable," Sullivan said. "And I think you and I will be responsible for it. I'm indirectly responsible by suggesting to you and Isabel the 'needs study' option. You, Jack, are directly responsible by forcing the judge to implement it. As soon as the word gets out, every surveyor and worker on the planet is going hunting for the fuzzys. They're going to try to kill them before their sentience can be proved one way or another. If they kill them now, there won't be any left to prove their sentience one way or another."

"If they're wiped out, no one could be charged with murder," Holloway said. "Because as far as anyone could prove, they were just killing animals."

Sullivan nodded. "We've marked them for extinction. Pure and simple," he said. "That's why I needed to know how you felt about them. Because right now, you, me, and Isabel are the only friends they have."

From Holloway's jacket pocket a tone rang out. It was his pocket infopanel. Holloway fished it out, read it, and stood up.

"What is it?" Sullivan said.

"It's the emergency alert system at my cabin," Holloway said. "My house is on fire."

Chapter Twenty

Holloway saw the tendrils of smoke rising while he was still twenty kilometers out. They were thin pencil lines against the sky.

"Crap," Holloway said, to himself. The good news is a thin line of smoke meant the worst of the fire was over and that the damage was contained to his own house and tree compound; the spikewoods had not gone up and the rest of the forest was not burning to the ground. The fire-suppression system he'd installed had done its job well enough.

The bad news was, his cabin was still almost certainly a smoking ruin. He was glad he left Carl with Isabel for this trip. Carl wasn't mentally equipped for figuring out fire damage.

He was also mildly worried about the Fuzzys, but only mildly. They might be sentient or they might not be, but either way he figured they knew how to run from a fire.

Several minutes later Holloway was circling his compound, assessing the damage. As he expected, the cabin was a mess, made as it was of relatively cheap plastics and woods. The storage sheds and landing area, made of less flammable metals and composites, showed smoke and outward fire damage but no charring or apparent structural damage. Holloway decided to go in, setting his skimmer to hover a meter over the landing pad rather than put its full weight on it. There might not be any apparent structural damage to the pad, but for the moment he'd rather not test the assumption. He felt confident the structure would bear his weight; less so that of a large flying machine.

He got out of the skimmer and put his weight on the landing pad. It held just fine. He took a step and nearly landed on his ass—not because of fire damage but because of the residue of the fire-suppressing foam that had shot out of several outlets to coat the compound as soon as the emergency system had registered a burn. Holloway's compound was in the trees, and on thundery days it was not all that unusual for lightning to find its way down for a visit. Holloway had his weathervanes and lightning harvesters, but despite all that, this wouldn't be the first time some part of the compound caught fire. After the first fire, Holloway had prepared for the next.

Holloway's first stop was not the wreck of his cabin. Instead he made an immediate beeline to the larger of the storage sheds. He gingerly touched the door. It was a couple hours after the initial burn, but the door might still be hot.

It wasn't. Even better, the electronic lock was undamaged. Holloway keyed the entry combination, stood to the side to avoid any escaping blast of superheated air, and slid open the door.

There was a gaping hole in the floor where his surveying explosives were supposed to be.

Holloway grinned. There was *supposed* to be a gaping hole in the floor where his explosives used to be. If there wasn't, there likely wouldn't have been a platform for him to land on, and possibly not a forest for him to fly to. Holloway did not keep an excessive amount of surveying explosives, but what he had on hand was more than enough to flatten the neighborhood.

He walked over to the hole. The hole was a trapdoor laid into the floor of the storage shed, over which Holloway placed his explosives, in sturdy cases. In case of a fire emergency or a direct lightning strike on the storage shed, the trapdoor would open and cases would tumble the many meters to jungle floor. The cases were designed to be tossed out of aircraft and survive a fall of up to three hundred meters; it was considerably less than that to the jungle floor. The explosives inside were susceptible to being triggered by heat but not by jostling.

Holloway looked down. The cases were visible on the ground, a couple directly underneath him but others knocked haphazardly by the branches of the spikewoods below. Holloway would have to reset the trapdoor and then retrieve the cases. That would be a pain in the ass as well as slightly dangerous—there was always the chance of predators—but it was better than having the explosives go off in a fire and turning the entire jungle into a conflagration.

In the branches below him, Holloway caught a flash of white. It looked like Pinto Fuzzy, lounging about. "You couldn't have tried to put out the fire?" Holloway yelled down to the fuzzy. The creature didn't answer, but then Holloway really didn't expect it to.

Back out of the shed and toward the cabin, then.

The cabin, complete with caved roof and gaping wall, was a total loss. The fire appeared to have started here; Holloway suspected the surge from a lightning strike might have caused a spark, probably to the cooler's or the air conditioner's heat pump. The cabin had fire suppression equipment too; ironically much of its use was predicated on Holloway being in or near the cabin at the time to operate it. Basically, having paid out substantially for suppressing fire everywhere else at the compound, Holloway skimped on his own living quarters. He assumed it was a reasonable personal risk; outside of his law school hat, there wasn't much of personal or financial value there. It could all be replaced with an extended shopping trip in Aubreytown.

Holloway looked through the ruins for his hat. He found it on his collapsed desk, charred and melted against his security camera.

That's one more thing from law school I don't get to use anymore, he thought. There was nothing for it now. Everything else was likewise black, melted, and crumbled. He sighed and headed back to the skimmer.

First, a test to see if the landing pad could hold the skimmer. It could. Holloway lifted off and landed three more times to be sure. It held. It seemed outside the cabin, the rest of the compound really was structurally all right. That was a small relief. The Aubreytown store had the prefab cabins in stock, but the rest of the compound would have been harder to replace.

That taken care of, Holloway returned to his storage shed and winched his trapdoor back into place. He would then additionally have to fly his skimmer under the platform and redo the supporting bolts and beams before he could set his explosives on top of it again. Holloway did that next, but not before using his infopad to order additional canisters of fire suppressant to replace the ones that were used. They weren't cheap, but Holloway figured he was coming into some money anyway.

The trip to the jungle floor was next. Holloway wasn't looking forward to dragging the explosives cases onto the skimmer; individually the cases were no larger than a large travel chest, but their indestructibility made them heavy and the explosives inside weren't exactly featherweight, either. The one good thing about it all was that now that Holloway knew the trick about blasting the high frequency noise, he could land the skimmer and get all the cases in one go, rather than landing, setting up the emergency perimeter, dragging the one or two cases inside the perimeter into the ship, disassembling the perimeter and doing it again a few yards over. Out of consideration for Pinto, however, who Holloway assumed was still loitering in the branches, he waited until he landed before setting off the high-frequency loop in his sound system.

Fifteen minutes later, Holloway had a blinding headache and was drenched in sweat from dragging cases across the ground in the heat. It was probably the most he'd exercised in years, and he was reasonably sure that between the last time he'd moved this much material and right now, his heart had been replaced by two flabby slices of ham slapping futilely back and forth against each other. He hauled the last of the cases into the skimmer and then slid up against the side of vehicle, panting. As he looked up he saw Pinto, several meters up in his branch, looking down at him almost directly from above.

"Thanks for your help," Holloway shouted up to the fuzzy. "It was really appreciated." Again, not that Holloway had actually expected help from the thing. It just made him feel better to say it. Holloway bent over, hands on his knees, and practiced breathing slowly and deeply to help get himself over his light-headedness.

A couple of seconds later a small splash of something landed on the back of his head, followed by a slightly larger splash of something on his neck. He looked up and saw Pinto still staring at him from above.

Holloway grinned. The little bastard was spitting on him. Well, it was better than what a monkey would do, he supposed. He wiped off the back of his neck and was about to wipe the spittle on his pants when his peripheral vision picked up on something.

Holloway stopped his hand and brought it directly in front of his face.

Pinto hadn't been spitting on him.

Holloway looked up again just in time to catch a spatter of blood across the cheek.

"Oh, no," he said. "Oh, shit." He wiped his face, got into the skimmer, slapped off the sound system, fired the skimmer's rotors, and launched the thing straight up.

• • •

Holloway landed the skimmer hard, popped it open, and as gently as he could lifted Pinto out of the skimmer and onto the landing pad. The fuzzy lay there, limp and unresponsive. Holloway went back inside the skimmer and grabbed his first aid kit, nearly slipping again as he came out of the craft in a hurry.

Pinto's abdomen was red and matted with blood. Its back and extremities were not, save for a single rivulet that streamed from its abdomen to its front left limb, which had dangled from the branch above Holloway. Holloway recognized that the fuzzy had been in the same position from the first time he had seen him until he felt the blood on his neck. It was possible the fuzzy had been dead that whole time. Or that it had been alive and Holloway had been jovially yelling at it when he could have been helping it, if he had just paid attention.

Pay attention. Holloway shook away irrelevant thoughts and focused on the creature in front of him. Holloway looked at Pinto's abdomen and realized there was too much blood; he couldn't see where it was coming from. He went back into the skimmer and found the water bottle he carried with him in the vehicle. It was about two thirds full. He brought it back to the fuzzy and as gently as he could poured it over the creature, washing away the clotted mess.

The wound made itself evident almost immediately; a hole the width of a finger in the fuzzy's lower left abdomen. Holloway briefly wondered if it could have been caused by one of the tree spikes, but as he washed the wound he saw something gray and dull inside it. He washed the wound again, clearing away as much of the blood as possible, and saw it again.

It was a bullet.

We've marked them for extinction, Sullivan said. *Pure and simple.*

Holloway seized up, but fought it back and reached into the first aid kit for a gauze pad. He ripped open the packaging and placed it on the bullet wound, pressing firmly but gently to stop the flow of any more blood out of the small creature.

There was no more blood flowing out of the fuzzy. It was dead.

Holloway leaned his cheek to the fuzzy's mouth, to feel for breath, and stroked the creature's fur as if to will it back to life with a touch. There was no breath or life. If there had been a time to save Pinto, it had passed, a minute, an hour, or several hours ago. There was nothing Holloway could do but to remain hunched over the creature, silent, hoping to be wrong.

He was not wrong. It took him several minutes to admit it to himself.

When he looked up, he was not alone. Papa, Mama, and Grandpa Fuzzy stood in front of him, watching him grieve over the body of Pinto.

Holloway looked at the three of them blankly, the gears in his brain spinning fast and free before they jammed together with a jolt Holloway felt clear down his spine.

"Where's Baby?" Holloway asked, to no one of them in particular.

Holloway didn't know whether they understood him or not.

What he did know is that when he asked the question, they all turned to the ruin of the cabin.

"Oh, God," Holloway said. He leapt up and ran toward the cabin, stopping outside it because of the heat and smoke it was still giving off. He looked through the caved-in wall, searching for Baby and hoping not to find the creature.

He found what was left of Baby by the door.

In spite of everything, Holloway was momentarily confused. Baby hadn't been in the cabin when he'd left, and he'd closed all the windows to keep out the lizards as well as the Fuzzys. It didn't make sense for Baby to have died in the cabin.

Then he remembered the bullet in Pinto. Baby didn't go into the cabin. The fuzzy had been *put* there.

Holloway glanced down and saw the remains of his hat, melted against the security camera.

The gears in his head jammed down hard again. Holloway stalked away from what was left of his cabin and went directly to his skimmer, snatching his infopanel almost violently from its cradle before forcing himself down into his chair. He played his fingers across its surface and opened up the feed for his security camera. The last few hours of recording would be cached there. And the last time Holloway had touched the security camera, he'd tilted the hat so the security camera could see outside.

The security feed popped up, the interior view of the camera obscured by the hat but the view out the window clear and open. Holloway impatiently fast-forwarded through an hour of nothing going on and had to backtrack when a skimmer landed on the pad, and a man got out.

Holloway froze the frame and zoomed into the man's face. Nothing; it was obscured by a ski mask. Holloway wondered who the hell would have a ski mask on a planet dominated by jungles, but then remembered that ZaraCorp did have alpine-level mining operations far south. You could get ski masks at the store, as this man must have. Holloway unfroze the video.

The man strode across the landing pad toward the cabin and stopped at the door, going partially out of frame as he did so, the wall of the cabin blocking the view. The man moved back and forth slightly, clearly trying the door, which was locked. He then moved over to the desk window, which was also locked. The man's bulk obscured most of the camera's view, but behind him Holloway saw movement, and then in the extreme right of the frame, Holloway saw Baby walking across the compound toward the man.

Holloway ached at the sight. Of all the fuzzys, Baby was the one who was the most trusting of humans. The other fuzzys seemed to grasp the idea that humans, like any other animals, could be dangerous. But Baby, for whatever reason, lacked that intuition. Baby liked people. Holloway, his heart falling, knew what it was about to lead to.

The man turned for whatever reason and saw Baby walking toward him. He broke off from his attempted breaking and entering and instead walked toward the fuzzy, eventually stopping and kneeling down in front of the smaller creature, reaching out eventually to touch and pet the fuzzy, who cuddled right into his hand. Holloway couldn't hear what he was saying—he had never gotten around to unmuting the security camera's microphone— but he could guess well enough. The man was a predator luring his prey into a sense of trust.

The man suddenly stood up and raised his boot.

Holloway had to turn away.

But he turned his face back in time to see what happened next: something flinging itself out of the trees and onto the man's face, tearing and biting into him through the eyeholes and mouth hole of the mask. The man howled, soundlessly on the video but no doubt loudly in real life, trying to fling off whatever it was attacking him.

It was Pinto.

Holloway let out a small cheer in spite of himself. Pinto, the reckless fuzzy, hadn't hesitated a single moment to defend Baby—its sibling? Its friend? Its mate?—and was now wreaking holy Hell on the man, taking vengeance on the human for its inhuman act.

The man flailed and hit at the fuzzy, but Pinto danced and held fast, constantly tearing at the man's head and face. There wasn't any doubt that the little fuzzy was making the man pay for his actions.

The man finally got a grip on Pinto and lifted the fuzzy off his face. Pinto scratched and bit at the man's hands. The man raised his hands and with full force hurled the fuzzy to the floor. Holloway felt the fuzzy's impact in his gut.

Pinto scrambled up from the ground and prepared to attack the man again.

The man pulled a handgun out of his waistband and shot the fuzzy.

The little creature spun around from the impact and was flung across the compound floor. Alarmed and running on whatever was the fuzzy equivalent of adrenaline, Pinto sprinted away, running past the cabin to the spikewood behind, the man shooting after the fuzzy. One of the bullets punched through the window; it was possible it further ricocheted inside the cabin, setting up the conditions for the fire. Holloway found he was utterly unconcerned about any of that now.

The man dropped his handgun and then clutched his face, dancing in pain. He stopped when he saw Baby lying there, unmoving from his earlier attack. He stormed up to the fuzzy, brought his boot down on it twice more, then grabbed the handgun off the ground and shot it. Then he yelled at it, silent and furious.

Holloway realized he knew exactly who this man was.

By this time smoke from the cabin was beginning to obscure the camera feed. Nevertheless, Holloway saw the man reach down, grab the body of Baby, and stomp over toward the cabin door, once again going partially out of frame. The man's body jerked spasmodically, and Holloway had a couple seconds of confusion before he realized what was happening: The man was kicking in the dog door. It must have given way, because the man's body moved in a different way. He was flinging Baby's body through the door, to burn up in the fire.

That accomplished, the man moved away from the door, holding his face, heading toward his skimmer. He got halfway there before the fire suppression foam kicked on, blasting out of its canisters to coat the landing pad and whatever was on it, including the man and his skimmer. The man jumped away from the foam, tripping over himself as he did so and falling to the floor, coating himself with more foam. It would have been comical, had the man not just killed two people. Eventually the man made it to his skimmer and launched off, going out of frame nearly simultaneous to the charred remains of Holloway's law school hat draping themselves over the camera, obscuring its view just before it was destroyed in the heat.

* * *

Holloway set down the infopanel and burst out of the skimmer, seeing nothing but Pinto's body. He knelt down next to the body and reached out to the fuzzy's hands, looking at their very ends, to the nails there, sharper and more conical than human nails, probably the better to catch insects and pry open fruit.

There was blood on them, and tiny shreds of skin.

"Yes," Holloway said, holding Pinto's hand. "I've *got* you, you son of a bitch. I've got you and you don't even know it."

Holloway looked up at Papa, Mama, and Grandpa Fuzzy, who were looking at him strangely, or at least in a way that Holloway thought was strange.

"I know you can't understand me," Holloway said to the three fuzzys. "But I know who did this. I know who did it and I am going to punish him for it. You have my word on it. I am going to get this son of a bitch. I promise you that."

And then Jack Holloway let go of Pinto's hand, collapsed on the floor on the skimmer pad, closed his eyes, and cried.

He cried because he knew, beyond certainty, that his maneuvering and plots had killed Pinto and Baby, two creatures who no matter what else they might or might not have been, were innocents. Sentient or not, it didn't matter to Holloway. No one deserved the deaths they were given, by his actions. Jack lay there and cried, racking his body in his guilt and shame.

He knew the other fuzzys were watching him. He didn't care. He lay there for a good long time.

Eventually, there was a touch on Holloway's cheek. Holloway opened his eyes and saw Papa Fuzzy staring down at him. Holloway looked at him, curious.

Papa Fuzzy pointed up.

Holloway looked up.

Above him, the spikewoods were filled with fuzzys. Dozens of them.

"Holy God," Holloway said, and sat up.

The fuzzys started climbing down from the trees, dropping down into the landing pad until it was packed with the creatures. Holloway looked at them all, partly amused at the convention of creatures, and partly apprehensive. A human had just killed two of their number. It was entirely possible the fuzzys were planning to take it out on him. He couldn't say that he would blame them.

On the periphery of the landing pad, one of the smaller fuzzys caught his eye. Holloway stared at it for a few seconds, wondering why this particular fuzzy was so interesting, when it occurred to him that it wasn't a fuzzy at all.

Holloway peered at it intently.

It was a capuchin monkey.

"You have *got* to be shitting me," Holloway said.

Papa Fuzzy looked at Holloway curiously. Holloway pointed at the monkey. "I know that monkey," he said. "Damn thing stole my wallet once. I can't believe it's still alive. I can't believe it's been with you guys."

Papa Fuzzy followed Holloway's pointing finger toward the monkey, and then looked back at Holloway with what for all intents and purposes was a noncommittal shrug. *Yes, so, it's a monkey,* it seemed to be saying. *What about it?*

"This has become a very strange day," Holloway said.

An object was moving forward through the crowd to Holloway, carried by a single fuzzy who held its arms outstretched, and sort of wobbled its way through the group, other fuzzys parting to let it through. The fuzzy came up to Papa Fuzzy, who squeaked something at it. The other fuzzy offered the object to Holloway, who took it.

It was an infopanel.

Holloway wondered for a second if it wasn't his spare panel, saved from the cabin fire, when he realized that it was a different make and model. This one was a lower-end model than any of Holloway's, but featured one high-end feature: solar panels on the non-display side. Leave it out in the sunlight for an hour, it'd be charged up for a week. Useful, actually, for people who spent most of their time out surveying.

Holloway turned on the display.

Andy Alpaca, the mascot of the Super Reading Adventures line of skill-adaptive electronic reading primers, beamed back at him, making eye contact with Holloway by way of facial identification software tied into the infopanel's camera.

"Hi there!" it said. "I'm Andy Alpaca! Would you like to go on a reading adventure with me?"

It was Sam Hamilton's infopanel, all right. Poor, semi-literate Sam, whose skimmer went down years ago. The monkey quite obviously survived. It didn't seem too likely Sam did.

"Should have bought that emergency fence, Sam," Holloway said.

He looked down at the infopanel again, where Andy Alpaca waited for him to respond. Then he looked out at the fuzzys, who stared up at him, patiently.

For the third time that day, the gears in his brain engaged, hard.

Chapter Twenty-one

Joe DeLise was mightily displeased when he walked through the door of Warren's Warren and found someone occupying his favorite stool. He was even more displeased when the man turned toward him and DeLise recognized who he was.

"I don't care what that son of a bitch lawyer said," DeLise said, from the door. "If you're not off of my stool by the time I get over there, I'm breaking your face."

"You should know that son of a bitch lawyer is right over there," Holloway said, pointing to Sullivan, who was shooting pool by himself.

DeLise paused. "Can't go anywhere without your protection, Jack?" he said, after a second. He started walking toward his stool again. "I guess I got you that scared, don't I."

Holloway peered at DeLise. "Jesus, Joe, what happened to your face?" he asked. "You look like you tried to tongue-kiss a cat and the cat objected."

"None of your damn business," DeLise said.

"Mind you, I don't blame the cat," Holloway said, and looked again. "How long ago did that happen, anyway? Looks like maybe four, five days ago."

"Kiss my ass," DeLise said. He was hovering over Holloway now. "And get off my stool."

"I was planning to," Holloway said. "It smells bad. All those years of you farting into it, I suppose."

"That's right," DeLise said. "Keep it up."

"But before I do that, I've got something for you," Holloway said.

"What?" DeLise said.

"This," Sullivan said, slapping a court notice against his shoulder. He had walked up behind DeLise while the man had been threatening Holloway. "You've got a court date. Preliminary hearing."

DeLise looked back at his shoulder but didn't touch the notice. "What for?" he said.

"For burning down my house, you asshole," Holloway said.

"I don't know what you're talking about," DeLise said. "I've been here or I've been working. And I have people who will tell you that in both places."

"Well then, you have nothing to worry about, do you?" Sullivan said. "You can show up in three days with some of your witnesses and let them chat with Judge Soltan and then you'll be free to go."

"I don't recall you calling in your little fire to security," DeLise said.

"Funny about that," Holloway said.

"Considering the possible involvement of a ZaraCorp security officer, Mr. Holloway asked the judge to allow him to file a request for a preliminary hearing directly," Sullivan said. "And I, as legal representative of ZaraCorp, indicated to her that the company wouldn't have a problem with that. And here we are."

"Surprise," Holloway said, to DeLise.

DeLise sneered at Holloway and looked back to Sullivan. "Even if it's true, which it's not, what do you care?" he asked Sullivan. "You're ZaraCorp's lawyer, not his. He's not a ZaraCorp employee. His house isn't ZaraCorp property. Shit, I'm the one who works for ZaraCorp, not this schmuck."

"You're not working for ZaraCorp when you're allegedly burning down someone's house, now, are you, Mr. DeLise?" Sullivan said. "That's on your own time."

DeLise smirked at that. "I don't think you really want to serve that notice to me, Counselor," he said.

"A tip for you, Mr. DeLise," Sullivan said. "Just because you haven't touched the notice with your fingers doesn't mean it hasn't been served to you."

DeLise snorted, took the notice, and set it on the bar. He turned to Sullivan. "This is going to be a waste of everybody's time," he said. "And I don't take very kindly to being made to look like an asshole, Counselor." He jerked a thumb at Holloway. "You think you're doing yourself a favor latching on to this piece of shit, but between you and me, Sullivan, I think you've picked the wrong horse this time. I don't think you're going to like where he's going to end up taking you."

"Well, Mr. DeLise, coming from a man I once had to stop from killing Mr. Holloway in a ZaraCorp holding cell, that's certainly an ironic slice of food for thought," Sullivan said. "You can be assured I'll give it the consideration it deserves."

"Yeah, I'm sure you will," DeLise said. "But he's not in the holding tank this time. He's not the untouchable you made him out to be. And when this is all done, we'll just see who the asshole is, won't we." He turned toward Holloway, who blinded him with a flash.

"What the hell?" DeLise said.

"Just taking a picture," Holloway said, lowering the camera. "Your scratched-up face amuses the crap out of me, Joe."

"Get off my stool, asshole," DeLise said. *"Now."*

"All yours," Holloway said, getting up. "Enjoy it while you can."

DeLise grunted and sat.

• • •

"Have I told you today how much I hate you?" Chad Bourne said, to Holloway. The two of them were walking Carl, who snuffled happily down one of the side streets of Aubreytown. Bourne had called Holloway to meet with him in his cubicle, but Holloway refused. A little bit of yelling later and they were walking down the street with a dog. It was muggy and hot. Bourne was not dressed for a walk and was already sweating profusely.

"I haven't done anything today to make you hate me," Holloway said.

"You made me walk your dog with you," Bourne said.

"That's not hate worthy," Holloway said. "And anyway, you like Carl."

"My cubicle is air-conditioned," Bourne said.

"Your cubicle is probably bugged," Holloway said.

"So now in addition to being annoying, you're paranoid," Bourne said.

"In the last few weeks I've had my skimmer sabotaged and my house burned down to its floor panels," Holloway said. "I've earned a little paranoia, I think. And anyway, I have things I need to say to you that I don't want anyone else to hear."

"Aside from your voices," Bourne said.

"Cute," Holloway said. He stopped while Carl examined a particularly interesting sapling. "Chad, look. We have our problems, you and I. And I'm willing to admit lots of those problems are my fault. And I know that there have been times when you've gone out of your way to make a little bit of trouble for me, because I've gone out of my way to make a lot of trouble for you. Fair to say?"

"Fair to say," Bourne said, after a minute. Carl had finished his examination of the sapling and left behind a note for future dogs. The three of them started walking again.

"Fair to say," Holloway said again. "So: ups and downs. But there's one thing that I respect about you, Chad. It's that you're fundamentally a decent human being. There are times when you've hated me, but you always invited me to that stupid holiday thing you hold for the contractors you rep. You've always been fair in our dealings—and I know not every ZaraCorp contractor rep is. Hell, you even like my dog."

"He's a good dog," Bourne said. "Better than you deserve."

"Well, that's the thing, isn't it," Holloway said. "One thing I've always been blessed with is better people than I deserve. Carl. Isabel. Sullivan, even though he's dating my ex. Even you, Chad. In your own annoying way, you've been better than I deserve. It's clear I've been pretty lucky."

"It's a mystery to me," Bourne said. "It really is."

Holloway smiled at this. "It's because you've been fundamentally decent to me that I wanted to tell you something. I think you're about to get royally screwed."

Bourne stopped. "What the hell is that supposed to mean?" he said.

"You have a skimmer," Holloway said.

"I have a company skimmer," Bourne said. "So what?"

"So I think by the time you get back to your cubicle today, you're going to find it's been impounded," Holloway said.

"What?" Bourne said. "Why? By who? You?"

"Not by me," Holloway said. "I suspect you're going to find

it's been impounded as evidence by whoever's representing Joe DeLise in the preliminary hearing I've filed against him for burning down my house."

"What does Joe DeLise have to do with my skimmer?" Bourne said.

"As far as anybody knows, not a thing," Holloway said. "And that's the point, Chad. When they impound it, they're probably going to run some tests on it, and I suspect they're going to find that there's residue of fire suppressant on it. The same sort of fire suppressant I have at my place."

Bourne looked confused. "How did it get there?" he said.

"Because your skimmer was at my place when it burned down, obviously," Holloway said. He started the three of them walking again; he didn't want to stay in the same place too long. "There might be some other physical evidence as well, I suppose, but I'm guessing that's the one DeLise's lawyer is going to use to introduce reasonable doubt to my assertion that he was the one who set fire to my place."

"I didn't drive it the day your place burned down," Bourne said.

"Where were you?" Holloway said.

"I had the day off," Bourne said. "I was supposed to go to that hearing about those fuzzy creatures of yours, but I woke up feeling sick and decided to chuck it. I stayed in my apartment all day."

"Anyone with you?" Holloway asked.

"No," Bourne said.

"So no corroborating witnesses to you sleeping through the whole day," Holloway said.

"So?" Bourne said.

"So, DeLise has already assured us that he's got numerous witnesses who will swear they've seen him, either at work or at that piece of shit bar he hangs out in," Holloway said. "He's got enough people scared of him that they'll testify in court he was where he says he was, instead of where he really was, which was at my house, burning it down."

"But it doesn't make sense," Bourne asked. "There's no way for DeLise or anyone else to get access to the skimmer. I keep the key fob in my pocket."

"Has DeLise ever been in your skimmer?" Holloway asked.

"You know he has," Bourne said. "He was Aubrey's security detail when we came to visit you."

Holloway looked at Bourne, counting off the seconds while the tumblers in his rep's brain clicked into place.

"Oh, *crap,*" Bourne said.

"You left the key fob with DeLise because I wouldn't let him out of the skimmer," Holloway said. "More than enough time for him to crack the encryption and make a copy, if he knows how or if he had help. Then later he could pick up the skimmer any-time and when it left the garage, it would be your key fob signa-ture registered as checking it out."

"Why me?" Bourne asked.

"Because you're *my* rep, Chad," Holloway said. "Everyone knows you have your troubles with me. Everyone knows I'm a pain in your ass. There is record after record of you and me wran-gling about one thing or another. There are lots of examples of me ignoring you or bypassing you or otherwise running right over you to get what I want. Now with Judge Soltan's ruling to get more study on the fuzzys, I've threatened your job along with the job of every other person on the planet. After everything, it's not entirely unreasonable for you to snap and decide to take it out on me. You assumed I returned to my cabin immediately after the hearing and decided to burn it down around me. It makes perfect sense."

Bourne stopped and sat down on the curb, wordless.

"It makes perfect sense," Holloway said. "Unless someone actually knows you, Chad. Someone like me. You and I have had our moments. But I know you're a decent person. That's why I'm warning you about this ahead of time."

Bourne just sat there and shook his head.

"Come on," Holloway said eventually, nudging him. "We've got to get you back."

"You could be wrong about this," Bourne said, after several moments of silence.

"I might be," Holloway said. "You might get back to your cubicle and then go out to the garage to get your skimmer and find it there waiting for you. In which case, I suggest you give it a thorough washing. On the other hand, you might get back to find I was right—and that you've been called to testify in front of the preliminary hearing. In which case, you're going to find the circumstantial evidence combined with your lack of an alibi is going to get someone off the hook and you on it."

"You're telling me all this is going to happen but you're not telling me how to clear myself," Bourne said.

"I can't tell you that," Holloway said. "I'm already telling you more than I should, and the only reason I can do that is because as far as either of us knows, they *haven't* impounded your skimmer or called you to testify. You're not on the docket yet. But you will be. And between now and then, you need to figure out some things for yourself."

"Like what?" Bourne asked.

"Like who it is that's decided keeping DeLise out of trouble is worth throwing you to wolves," Holloway said. "Because whoever it is has decided that there's nothing you can do to them that could possibly hurt them. So when you *do* figure out who it is, that's your next step. Finding out what's going to hurt them the most."

"There's no point in that if it's not going to help me," Bourne said.

"Chad, this is what I mean about you being a fundamentally decent guy," Holloway said. "Let me put it to you this way: Sometimes in life you're going to win and sometimes you're going to lose. But just because you lose doesn't mean the other guy needs to win. Do you understand me?"

"Not really," Bourne said.

"Well, think about it anyway," Holloway said. "Maybe it will come to you." The three of them turned a corner and stood in front of the ZaraCorp administration building.

"Your stop," Holloway said.

"I still don't like you very much," Bourne said, to Holloway.

"I haven't ever given you any reason to like me, Chad," Holloway said. "And I'm not going to pretend I like you all that much either. Just know that I think you're a good guy. You're a good guy and you don't deserve to get screwed. And as much as I can, I'm going to try to keep that from happening. All right?"

"All right," Bourne said. Impulsively he stuck out his hand to Holloway. He took it.

"Thanks," Holloway said.

Bourne nodded and entered the building. Holloway watched him fade into the murk of the lobby and then maneuvered Carl across the street, where Isabel and Sullivan were waiting for him. Carl made a beeline for Isabel, who patted him happily.

"How is he?" Sullivan asked, of Bourne.

"He's now completely scared shitless," Holloway said. "Which was the plan."

"Any idea what he'll do when he gets called to testify?" Sullivan asked.

"Not a clue," Holloway said.

"Should be interesting," Sullivan said.

"That's a word for it," Holloway said.

"Stop it, both of you," Isabel said. "Poor Chad. He is an actual human being, you know. Not just a chess piece for the two of you to play with."

"He's definitely a pawn," Holloway said. "The question is whether he's ours or someone else's. And at the very least, we're trying to keep him from getting framed for arson. Or attempted murder, come to think of it."

"He's a good guy, Jack," Isabel said.

"I know it, Isabel," Holloway said. "I really do." Isabel did not look terribly convinced.

"While the two of you were off having your little chat, both Isabel and I got some interesting news," Sullivan said.

"What is it?" Holloway asked.

"We're being transferred," Isabel said. "Both of us. Mark's been given a general counsel position on Zara Eleven and I'm being sent back to Earth to head up a lab there."

"Effective when?" Holloway asked.

"Effective immediately," Sullivan said. "We've both been relieved of our duties and have been given three days to pack. Our beanstalk transport is scheduled to leave while you're having your preliminary hearing."

"How unsurprisingly coincidental," Holloway said.

"It's not just us," Isabel said. "Arnold Chen's paperwork snafu has magically cleared itself up. He's headed for Uraill on the same beanstalk transport we are."

"He must be excited," Holloway said.

"He's miserable," Isabel said. "He called me about it and was wailing. He's waited his whole life to decipher the language of a new sentient being, and they won't let him. They've locked him out of his files entirely. They locked me out of mine, too."

"I still have copies of yours," Holloway said.

"Which is the only reason *I'm* not wailing," Isabel said.

"They're clearing us out before the CEPA xenosentience team can get here," Sullivan said. "Anyone who knows anything about the fuzzys. Except for you, Jack."

"You figure that's ominous," Holloway said.

"Don't you?" Sullivan asked.

"I've been in ominous mode since my skimmer fell out of the sky," Holloway said.

"We're worried about you, Jack," Isabel said. "Both of us are."

"You can't fool me," Holloway said. "You're more worried about Carl."

"I'm serious, Jack," Isabel said.

"I'm more worried about the dog, myself," Sullivan said.

"There we go," Holloway said.

"Mark," Isabel said.

"Isabel, Mark," Holloway said. "Your new assignments don't change anything. None of this changes anything. When we woke up this morning we had three days to prepare. We still have three days to prepare. If we pull it off, three days is all the time we're going to need. If we don't, then it's not going to matter one way or another. For now, let the future take care of itself. We've got three days. Let's get to work."

Chapter Twenty-two

Judge Nedra Soltan took her seat and peered out into her courtroom. "This looks familiar," she said to Holloway and Janice Meyer, who were standing at their respective tables. "We talking fuzzy creatures again, Counselors?"

"No, Your Honor," said Meyer, who was representing De-Lise, who was standing with her at the defense table.

"I think the defendant is bit of an ape, Your Honor," said Holloway.

"Watch it, Mr. Holloway," Soltan said. She held up a sheet with her notes on it. "It says you are acting as your own counsel."

"There's someone else I might have asked, but he's being deported off-planet today," Holloway said. "So I'm stuck with myself."

"You know what they say about the man who represents himself in court, Mr. Holloway," Soltan said.

"Yes. I do know it," Holloway said. "But I also know the law. I even used to be a lawyer."

"Disbarred," Meyer said.

"Not for not knowing the law," Holloway said.

"Yes, I know," Soltan said. "After your performance the last time you were here, I looked up your file. You punched your own client."

"He deserved it," Holloway said.

"Maybe so," Soltan said. "But do anything like that here, and being disbarred will seem like a cakewalk in comparison. Do you understand me, Mr. Holloway?"

"I give you my word I will not punch my client," Holloway said.

"Very droll, Mr. Holloway," Soltan said. "Sit."

Everyone sat.

"This is a preliminary hearing before a judge," Soltan said in a tone of voice that suggested she had said the same bit of verbiage innumerable times before, in front of people who knew exactly what she was going to say. "In cases where the nature of a colony makes it difficult or impossible to convene a grand jury, the plaintiff and defense may jointly agree to have evidence for a potential suit examined by a judge, and to have witnesses examined by the same, who will then determine if there is sufficient cause to bring the matter forward into a full court trial, either civil or criminal. Do the plaintiff and the defense so request?"

"Yes, Your Honor," said Meyer.

"Yes, Your Honor," said Holloway.

"Does counsel understand that this hearing is for the benefit of the judge alone for determining the adequacy of the evidence to move forward to a trial, and not the trial itself, and that as such customary trial rules concerning discovery do not apply?" Soltan said. "That is to say, one or the other of you, or both, may not be aware of the evidence or witnesses called by the other."

"Understood," said Meyer.

"Yes," said Holloway.

"Does counsel understand that the determinations and rulings of the judge in this preliminary hearing are binding pending full trial, provided there is one?" Soltan said.

Meyer and Holloway both gave their assent.

"Fine," Soltan said. "Then let's get on with this. Mr. Holloway, what are you accusing Mr. DeLise of?"

"He burned down my house," Holloway said.

"So, arson," Soltan said.

"Arson, yes," Holloway said. "Also attempted arson for attempting to burn down my outbuildings and failing, destruction of personal property, and attempted murder."

"You weren't home when your house burned down," Soltan said.

"He didn't know that before he got there," Holloway said.

"Let's not stretch ourselves too far, Mr. Holloway," Soltan said. "I'm going to proceed for the moment with arson and destruction of personal property. If attempted arson and attempted murder become evident in the evidence you present, I'll reinsert them."

"Fine, Your Honor," Holloway said.

"Ms. Meyer, by any chance would your client like to cop to these allegations?" Soltan asked.

"No, Your Honor," Meyer said. "My client has a roster of witnesses who will account for his whereabouts for the entire day in question."

"Of course," Soltan said. She made a note and then looked up. "All right, Mr. Holloway, plaintiff first."

"Thank you, Your Honor," Holloway said, and picked up his infopanel, to connect it to the larger monitor in the courtroom. "The first piece of evidence I'd like to show you is a security camera video from my house. I have a camera on my desk that is constantly running, and the video caches onto my infopanel storage space, which is convenient in this particular case, since the actual camera was destroyed in the fire."

"Is this video from a secure camera?" Meyer asked.

"No," Holloway said.

"So it's possible you could have tampered with it," Meyer said.

"I'm perfectly willing to file an affidavit with the court that the video is unaltered and unedited, and to testify so on the matter in open court," Holloway said.

"Later," Soltan said. "For now, show me the video."

"Yes, Your Honor," Holloway said. He started the video. It unspooled in the monitor: The skimmer landing at Holloway's compound, the man stepping out of the skimmer, him trying the door and window, and him meeting the fuzzys, stomping Baby, and fighting with Pinto. Holloway glanced over at Meyer, who looked horrified at what the man had done to Baby, and then at DeLise, who sat there motionless.

"Pause this," Soltan said, suddenly. Holloway paused the video. The judge turned to him. "Is this a joke, Mr. Holloway?"

"In what sense, Your Honor?" Holloway asked.

"This video has yet to show anything related to arson," Soltan said. "Instead I'm watching some man fight and kill small animals. It's sickening, but it doesn't have anything to do with your claim."

"First, I would note to Your Honor that we're in the process of determining whether the fuzzys which you see being killed here are animals or if they're people," Holloway said. "And if they do turn out to be people, then whoever it is setting fire to my house—I am claiming Mr. DeLise—will also have at least one count of murder to contend with."

"Mr. Holloway," Soltan began.

"However, that is neither here nor there to my claim, and I

am not alleging murder," Holloway said, quickly. "Nevertheless the man's actions with the fuzzys are relevant, as you are about to see."

"I had better," Soltan said.

"Yes, Your Honor. In fact, it's just about to happen." Holloway resumed the playback. The man threw Pinto to the ground and shot the fuzzy. "There's the gun. Now, you see the fuzzy runs away, in the direction of my cabin. The man keeps firing. And there, a bullet enters my cabin. This I suspect is what initially started the fire. If you wait a minute, you'll start to see smoke." The courtroom waited for the smoke to arrive, and as it did so watched the man kick and shoot Baby, and throw the corpse into the burning cabin. Meyer looked like she was about to be sick. *Good,* thought Holloway.

Holloway stopped the playback when the camera failed.

"Ms. Meyer," Soltan said, after a minute. "Any rebuttal?"

Meyer blinked and then coughed to hide the fact she was trying to get her focus back. "The video shows that a man accidentally set fire to Mr. Holloway's cabin, but it doesn't show that it was Mr. DeLise," she said.

"The man set fire to the cabin after trying to break into it, which means it was an action associated with a crime," Holloway said. "By Colonial law, that's third-degree arson."

"The man in question could have been there for another reason," Meyer said.

"In a *ski mask,*" Holloway said. "In a jungle. On a sweltering day. Besides that, look. The first thing this guy does on encountering someone else—human or not—is to stomp and shoot them to death. If the fuzzys were people, that would be murder. He's not there for a social call, Your Honor. And now you can see why I think my murder was one of the goals of the visit."

"Attempted murder's not coming back in on the basis of this

video," Soltan said. "But I agree that there's reasonable claim for an arson charge, as well as destruction of property."

"Nothing on the video proves that the man in it is my client, however," Meyer said. "And in point of fact, there's something in it that points against it. Mr. Holloway?" Meyer held out her hand, requesting the infopanel. Holloway gave it. Meyer ran the video back to the beginning, to the skimmer landing. "There," she said. "The skimmer."

"What about it?" Soltan said.

Meyer pointed. "Look at the serial numbers on the side," she said. "That's a Zarathustra corporate number. This isn't a security skimmer, which is the sort my client usually has access to. It's a model given to ZaraCorp's contractor representatives so they can visit their contractors out in the field."

"So run the number through the ZaraCorp database, and tell me whose skimmer it is," Soltan said.

"We don't have to," Meyer said. "We already know. He's outside the courtroom right now, waiting to be a rebuttal witness."

* * *

"You understand you are under oath," Soltan said.

"I do," said Chad Bourne.

"Your name and occupation, please," Soltan said.

"Chad Bourne, Contractor Representative for Zarathustra Corporation," he said.

"You're up," Soltan said, to Meyer.

"Mr. Bourne, are you Mr. Holloway's contractor representative?" Meyer asked.

"Yes, I am," Bourne said.

"And you have been so for how long?" Meyer asked.

"I've been his rep for as long as I've been here on Zara Twenty-three," Bourne said. "That'd be about seven years now."

"What's your general opinion of Mr. Holloway?" Meyer asked.

"Am I allowed to use profanity?" Bourne asked.

"No," Soltan said.

"Then it's best to say that our relationship has been a tense one," Bourne said.

"Any particular reason?" Meyer asked.

"How much time do you have?" Bourne said.

"Just hit the highlights," Meyer said.

"He's lax with CEPA and ZaraCorp regulations, he's argumentative, he tries to lawyer everything, he ignores me when I tell him he can't do things, and he's just all-around a jerk," Bourne said, looking at Holloway.

"Any positive qualities?" Meyer asked, slightly bemused.

"I like his dog," Bourne said.

"Have you ever said that you hate Mr. Holloway?" Meyer asked.

"On a regular basis," Bourne said.

"Mr. Bourne, are you aware that your skimmer may have been used in the furtherance of a crime?" Meyer asked.

"I guessed that when my skimmer was impounded the other day," Bourne said.

"Yes," Meyer said. "We found fire suppressant residue on the skimmer. The same brand that Mr. Holloway used to keep his compound from burning down."

"Okay," Bourne said.

"We've also now seen a video where your skimmer's number is visible," Meyer said.

"All right," Bourne said.

"Mr. Bourne, can you account for your whereabouts the day Mr. Holloway's cabin burned down?" Meyer asked.

"I was at home sick most of the day," Bourne said.

"So you didn't see any one, and no one saw you," Meyer said.

"No," Bourne said.

Meyer turned to Soltan and prepared to introduce an alternate theory of the crime.

"Oh, wait, that's not quite right," Bourne said. "I did see someone."

Meyer swallowed her intended speech. "How is that again?" she said.

"I did see someone," Bourne said.

"Who?" Meyer asked.

"Him," Bourne said, pointing at Holloway. "I needed to tell him I had made a small error regarding that sunstone find of his. Turns out ZaraCorp doesn't own it. He does."

"What?" Meyer said.

"What?" Soltan said.

"Yep," Bourne said. "Just before he discovered it, I terminated his contract. For cause, I might add. But when he told me about his find, I guess in all the excitement, I forgot to reactivate his contract, which would have ceded the find back to ZaraCorp. While I was at home, I was reviewing contracts and I noticed his was missing. So I did a little digging. Turns out that by both *Butters versus Wayland* and *Buchheit versus Zarathustra Corporation,* he's the actual owner of the seam. I thought maybe ZaraCorp could try to take it from him, but then we'd be running up against *Greene versus Winston,* and given what happened the last time ZaraCorp went up against that, I didn't want to risk it. So I felt obliged to inform him. I knew he was in Aubreytown that day, so I went and told him about it. I figured he might want to know he's worth one-point-two trillion credits. I would. Who wouldn't?"

There was dead silence in the courtroom.

"Oh, come on!" Meyer said, eventually. "You can't seriously believe Holloway owns that seam."

"He does," Bourne said. "Oversight on my part. Sorry."

"Sorry?" Meyer said. "The only witness to your whereabouts

is the plaintiff, who you just happen to be giving a trillion credits of ZaraCorp's money to? *Sorry* is the word I would use for that, indeed."

"Am I allowed to make objections here?" Holloway asked, raising his hand.

"What is it, Mr. Holloway," Soltan said.

"Is it just me, or did the defense go from implying it was the witness who set fire to my cabin to suggesting he and I are teaming up to rob ZaraCorp, all in a single sentence?" Holloway asked.

Soltan looked over to Meyer. "He has a point, Ms. Meyer," Soltan said.

"Your Honor, regardless of the content of the statement, it's highly suspect," Meyer said. "Mr. Holloway is accusing my client of arson, and he's the only person here who can give Mr. Bourne an alibi."

"Well, Mark Sullivan was there, too," Holloway said.

"Excuse me?" Meyer said.

"I was at Sullivan's when Chad tracked me down about this," Holloway said. "He should be a credible witness. He was Ms. Meyer's underling, after all."

"Fine," Soltan said. "I'll have a clerk go get him."

"That's not possible," Meyer said.

"Why not?" Soltan said.

"He got promoted over her," Holloway said. "He's the new ZaraCorp General Counsel on Zara Eleven. He's leaving today."

"Leaving, or left?" Soltan said, looking back and forth between Meyer and Holloway.

"Left," Meyer said.

"Leaving," Holloway said. "His transport ticket is for three hours from now. He's probably loitering at the beanstalk passenger waiting area."

Soltan looked at Meyer narrowly. "For future reference, Ms. Meyer, if someone is in fact still on-planet, they have not left it."

"Yes, Your Honor," Meyer said.

"I'll have one of my clerks stop Mr. Sullivan's ticket and re-book him on the next transport," Soltan said. "I'm having the other retrieve him and bring him here. That should take a half hour or so. We're in recess until then." She stood and looked at Bourne. "You're excused, but don't go anywhere." she said. Bourne got up.

"May I approach the bench, Your Honor?" Meyer asked.

Soltan blinked. "What part of 'we are in recess' are you having a problem with, Ms. Meyer?" she asked.

"Please, Your Honor," Meyer said. Soltan sat, grumpily, and motioned Meyer and Holloway forward.

"We need to talk about the disposition of the sunstone seam," Meyer said.

"No, we don't," Soltan said. "Aside from establishing an alibi for Mr. Bourne, it's not relevant to this case."

"It's relevant for every single other thing on the planet," Meyer said. "Mr. Bourne testified in open court that ZaraCorp has no claim on that seam. That puts us on dangerous ground. We need to get a preliminary ruling."

"After this hearing," Soltan said.

"The longer they wait, the worse their legal ground is going to get," Holloway said. "Speaking as an interested party, I'm up for a preliminary ruling as well. The sooner the better."

Soltan narrowed her eyes again. "Fine," she said. "Both of you, in my chambers. Ten minutes. Make whatever case you want, but make it quick, because the minute Mr. Sullivan steps into this courtroom, *this* preliminary hearing is back on."

● ● ●

Soltan's chambers, cramped when it was just her in them, were positively claustrophobic with six people. Soltan, Meyer, and Holloway were there, along with Chad Bourne, Brad Landon, and Wheaton Aubrey VII, whom Meyer had frantically summoned.

"This is cozy," Holloway said, jammed up against a wall.

Soltan, sitting behind her desk, gave him a look, then turned to Meyer. "Go," she said. "Fast."

"Mr. Bourne doesn't have the authority to grant Holloway control of that seam," Meyer said. "He's a contractor rep, he's not the board of directors."

"A point that's completely irrelevant," Holloway said. "Bourne never said he had the authority. He pointed out that he voided my contract. The second he did that, *Butters* applied. It's my seam."

"If your contract is void, then you've been on-planet illegally since then," Meyer said, to Holloway.

"I'm aware you're loyal to your company and all, Ms. Meyer," Holloway said. "But in point of fact ZaraCorp regulations are not the same as Colonial law. It's against regulations for noncontracted surveyors to be on Zara Twenty-three, yes. But it's not against the law. And in any case, it's up to ZaraCorp to enforce its own regulations. I can't be blamed if the company never bothered to escort me to the door."

"We'll be fixing that," Aubrey said. Landon winced at this almost imperceptibly.

The reason why became evident immediately when Soltan straightened her spine. "Do that in front of me again, Mr. Aubrey, and you're going to be spending time in your own company's holding cell," she said.

"It's fine, Your Honor," Holloway said. "Although I should note that I'm not going to allow any exploitation of my seam unless I'm around to supervise it. Good help is hard to find."

"Quiet, Mr. Holloway," Soltan said. She turned to Bourne. "Mr. Bourne, are you certain you voided Mr. Holloway's contract prior to his discovery of the seam?"

"Yes, Your Honor," Bourne said. He handed her his infopanel. "Here's the order for the termination of the contract. You'll note several moments later both Mr. Holloway and I signed off on a rider to the original contract, having negotiated some new terms for his find. However, since the contract the rider was meant to be attached to was never reactivated, the rider itself is null and void."

Soltan looked at the infopanel for a few minutes, then looked up at Meyer. "No one thought to double-check this?" she said.

"All contracts are standard and handled through the reps," she said, tightly. "Legal looks at them only if they're flagged by the rep."

Soltan looked back at Bourne. "And you didn't flag the contract," she said.

"I flagged the rider," Bourne said, and took back the infopanel for a second to pop up the document history. "It was the rider that had the unusual bits in it. There was no need to flag the standard contract, because it was standard."

"Except for the fact you forgot to activate it again," Soltan said, taking the panel again.

"Yes, Your Honor," Bourne said.

"The sign-off on the rider is yours, Ms. Meyer," Soltan said.

"Yes," Meyer said.

Soltan set down the infopanel. "This isn't complicated," she said. "If there was no contract, *Butters* applies."

"Mr. Holloway believed he had a contract," Meyer said.

"Are you suggesting Mr. Holloway is now somehow legally obliged to honor a contract that doesn't exist, merely because he believed it did?" Soltan said. "No, Ms. Meyer. It's ZaraCorp who's been getting the free ride here. In any case, you wanted an immediate preliminary ruling. Here it is: I'll be issuing a ruling in favor of Mr. Holloway and putting the full court case on the docket. It's a civil case, and you have a few ahead of it, if I recall. So I'll hear it in about a year."

"I ask that you move it up on the schedule, Your Honor," Meyer said.

"I'll consider it," Soltan said. "But not today."

"This decision will bring operations on Zara Twenty-three to a standstill," Brad Landon said. "Tens of thousands of people will be out of work. Are *already* out of work because of your preliminary ruling. They just don't know it yet."

"That all depends on Mr. Holloway, doesn't it?" Soltan said. She looked at Holloway.

"I have to say I'm deeply moved by ZaraCorp's concern for its common worker," Holloway said. "So I'm more than happy to keep operations going at the seam. All I ask is for half the gross revenue."

Landon blanched. "Half," he said.

"Unless you think I should have more," Holloway said.

"Meanwhile, ZaraCorp carries the load for the cost of machines and the workers," Aubrey said.

"Ms. Meyer said it," Holloway said. "Only ZaraCorp employees and contractors are allowed on-planet. Anytime you want to change that, you let me know. Until then, that's your cost to sink."

"That's not exactly an equitable division of cost," Landon began.

"Half the gross or nothing," Holloway said, cutting him off. "That's the deal. Take it or don't."

Landon looked at Aubrey, who nodded imperceptibly. "Done," Landon said.

"Good, everyone's happy," Soltan said, and stood up. "Now please leave. I have some other issues to attend to." She opened the door to her small private lavatory and disappeared into it.

Aubrey looked over at Bourne, sitting in one of the clerks' chairs. "Little worm," he said. "You will never work again. I promise that."

Bourne returned the stare. "Yes, well," he said. "Your lawyer was already working on that out there, wasn't she? The only difference between now and then is that deciding to screw up my career and my life just cost you six hundred billion credits. Hope it was worth it, you arrogant prick." He stood up and left the room.

●   ●   ●

"Name and occupation," Soltan said.

"Mark Sullivan," Sullivan said. "I'm a lawyer. Currently between jobs."

"Mr. Sullivan, on the day Mr. Holloway came to visit you, did you receive visitors?" Soltan asked.

"Aside from Mr. Holloway, you mean," Sullivan said.

"Yes," Soltan said.

"I had two," Sullivan said. "Three if you count Jack's dog. Besides Jack and the dog, there was Isabel Wangai, who is a mutual friend of ours. And then Jack briefly had a visit from Chad Bourne."

"Do you know what they spoke about?" Soltan asked.

"No," Sullivan said. "They were talking quietly, and Jack did not discuss it with me afterwards. Then Isabel arrived and we talked of other things."

Soltan looked at Meyer. "Any questions?"

"No, Your Honor," Meyer said. "We will still be supplying witnesses who will testify to Mr. DeLise's whereabouts on the day of question. All we've done here is clear Mr. Bourne of any involvement."

"I would guess he'd say that was enough," Soltan said. "Mr. Sullivan, you may step down. My clerk will take you back to the beanstalk terminal."

"If I may, I'd like to stay," Sullivan said. "My transport doesn't leave for twelve hours."

"Your choice," Soltan said. "Now, Mr. Holloway. Your second piece of evidence, please."

Chapter Twenty-three

Thank you, Your Honor," Holloway said. "Now, as Ms. Meyer has astutely noted, the last piece of evidence showed only that arson had occurred. It did not identify the man who landed at my compound, beat and killed those fuzzys, and in the process of doing so managed to set fire to my cabin. The man in question was careful to conceal his identity, whether or not he knew the security camera was there. He wore a ski mask. He wore gloves. He wore common boots sold in the general store to thousands of ZaraCorp workers and contract surveyors. He quite intentionally intended to evade identification.

"But," Holloway said, "then something happened the man didn't intend."

Holloway queued up a shorter excerpt from the previous video. It was of the man suddenly getting a faceful of Pinto.

"The man clearly did not intend to get the crap beat out of him by a fuzzy," Holloway said. "Look how he's taken by surprise, completely unprepared to deal with a small creature bent on tearing off his nose and popping out his eyes." Holloway looked directly at DeLise, who was grinding his teeth. "It must have been some surprise to get schooled so completely by something the size of a cat. Here, let's look at it again."

"Not unless you have a point to make, Mr. Holloway," Soltan said.

"Quite right, Your Honor," Holloway said. "And indeed, I do have a point to make." Holloway played the video once more, this time in slow motion. "Color commentary aside, the fuzzy is doing some very real damage to the man's face: There are some serious scratches, bites, and cuts going on there. This happened a week ago."

Holloway paused the video mid-gouge and then went to his table and pulled a picture out of his folder and gave it to Soltan. "This is a picture I took of Mr. DeLise three days ago, using a secure camera. You can see how scratched up his face is. In fact"— He pointed to where DeLise was sitting. —"you can still see scratches on his face a week after the attack."

Soltan looked over to Meyer. "I assume you have an alternative theory of the scratches," Soltan said.

"We do, Your Honor," Meyer said. She glanced over to DeLise and nodded.

"I got drunk," DeLise said. "I had too many to drink at Warren's and on the way home I fell facedown into a bush."

"Congratulations," Soltan said.

DeLise shrugged. "I'm not proud of it. But that's the reason," he said.

"Mr. Holloway?" Soltan said.

"Well, since I know how much Joe likes his drink, normally I'd be perfectly willing to believe him," Holloway said. He walked back to his table and pulled out a sheet with graphs and text on it. "But there is the little case of the DNA evidence."

Soltan took the sheet, frowning. "The man who set fire to your cabin left DNA," she said.

"He surely did," Holloway said. He walked back to the table. "As you might imagine, there was a lot of blood when the man attacked the fuzzys, and the fuzzys attacked back. I had it tested. Most of it was fuzzy blood, of course, considering the gunshots and the vicious physical attack. But enough of it was human."

"Ms. Meyer?" Soltan said.

"The plaintiff is collecting and processing his own DNA evidence, Your Honor?" Meyer asked.

"I'm accusing a ZaraCorp security officer of arson and destruction of property," Holloway said. "And it's a small security detail here. I have good reason to doubt that any material collected and processed by them will be compromised. And in point of fact the DNA evidence was collected and processed by the same ZaraCorp biology lab that would process DNA evidence for the security office, not by me. I just eliminated the middleman."

"Was the blood taken from the floor of Mr. Holloway's compound?" Meyer asked.

Soltan looked at Holloway. "Yes," he said.

"The compound floor was flooded with fire suppressant," Meyer said. "The chemicals in the suppressant would dilute and degrade the blood. Any DNA report from that source would be suspect."

"My colleague is absolutely correct," Holloway said, and noted the slight flare Meyer had at the implication that he was her colleague. He reached under the table, where he had stored a sturdy cooler. He hauled it up on the table. "Fortunately, we also have DNA from tissue samples." Holloway started undoing the lid latches.

"Tissue samples from what?" Soltan asked.

"Not from what," Holloway said. He opened the lid. "From whom."

And with that Holloway reached into the cooler and gently removed Pinto. He placed the fuzzy's corpse on the table. Meyer gasped in spite of herself.

"Bringing a corpse into the courtroom was *not* necessary, Mr. Holloway," Soltan said, sharply.

"With all due respect, Your Honor, I disagree," Holloway said. "If I had not, I doubt Ms. Meyer would accept the authenticity of the evidence, of which there are two types." Holloway held up Pinto's small hand. "First, human skin and blood underneath the fuzzy's nails." Holloway set the hand back down, gently, and then reached into the cooler again, taking out a small jar. "Second, this bullet, taken out of this fuzzy." He reached into his folder and extracted a third paper, then walked the bullet and the paper over to the judge. "Here's my request to impound any and all handguns in Mr. DeLise's possession, to perform a forensic analysis of their ballistics." Soltan took both the bullet and the jar.

"That bullet could have come from anywhere," Meyer said. "A bullet hole in the creature does not mean that particular bullet caused it."

"The bullet was extracted by ZaraCorp's own biologist," Holloway said. "She also ran the DNA tests and compared the results against samples in the employment database. I'm certain she would have been happy to testify."

Soltan looked up. "Would have been happy?" she asked.

"She's been transferred Earthside," Holloway said. "She's on the same transport Mr. Sullivan was."

Soltan looked over to Meyer. "Ms. Meyer, is there any particular reason that the all the people who would be really useful to

Mr. Holloway have suddenly been transferred off the planet?" she asked.

"I'm sure it's coincidental," Meyer said.

"Uh-huh," Soltan said. "I'll be having my clerks do another search and rescue so she can testify. In the meantime, Mr. Holloway, please put that body back into your container. I'm going to have to impound it for the time being."

"Yes, Your Honor," Holloway said. He walked back to Pinto and gently returned the fuzzy to the cooler, the condenser of which hummed quietly after he closed the lid again. He walked the cooler over and set it down next to the judge.

"We should note that the biologist in question is Dr. Isabel Wangai," Meyer said. "She has a past relationship with Mr. Holloway."

"Noted," Soltan said. "It's one reason I'm impounding the animal."

"Not an animal," Holloway said.

"The creature," Soltan corrected. "Happy, Mr. Holloway?"

"Yes, Your Honor," Holloway said.

"I will order an independent study of the DNA under the creature's nails, and of the ballistics of Mr. DeLise's weapons," Soltan said.

"The body of the . . . creature has been in Mr. Holloway's possession all this time," Meyer said. "The evidence is almost certainly tainted."

"How?" Holloway asked, incredulously. "I somehow arranged to have Mr. DeLise's flesh clawed off his body and then stuffed it under the fuzzy's nails? That's a little *elaborate*."

"The body is in my possession now and will be examined for any sign of tampering," Soltan said. "Unless you have an objection with my doing so."

"No, Your Honor," Meyer said.

"Now you see why I brought the body, Your Honor," Holloway said. "Imagine what Ms. Meyer's objections would have been without it."

"Stop grandstanding, Mr. Holloway," Soltan said.

"Apologies, Your Honor," Holloway said.

"We'll take another half hour break while my clerk retrieves Dr. Wangai from the beanstalk," Soltan said. She stood. "See you in thirty." She returned to her chambers. Holloway sat at his table and watched Meyer and DeLise confer furiously.

Sullivan came up to the audience area directly behind the plaintiff table. "He doesn't look very pleased," he said to Holloway, nodding over to DeLise.

"That's because he's realized that the fuzzy he thought got eaten by a zararaptor has come back to haunt him," Holloway said. "It's finally getting into his thick skull that he just might have to go to trial on this, and if he actually goes to trial, he's going to lose."

"And you're enjoying that fact," Sullivan said.

"Shit, yes," Holloway said.

Sullivan smiled. "That's the Jack Holloway I've come to know," he said. "Always ready to revel in the cheap dig."

"It's not cheap," Holloway said. "It's cost ZaraCorp six hundred billion so far."

"Not bad for a morning's work," Sullivan said.

"The day's still young," Holloway said.

"Here comes Janice," Sullivan said. Holloway looked up. Meyer was standing over him.

"Let's talk," Meyer said.

"Of course," Holloway said. He stood up, and the two of them walked out of the courtroom, leaving DeLise and Sullivan behind.

"This whole thing is getting out of hand," Meyer said, as they stepped into a vacant conference room.

"You're just saying that because I'm kicking your client's ass with the evidence," Holloway said.

"Don't flatter yourself," Meyer said. "Making a show of an animal corpse in a preliminary hearing is one thing. But it's the sort of thing I'm going to demolish in an actual trial. Shit, Holloway. You hanging on to that thing for a week? You really think I'm going to have a problem introducing reasonable doubt on that? Not to mention it's morbid as hell."

"I see," Holloway said. "So you want to do me a favor and save me the embarrassment of falling on my ass in a big-boy trial."

"Don't do that," Meyer said. "I know about you, Holloway. I know you used to do this for a living. I know you were good at it too, until you punched your client. And I know that you didn't exactly punch your client out of passion, either. You did it for effect, and you got paid well for it, and that your time on this planet has been a sort of extended vacation for you. So, yeah, Holloway, I know you're good. All right?"

"Okay, better," Holloway said.

"But we both know this is all bullshit anyway," Meyer said. "You and DeLise have a history. Fine. He finally went over the line with it. Fine. Let's all agree he's an asshole and just settle this."

"What's the offer?" Holloway said.

"Drop the suit," Meyer said. "DeLise apologizes without admitting guilt. ZaraCorp fires DeLise and puts a note in his employment record that keeps him from working security again—but no criminal record. We ship him off and he spends the rest of his life washing dishes somewhere and is grateful for it. And not that it should matter to you at this point, Mr. Billionaire, but ZaraCorp also reimburses you for your cabin and anything else damaged by the fire."

"How much total?" Holloway asked.

"We're not exactly going to be pinching pennies," Meyer said.

"And what about for the fuzzys?" Holloway asked.

"What about them?" Meyer said.

"Your boy stomped one, shot another, and killed both," Holloway said. "That has to be worth something."

"Name your price," Meyer said. "But don't go crazy about it."

"It's not a bad deal," Holloway said.

"It gets you what you want," Meyer said. "Hell, it gets everyone what they want—DeLise out of security. He's a menace. You'd be doing the universe the favor."

"That is, if you can get him to accept it," Holloway said.

"Don't you worry about that," Meyer said. "That's my job, and I'm good at it."

"I'm sure you are," Holloway said.

"So we have a deal," Meyer said.

"Absolutely not," Holloway said.

"No deal," Meyer said.

"No way," Holloway said. "Not a chance in Hell."

"Can I ask why not?" Meyer asked.

"Because, Ms. Meyer," Holloway said, "with all due respect for your considerable skills and intellect, the fact of the matter is you have absolutely no clue what it is I want out of this."

• • •

Isabel's testimony was anticlimactic. Yes, Your Honor, Jack brought me the body to examine. No, Your Honor, it was not tampered with in any way I could see. Yes, I dug the bullet out myself. No, I am not a licensed forensic examiner. Yes, the DNA work was only preliminary; I was locked out of the lab for half the week when they informed me I was being transferred. No, I don't know why they should have locked me out of the lab. Holloway smiled at Isabel as she walked out of the witness stand. Now the whole gang was here.

"Mr. Holloway, any other evidence for me before I get to the defense exhibits?" Soltan asked, after Isabel had sat down in the audience area.

"No more physical evidence, Your Honor," Holloway said. "But I have a witness to the arson. Someone who can definitively identify Mr. DeLise as the man in the mask."

"Very well," Soltan said. "Bring in your witness, Mr. Holloway."

"The witness is in my skimmer, Your Honor," Holloway said. "It's in the parking area."

"Send someone, then," Soltan said.

"Mr. Sullivan knows what my skimmer looks like, if that's all right," Holloway said.

"Fine," Soltan said, irritably. "Make it fast." Holloway nodded to Sullivan and handed him his key fob. Sullivan left.

"Is there a reason you left your witness in the skimmer, Mr. Holloway?" Soltan asked, while they waited.

"The witness wanted to spend time with my dog," Holloway said.

"Is the witness someone you have a personal relationship with, Mr. Holloway?" Meyer asked.

Holloway smiled. "You could say that, Ms. Meyer."

The door to the courtroom opened and Sullivan walked through, followed by something small.

It was Papa Fuzzy.

Chapter Twenty-four

That's it," Soltan said. "Mr. Holloway. Approach the bench. *Now.*"

Holloway approached. Janice Meyer, making a unilateral decision, approached as well.

"You're in contempt, Holloway," Soltan said, spitting out the words.

"For calling a witness, Your Honor?" Holloway asked.

"For trying to make a fool out of me," Soltan said.

"I am not trying to make a fool out of you," Holloway said.

"Really," Soltan said. "Because from where I'm sitting, that's exactly what you seem to be doing. Otherwise you wouldn't have been inserting these animals into the hearing at every opportunity."

"They're not animals," Holloway began.

"Don't start that with me now, Mr. Holloway," Soltan warned. "I am really not in the mood."

"Nor have I been *inserting* them into the hearing," Holloway continued, risking Soltan's additional wrath. "The video of the attack and the corpse of the attacked fuzzy had material bearing on the charges."

"But you haven't exactly been shy about using the creatures as an attempt to play off our emotions, have you," Meyer said.

"I don't particularly care about your emotions, Meyer," Holloway said.

"And I don't particularly care for you attempting to play off of mine," Soltan said, to Holloway. "We're here to look at the facts of the case, Mr. Holloway. I've given you slack on your rope because I thought you were getting to these facts, but this"— Soltan nodded her head dismissively in the direction of Papa Fuzzy, who by now had reached the well of the courtroom and was watching the three of them curiously—"makes it clear that you're not here to present those facts, you're here to do something else entirely. It's bad enough you brought a dead one of these creatures into this courtroom to showboat. I'm not going to allow you to bring in a live one to make a fool out of me. You've taken that rope I gave you and hanged yourself on it."

"This creature is a witness, Your Honor," Holloway said, grimly. "If you want the facts as you say you do, then you will let me call it to testify."

"And how are you going to do that?" Meyer said. "Have you suddenly become an expert on their communication, Holloway? Or are you planning to call Dr. Chen to translate? Because calling in a xenolinguist who has an entire career to gain by asserting these animals have language isn't going to be problematic at all."

"I find it interesting the concern you have for my potential witnesses, considering how ZaraCorp's gone out of its way to try to make sure I didn't have any to call," Holloway said.

"He's not calling Dr. Chen, Ms. Meyer," Soltan said. "He's not calling anyone. I reiterate, Mr. Holloway: You are in contempt of court. Recess is called until such time as you find new legal representation for the remainder of your case. When we resume, you will be allowed into the courtroom and you will be allowed to communicate with your new legal representative, but that's it. When the preliminary hearing is through, you'll be taken into custody."

"You're going to place me into the loving hands of Zara-Corp's Security force?" Holloway said. "You really *are* trying to get me hanged."

"That is *enough,* Mr. Holloway," Soltan said, and stood.

"I have a witnesss, Your Honor," Holloway said, loudly. "You need to let my witness talk."

"Stop wasting my time, Mr. Holloway," Soltan said. "The answer is no."

"So I will not talk?" Papa Fuzzy asked, in a high, thin but distinct voice. "I have come to talk. I have come to tell my story. Will I not talk now?"

• • •

Holloway counted in his head the seconds before anyone else spoke. He got to nine.

"Tell me I just heard what I think I heard," Judge Soltan said, still standing.

"This is what I've been trying to tell you, Your Honor," Holloway said, quickly. "I have a witness. It is ready to testify." He turned to Meyer. "And it doesn't need a translator." He looked at Papa, who was eyeing him curiously. "Please say hello to Judge Soltan," he said.

The fuzzy turned and looked back at the judge. "Hello, Judge Soltan," said the fuzzy, slowly.

Judge Soltan sat.

"So he's taught the thing to recite a phrase," Meyer said, scrambling to regain ground. "That proves it's as smart as a parrot."

"Mr. Holloway," Soltan began.

"*Talk* to it, Your Honor," Holloway said. "If you think I'm trying to trick you, talk to this fuzzy here. Ask it a question. Any question. But if I may suggest, keep your words simple. Its vocabulary is not extensive."

"This is ridiculous, Your Honor," Meyer said.

"Your Honor, I may showboat, but I'm not stupid," Holloway said. "Do you honestly think I'd bring this creature in front of you if all I could get it to do is recite spoon-fed words and phrases? How long would that trick work? One round of questions, maybe two, before everything went off the script. There's no possible way I could account for every comment or question you would have to ask it. And then what? What good would it do me and my case against Mr. DeLise to attempt to con you?"

Holloway pointed a finger at DeLise. "All I would get out of it is time in a security holding cell with *his* buddies watching over me," he said. "So, no. It's not a trick. Ask it whatever you like, for as long as you like, until you're convinced."

"That doesn't prove a thing," Meyer said. "A transmitter could feed the thing lines."

"Examine it however you want," Holloway said, to Meyer. "Run any sort of scanner you have over its body. You'll be wasting your time, but if that's what it takes, be my guest."

"Your Honor, this mockery needs to stop now," Meyer said, to Soltan.

"Quiet, Ms. Meyer," Soltan snapped. Meyer quieted, and shot a poisonous look at Holloway. Holloway kept his face blank. Soltan sat silently at her desk, chewing over recent events.

"Your Honor," Holloway prompted, after a minute. "You need

to tell us what we're doing now. And I need to know if I'm still under contempt."

Soltan looked over at Holloway. "Mr. Holloway, if I find a single bit of evidence that this witness is anything but what you say it is, contempt charges are going to be the least of your problems."

"Fair enough," Holloway said. "But at least try to talk to the fuzzy first." He and Meyer returned to their tables.

Soltan glanced down at the fuzzy, who still stood there, staring impassively at her. Soltan opened her mouth to speak, closed it, and got a look on her face that said, *I can't believe I'm doing this*. She looked up again at Holloway.

"Does it have a name, Mr. Holloway?" Soltan asked.

"Why don't you ask the fuzzy," Holloway said.

Soltan looked back to the fuzzy. "Do you have a name?" she asked slowly.

"Yes," the fuzzy said.

There was a pause after this before Soltan figured out that she might have to be more literal. "Please tell me your name," she said.

"My name is," and here there was a pause. "Jack Holloway calls me 'Papa' but that is not my name. My name is."

Soltan looked up, confused. "I didn't catch the name," she said.

"You couldn't," Holloway said. "Fuzzy speech is spoken above the range of our hearing, remember. When it's speaking to you in English, it's talking at the absolute bottom of its vocal range."

Soltan nodded. "May I call you Papa?" she asked the fuzzy.

"Jack Holloway calls me 'Papa.' You can call me 'Papa,'" Papa said.

"How do you feel, Papa?" Soltan asked.

"I feel with my hands," Papa said.

"You might want to try more direct questions," Holloway said.

"All right," Soltan said. "Papa, how do you speak our language?"

"With my mouth," Papa said, and gave Soltan a look, as if wondering how she didn't know either this, or how to feel.

"No," Soltan said. "Who *taught* you to speak our language? Did Jack Holloway teach you to speak?"

"I knew your language before I met Jack Holloway," the fuzzy said. "No man taught me to speak your language. Andy Alpaca taught us to speak your language. Andy Alpaca taught us from inside the flat talking rock."

"That makes no sense," Meyer said. "That makes no sense at all."

"What is a flat talking rock?" Soltan said.

Papa turned and pointed to Holloway's infopanel. "This is a flat talking rock," it said. "You use other words for it."

"That's an infopanel," Soltan said.

"Yes," Papa said. "The man and the monkey fell out of the sky and the man was killed by the" pause, as Papa used a fuzzy word. "We went into the skimmer to see what we could see and found the flat talking rock. It taught us your language."

Soltan looked at Holloway. "Translate," she said.

"There was a surveyor named Sam Hamilton," Holloway said. "He had a pet monkey. His skimmer went down. He was killed by zararaptors. The fuzzys checked out the skimmer wreckage and found his infopanel. Sam was nearly illiterate, so he was using kids' reading software to learn how to read. The software was adaptive, so it took into consideration the user's comprehension level and scaled from there."

"You're seriously suggesting these things learned to read and speak a human language from an advanced piece of technology," Meyer said.

"Yes, just like human toddlers," Holloway said. "Amazing, that."

"Unlike these things, toddlers are surrounded by other humans talking to them all the time," Meyer said.

"And unlike toddlers, the fuzzys who found this were adults, and smart enough to figure out what the infopanel was displaying to them," Holloway said. "You're still working under the impression these things are animals. They're not. They're as smart as you or I."

"Why didn't you mention any of this before?" Soltan asked. "You were in here last week arguing these fuzzys had language. If you had one come in and speak English, it would have made your case a lot better."

Holloway nodded toward the fuzzy. "That's a question for Papa," he said.

Soltan looked at the fuzzy. "You knew our language before you met Jack Holloway," she said.

"Yes," said Papa.

"You did not speak to Jack Holloway in our language when you met him," Soltan said.

"No," said Papa.

"Why?" asked Soltan.

"I did not want Jack Holloway to know," Papa said. "We did not know if Jack Holloway was a good man or a bad man. You have many bad men. Bad men take our homes and food from us and make us move away from other" pause. "We did not know if there are any good men. All the men we saw were bad. When we moved, we found where Jack Holloway lived. I wanted to see and went to see it. Jack Holloway and Carl came and I was scared. But Jack Holloway was good and gave me food. I went back to my people and said I had found a good man."

There was a snort from Janice Meyer at this.

"I wanted to go back but my people were scared," Papa said.

"I told them about Carl and how Carl was like the monkey who follows us. An animal who was not smart but who men liked. I said I would go and be quiet, to learn more about Jack Holloway and men. I would not speak your language. I would not let Jack Holloway know I could speak your language. I would see how Jack Holloway was with me quiet before I would see how Jack Holloway was with me smart. If Jack Holloway was a good man, then we could show who we are and that we are smart. If Jack Holloway was a bad man, we would hide and move, as we did before."

Holloway listened to Papa explain to Soltan and was amazed again by the creature. Papa's words were simple—even at its highest setting the particular software Sam had on his infopanel was not meant for complex adult concepts or reading levels, and Papa's language would be hampered by that—but the fuzzy spoke them confidently and fluently. It didn't know much of the English language, but the little part it knew, it knew pretty well. Well enough for this.

Papa turned to Holloway. "My throat hurts," the fuzzy said.

"Of course it does," Holloway said. "You've been orating in a very low voice."

Soltan looked at Holloway. "He's saying he was a spy," Soltan said. "Acting like a pet."

"Yes," Holloway said. "Although not entirely like a pet. It was clear Papa was smart, it just wasn't clear he was smart on the level of a sentient creature. Also, he's not really a he, he's an it."

Soltan frowned. "You call him 'Papa,' " she said.

"Biology mistake," Holloway said. "Patriarchal assumptions. What are you going to do."

"Well, whatever," Soltan said, and turned her attention back to Papa. "Do all of your people speak our language?" she asked.

"No," Papa said. "I do. Some others do. Not many. It is hard to learn. Only I did from those who came to be with Jack Holloway."

"Why did you want to learn our language?" Soltan asked.

"We want to know why you do what you do," Papa said. "When we found the flat talking rock we knew that it could help us learn to talk with men. We learn and we look for a man to talk to. We did not find good men. We found bad men."

"Who are the bad men?" Soltan said. "You said we had many of them."

"Yes," Papa said. "They have machines and tear the ground and trees and make the air stink. The trees are where we live and where our food is. When they come we do not stay. They do not see us because we see how they kill animals who come close. We go and we hide."

Soltan glanced up at Holloway at this. "I presume you haven't told your friend here what you do for a living, Mr. Holloway."

Holloway looked embarrassed at this. "It hasn't come up, no," he said.

"There are levels of irony to that," Soltan said.

"Granted," Holloway said. "But given who they are and how they live, it's easy to see why they see the surveyors and workers they come across as bad men. It also explains how they came to find me. Sam Hamilton's old territory was next to mine. Not too long ago, the new surveyor there found copper along the border of our territories, and ZaraCorp came in and tore up a good chunk of it. Papa's tribe of fuzzys must have gotten displaced. They've been moving through the trees ever since, looking for a new home. And if you want to hear something both funny and sad, ask Papa why it thought living with me might be a good idea."

Soltan looked at Papa. "Why did you want to live with Jack Holloway?" she asked.

"I do not think men will tear the ground and trees where they live," Papa said.

"Think about that, Your Honor," Holloway said. "Aside from the irony inherent in the statement, that's a fair feat of cognitive modeling. This fuzzy took what it knew about humans and guessed at what our behavior would be toward each other, and how it could work that to its own advantage and to the advantage of its own people."

"If that's true, then the thing's been using you all this time, Mr. Holloway," Soltan said.

"Another argument for their sentience, Your Honor," Holloway said.

"It doesn't bother you," Soltan said.

"Not really, Your Honor," Holloway said.

"Mr. Holloway, that doesn't surprise me in the least," Soltan said.

"Yes, Your Honor," Holloway said. "And now may I remind you that as enlightening as this has been for all of us, I brought Papa here for a specific reason, which is to testify for this preliminary hearing. If Your Honor is sufficiently convinced that Papa is neither a trick nor a parrot, I would like to put it on the stand."

"Your Honor, I have to strenuously object," Meyer said. "This creature has not yet been proven sentient. Any testimony it gives would be inadmissible in any court in the Colonial Authority or on Earth. If you allow the testimony, you're giving in to the sideshow you said you were hoping to avoid."

Soltan blinked at Meyer. "Ms. Meyer, have you been in the same courtroom I have been in for the last several minutes?" she asked. "I've just had a longer and more cogent discussion with this creature than I suspect you have ever had with your client. The question to me no longer is whether these creatures are sentient or not. That particular question was answered to my satisfaction several minutes ago. The only question now is whether or not this creature in particular is a credible witness. So I'm going to hear its testimony, Ms. Meyer, and make my decision after I hear what it has to say."

"Then I'd like to request a thirty-minute recess to prepare," Meyer said.

"Another recess," Soltan said. "Why not." She headed for her chambers.

Meyer was up like a shot and out the door of the courtroom. DeLise watched her go, openmouthed. He caught Holloway looking at him and glared.

"Looks like you're not your lawyer's main concern anymore, Joe," Holloway said. "I'd be worried if I were you."

DeLise crossed his arms, stared forward, and ignored Holloway.

Chapter Twenty-five

Zara Twenty-three's entire flotilla of ZaraCorp lawyers, along with Brad Landon and Wheaton Aubrey VII, was waiting for Judge Soltan when she emerged from her chambers.

"Well, I can't say this is a total surprise," Soltan said, as she took her seat.

Meyer approached the bench without asking and placed a folder in front of Soltan. "A request for the suspension of this preliminary hearing," she said. She dropped a second folder on the desk. "Request for change of venue for the preliminary hearing." A third folder. "Request for suspension and review of your previous determination for more study concerning the so-called 'fuzzys.'" A fourth folder. "A request to have you removed for legal malfeasance."

Soltan looked at the folders and then up at Meyer. "Someone's had a productive half hour," she said.

"Your Honor, it's become abundantly clear that your legal standards are dangerously and prejudicially lax," Meyer began.

"You're too late, Ms. Meyer," Soltan said, interrupting her.

"Excuse me, Your Honor?" Meyer said.

"I said, you're too late," Soltan said. "Because I am not actually stupid, Counselor, while you were off drafting this raft of legal chaff, I was in my chamber amending my determination for more study of the fuzzys. It's been amended to require ZaraCorp to file a Suspected Sapience Report, and not just in two weeks, Ms. Meyer, but immediately. You can pick one of your people here to write it up while we're listening to testimony, and file it with one of my clerks by the close of business today. So this"—Soltan lifted up the third folder—"is now outdated and irrelevant.

"As for the rest of these," Soltan said, motioning to the rest of the folders, "your request for the suspension of the preliminary hearing is denied, your request for change of venue is denied, and as for your request to have me removed, by all means file it with my clerk, who will send it along with every other request at end of the business day. Which means until then we continue on as planned."

"I'm afraid I can't do that," Meyer said.

"I beg your pardon, Ms. Meyer," Soltan said.

"I cannot in good conscience as a lawyer continue with these proceedings," Meyer said. "I feel it's impossible for my client to get a fair hearing from you."

"And which client would that be, Ms. Meyer?" Soltan asked. "Mr. DeLise over here, or ZaraCorp?"

"Either," Meyer said. "Both. I refuse to continue with this preliminary hearing, and I will not direct my staff to file the SSR. I believe you are not competent to continue with the first, or to require the second."

"I admire your willingness to throw a wrench into the wheels of jurisprudence on behalf of your employer, Ms. Meyer, but I've given you my decisions," Soltan said.

"You have given them," Meyer said. "I suppose now you'll have to enforce them."

"A pretty sentiment, Ms. Meyer," Soltan said. "Unfortunately for you, this isn't the United States Supreme Court or the 1830s, and you are definitely not Andrew Jackson. And as for enforcing my orders, I ask you to note the security cameras on the wall above my head."

"What about them?" Meyer said.

"Those security cameras don't just feed into the security office here on planet," Soltan said. "They also have a secure, encrypted wireless feed that goes directly to the Colonial Authority communication satellite and then into the databanks of the nearest Colonial Authority Circuit Court, in this case the Seventh CACC. The feed is mostly there to watch the judges, because judges on Explore and Exploit–chartered planets are historically prone to corruption and bribery. It's a nice reminder to us to stay poor, impartial, and on our toes.

"However, they also have another purpose," Soltan continued. "If and when a judge feels that an E and E corporation is trying to bigfoot its way around the courtroom, or if, say, a local general counsel gets it into her head to illegally override the orders of the court, or something even worse occurs, the judge can press a button, and the feed is ported, live, to the chambers of one of the sitting circuit court judges. It's just our little way of making sure that corporate executives on backwater worlds remember they are not actually above the law. I pressed that little button just before I came back into this courtroom.

"So, Ms. Meyer, you have a choice. You can continue with this preliminary hearing on behalf of your client Mr. DeLise, or I can have the Circuit Court order down some Colonial Marshals to haul you away for contempt of court and obstructing a judicial proceeding. You'll very likely be disbarred, serve jail time, and as you are an officer of the Zarathustra Corporation, a very heavy fine will be levied against the company.

"Likewise, if an SSR filing is not handed over to my clerk by the end of the business day, the Seventh Circuit will order the impounding of Zarathustra Corporation assets equivalent to the last ten years of gross revenues from this planet. As you are making this little power play of yours in front of the future Chairman and CEO of the company, who could stop you if he chose, there's little doubt you are carrying out a company order, so ZaraCorp will be on the hook for all sorts of penalties, up to and including jail time for you, for Mr. Aubrey over there, and for every single ZaraCorp lawyer in this chamber with the exception of Mr. Sullivan, who, as his good fortune would have it, no longer works for your department.

"So, Ms. Meyer. Smile for the camera, and tell me what it will be."

"She is *excellent*," Holloway whispered to Papa Fuzzy. Papa Fuzzy watched everything with curiosity. It might not understand the details, but Holloway suspected it got the emotional gist of what was going on.

"I'll comply for now," Meyer said, tightly, after a moment. "Your clerk will still be getting my request for your removal."

"At this point I'd be disappointed otherwise," Soltan said. "In the meantime, Ms. Meyer, back off my podium and get back to work."

Meyer backed off, glancing at the cameras while she did so.

"Now that today's insurrection has been quashed," Soltan said, briskly, "I believe we have a witness to hear from. Mr. Holloway?"

* * *

"Your name, please," Soltan asked Papa Fuzzy.

"You know my name," Papa said. He was at the witness stand, standing rather than sitting.

"Please say it again," Soltan said.

"I am" pause "who Jack Holloway and other men call Papa," Papa said.

"Your witness," Soltan said, to Holloway.

"Papa, you know the day Baby and Pinto were killed," Holloway said.

"Yes," Papa said.

"Who?" Soltan said.

"The two fuzzys who were killed," Holloway said. "I called them Baby and Pinto. Baby was the one that was stomped. Pinto was the one who was shot."

"Continue," Soltan said.

"Who were Baby and Pinto to you," Holloway said.

"The one you call Baby was my child," Papa said. "The one you call Pinto was to be the mate of my child in time."

"Tell us what happened that day," Holloway said.

"Your Honor, we have already seen what happened on video a number of times," Meyer said. "We can stipulate the events we've already seen."

"Your Honor, there's not much point in witness testimony if the witness isn't allowed to describe the events," Holloway said.

"Agreed," Soltan said. "But let's not dwell on details, Mr. Holloway."

"Yes, Your Honor," Holloway said. He looked back to Papa. "Tell us what happened that day," he said.

"You were gone," Papa said. "When you are gone, we leave your home and go to our people to talk and be with them. Baby heard the noise of a skimmer going to your home. Baby went to see. Baby wanted to see Carl. Pinto went with Baby. I was near but I was in the tree, eating. I did not go with them.

"I heard Pinto call to me to say that the man was not you, but some other man. Then I heard my child cry and then stop. Then I heard Pinto yell. Then the man yelled. Then Pinto called for help.

"I came from the trees and heard a very big noise. Then I came to the tree by your house and saw the man step on my child. I saw the man kill my child. I saw the man hold my child and put my child in your house. Your house was on fire. And then I heard the man speak."

"Tell us what the man said," Holloway said.

"I did not know some of the words," Papa said.

"Try," Holloway said.

"The man said 'jesiscris migodam face,' " Papa said.

"He said 'Jesus Christ, my goddamn face,' " Holloway said."

"Yes," Papa said. "Those are the words the man said. The man was very loud."

"Did you see his face?" Holloway said.

"I did not see the face of the man," Papa said. "I did not need to see a face. I knew the voice."

"How did you know his voice?" Holloway asked.

"The man had come to your house before," Papa said.

"When had he come to my house before?" Holloway asked.

"The man came with three other men," Papa said. "You let the three other men go to your house. You did not let this man go to your house. You did not let the man get out of the skimmer."

"How do you know it was the same voice?" Holloway asked.

"The man was very loud in the skimmer," Papa said. "Pinto went to look at the man and the man did not like that. I was in the tree and I heard the man yell."

"Did you see the man's face that time?" Holloway asked.

"Yes," Papa said, and pointed at DeLise. "This is the man."

Holloway glanced over at Meyer and then at Aubrey and Landon, who sat in the audience seats with their flotilla of lawyers. He smiled at each of them and picked up his infopanel.

"This is the day Papa is referring to," Holloway said, and loaded up the video of DeLise pitching a fit in the skimmer while Pinto rubbed his bottom against the glass. "Unfortunately there's no sound with the video, but I think it's pretty obvious that Mr. DeLise is being quite vocal."

"Mr. Holloway, you didn't mention that Mr. DeLise had been to your home before," Soltan said.

"It must have slipped my mind," Holloway said. "Probably because he didn't actually get into my house, he was stuck out in the skimmer. As you can see."

"Why was he there in the first place?" Soltan asked.

"Because he was allegedly Wheaton Aubrey's security detail," Holloway said.

"And what was Mr. Aubrey doing at your place?" Soltan asked.

"I'm not sure it's entirely relevant to the matter at hand," Holloway said.

"Let me be the judge of that," Soltan said.

"All right," Holloway said, and then looked over at Aubrey and Landon. "They were there to bribe me into throwing the hearing to determine the fuzzy's sapience. Offered me the entire northwest continent, they did."

" 'They,' " Soltan said.

"Yes. Aubrey and his assistant, Brad Landon," Holloway said. "Chad Bourne was there too, but I'm pretty sure he was just their cover for sneaking out to my place in the guise of one of Chad's official contract rep meetings. You could ask him. I'm sure at this point he'd be happy to talk."

"This is all allegation, Your Honor," Meyer said. "And for once, Mr. Holloway is right. This isn't the right venue for this line of questioning."

"I agree," Holloway said. "Although now that I think of it, it does offer an explanation for how DeLise got access to the skimmer. All that time alone in the skimmer would be a perfect time to duplicate the data off the key fob. That is, when DeLise wasn't busy yelling at fuzzys."

"There's no proof of that," Meyer said.

"Oh, he's definitely yelling at the fuzzy," Holloway said, intentionally misreading Meyer's comment. "It's the same fuzzy he shot later, in fact."

"That's enough, Mr. Holloway," Soltan said.

"This is a complete farce, Your Honor," Meyer said. "It's bad enough you just allowed Holloway to slander Mr. Aubrey and Mr. Landon, but entertaining testimony from this creature is beyond ridiculous. The creature can't make the visual connection between Mr. DeLise and the man in a ski mask. Instead we're asked to believe instead that this thing can recognize a voice it's allegedly heard only once, days after the initial encounter. This is a sham, Your Honor. Pure and simple."

"While I wouldn't call this a 'sham,' Ms. Meyer has a point, Mr. Holloway," Soltan said. "There's a reason they're called 'eyewitnesses,' not 'earwitnesses.'"

"Your Honor, do me a favor and order Mr. DeLise not to speak," Holloway said.

"Excuse me?" Soltan said.

"Please, Your Honor," Holloway said.

Soltan looked at Holloway strangely. "Mr. DeLise," she said. "You are not allowed to speak again until I tell you to. You can nod your understanding." DeLise nodded.

"You have your silent defendant, Mr. Holloway," Soltan said.

"Thank you, but it's worth noting he had been silent before," Holloway said. "In fact, Mr. DeLise has been silent the entire time Papa Fuzzy has been in the courtroom. So I propose a little challenge. Ms. Meyer says it's impossible that Papa could have recognized a voice it heard only once before. Fine. Let's do a lineup." Holloway waved at the small army of lawyers. "This courtroom is full of men. Pick as many of them as you want and put Mr. DeLise with them. Then turn Papa around so it can't see any of them. Have them speak the same sentence. If Papa picks the wrong one or can't identify the voice, throw out the testimony."

Soltan turned to Meyer, who looked about to object. "You were the one who objected to earwitnesses," Soltan said, shutting her down. "Pick four. Mr. Holloway, pick four as well. Gentlemen, if you are picked, go to the far wall of the courtroom, but don't line up yet. Mr. DeLise, you go back there as well."

Holloway and Meyer made their picks; DeLise shuffled back to the far wall. "I also have a pick," Soltan said. "Mr. Aubrey, walk to the wall, please."

"Your Honor, this is outrageous," said Brad Landon.

"Don't you start, Mr. Landon," Soltan said. "Your boss goes to the wall or he goes to a holding cell on a contempt charge. One or the other. I don't have all day."

Aubrey walked to the wall.

"Mr. Holloway, prepare your witness," Soltan said.

Holloway walked to the witness stand and turned Papa around. "Do not look," he said. "When the men speak and you hear a voice you know, say so. Yes?"

"Yes," Papa said. Holloway looked up at Soltan, who nodded. "Arrange your men, Ms. Meyer." Meyer arranged the men so DeLise was eighth, and Aubrey tenth.

"Swap the last one with one of the others," Soltan said.

Meyer bit her cheek and swapped Aubrey with the fourth man.

"What shall we have them say, Mr. Holloway?" Soltan asked.

"I think 'Jesus Christ, my goddamn face,' would work just fine," Holloway said.

"Number one, say the line," Soltan said.

"Jesus Christ, my goddamn face," said the man. Holloway glanced down at the fuzzy, who was motionless and silent.

"Number two," Soltan said, after a minute. The man spoke his line. Papa said nothing. It did the same with number three.

"Jesus Christ, my goddamn face," said Aubrey.

"I know this voice," said Papa. "It is one of the other men who came to the house of Jack Holloway. It is not the man who killed my child."

Soltan looked at Aubrey with a face that said *got you*. Aubrey did not seem particularly concerned.

"Number five," Soltan said.

The man said his line. Nothing from Papa. Man six, nothing. Man seven, nothing.

"Jesus Christ, my goddamn face," said DeLise.

Papa took in a sharp breath, held it, and let it out. "I know this voice," the fuzzy said. "It is the voice of the man who killed my child. It is the voice of the man who killed the mate of my child."

"Are you sure?" Soltan said.

"I know this voice," Papa said, and its voice was surprisingly forceful. Papa looked up at Soltan. "Do you not have a child? If a man killed your child, you would know about that man. You would know the face of the man. You would know the hands of the man. You would know the smell of the man. You would know the voice of the man. This is the voice of the man who killed my child. My child who I cannot see. Who I cannot hold. Who is gone. My child is gone. This man killed my child. I know this voice."

Papa fell to its knees in the witness stand and keened, silently, as far as the humans could hear.

The courtroom was absolutely still.

"Your Honor," Holloway said, quietly, after several moments.

"The testimony stands," Soltan said, also quietly. "Everyone, sit down again."

Chapter Twenty-six

Your Honor," Holloway said, after everyone had sat. "If Papa's testimony stands, we have another issue to address."

"And what issue is that, Mr. Holloway," Soltan said. She seemed drained.

"We have reasonably established Mr. DeLise at the scene of the arson," Holloway said. "Ms. Meyer may still attempt to call forward her list of so-called witnesses testifying to Mr. DeLise's whereabouts, but we have DNA evidence and a credible witness, and we have excluded other potential arsonists. I doubt any of Meyer's witnesses will stack up to the evidence I've presented to you today. And on top of that, we have more than reasonably established that the fuzzys are sentient. By accepting Papa's testimony, you have effectively declared its species so."

"I'm still waiting to hear about this other issue, Mr. Holloway," Soltan said.

"Quite obviously, I'm talking about murder," Holloway said.

"What?" DeLise roared. After glowering through the entire preliminary hearing, he was suddenly engaged.

"Murder," Holloway repeated, turning to look at DeLise. "You murdered those fuzzys, Joe."

"This is *bullshit*," DeLise said, standing up.

"No, not *bullshit*, Joe," Holloway said. He stalked over to DeLise. "Not this time. It's *deep shit* this time. Because you walked right up to a tiny sentient being, lifted up your boot, and stomped the life right out of it. And when its mate tried to defend it, you killed it too. That's two counts of murder, fair and square, pure and simple."

"Your Honor." Meyer looked around DeLise and Holloway to Soltan, to get her to stop the two men.

"Mr. Holloway," Soltan said.

"How do you think this is going to look, Joe?" Holloway said, ignoring the judge. "We discover a new sentient species, only the third one we've ever found besides ourselves, and the first thing you do is stomp one of them to death. How do you think that's going to play, Joe?"

"Get out of my face, Jack," DeLise said. "I'm warning you."

"Because you know what, Joe, murder's not the only thing they're going to throw at you. They're probably going to hit you with hate crimes against xenosentients, too. There's not much doubt you targeted that first little fuzzy because of what it was, is there? You came, you saw, you crushed it to death."

"Your Honor!" Meyer practically screamed.

"If it was just murder, maybe you'd get off with life in prison, Joe," Holloway said. "But it's not. With a xenosentient's hate crime rider, that's the death penalty. Two counts. You're going to die, Joe, because you stomped that little creature *just for the fun of it.*"

DeLise howled and launched himself over the defense table at Holloway. Holloway took the tackle and went down without resistance. Sullivan was up over the audience railing and pulling

DeLise off Holloway, but not before DeLise landed heavy blows to Holloway's face and head. Holloway didn't bother to block them. Sullivan was followed by a rush of ZaraCorp lawyers, who finally managed to pull DeLise up and off his quarry.

Holloway picked himself up and wiped some of the blood off his face with his jacket sleeve. He faced Soltan, who looked frankly appalled.

"As I was saying, Your Honor, two counts of murder," he said. He wiped off his eyebrow, from which the blood was drizzling into his eye. "And a side order of assault and battery while you're at it."

"This is bullshit!" DeLise said from behind a pile of lawyers. "I want to make a deal, Your Honor."

"What are you talking about, Mr. DeLise?" Soltan said.

"Shut up, Joe," Meyer said, to DeLise.

"Shut up yourself, Meyer," DeLise said. "No way I'm dying for your boys back there. And if I *am* dying, they're coming with me."

"Mr. DeLise!" Soltan said. DeLise shut up. "I repeat: What are you talking about?"

"I was at Holloway's under orders," DeLise said. "I was there to booby-trap Holloway's place and to kill any of those things I could find."

"Whose orders?" Soltan said.

"Oh, I think you can guess, Your Honor," DeLise said. "But I'm not saying a damn thing else until I get a deal."

Soltan stared at DeLise, and then at Meyer. "Your client wants to make a deal, Ms. Meyer."

"I must request to withdraw as Mr. DeLise's attorney at this time," Meyer said.

"I suspected as much," Soltan said. She looked around in the courtroom until she found who she was looking for. "Mr. Sullivan," she said. "You are by all accounts currently unaffiliated."

"That would be accurate, Your Honor," Sullivan said. "I quit the employ of Zarathustra Corporation roughly forty seconds ago."

"How wonderful," Soltan said. "Will you please represent Mr. DeLise, then, at least for the short term. I can offer you standard Colonial Authority public defender rates."

"Happy to oblige," Sullivan said.

Soltan turned to Papa Fuzzy, who was still in the witness stand, watching everything unfold with a sort of quiet fascination. "Papa Fuzzy," she said. "You are someone who speaks for your people."

"Yes," Papa said.

"Soon my people will need to speak to your people," she said. "It would help if you choose a man to help your people speak to my people. A man you like who is good to you and good to your people."

"I choose Jack Holloway," Papa Fuzzy said.

"Are you sure?" Soltan asked.

"I am sure," Papa said. "I do not know all the things your people know. But I am smart. I see what Jack Holloway has done here now. Jack Holloway has helped you see bad men have hurt my people and killed my child. Jack Holloway is a good man. I choose Jack Holloway."

"Mr. Holloway," Soltan said. "You understand the job you've just been nominated for."

"Defender general of the fuzzy nation, it seems like," Holloway said.

"Do you accept the job?" Soltan said.

"I do," Holloway said.

"Then congratulations," Soltan said. "Because as of this moment, you're effectively in charge of this entire planet."

"Wait a minute," said Wheaton Aubrey VII. "You can't do that. The Zarathustra Corporation has an E and E franchise with the Colonial Authority. A judge at your level can't just decide it doesn't apply. And you certainly can't hand over responsibility to a contract surveyor."

"Not that you have any standing whatsoever in this courtroom at the moment, Mr. Aubrey, but as your statement dovetails into my next announcement, I'll address it," Soltan said. "But first, everyone needs to *sit down*."

The courtroom slowly returned to order.

"Now, then," Soltan said. "As it happens, Mr. Aubrey, once a Suspected Sapience Report is ordered, as I have done, if *any* Colonial Authority judge finds compelling evidence that the native sentient life of a planet is threatened, he or she is required to report it to the planet's ranking judge. The ranking judge then becomes or appoints someone to the role of Special Master for Xenosapience, whose tasks include making sure the new possibly sentient life remains extant long enough for its sentience to be fully assessed. The Special Master not only can but *must* take steps to ensure the species' survival, up to and including instituting martial law and suspending all franchises.

"As you have so condescendingly noted, Mr. Aubrey, I am merely a common Colonial Authority court judge," Soltan said. "But, in part because of your own corporation's desire to have the absolute minimum judicial interference on your E and E franchise worlds, I am also the *only* Colonial Authority court judge here. This makes me the Special Master for Xenosapience, which means I can and *must* act to protect the fuzzys.

"After today, it is my *strong* belief that the fuzzys are in clear and present danger from the humans on the planet, and from your corporation," Soltan said. "I will not wait for the legal wheels to turn to prove a sapience I have already seen in abundance. A slaughter has already begun here. Two of these creatures are already dead, Mr. Aubrey. Whether by your instigation, or by your encouragement, or through your willful blindness, is not my concern at the moment. My concern is stopping it before there are more of them dead by human hands.

"Therefore, Mr. Aubrey," Soltan said. "By the power vested in me as the Special Master for Xenosapience, the Zarathustra Corporation's Exploration and Exploitation Charter for the planet known as Zara Twenty-three is immediately and provisionally revoked, pending further review. All exploration and exploitation is to cease at once. All employees and contractors are ordered off the planet within thirty days. I am declaring martial law. Colonial Marshals will be on-planet within two days to relieve Zara-Corp's Security forces, who will surrender all weapons and security authority at that time.

"Furthermore, I am appointing Jack Holloway as Assistant Special Master for Xenosapience, with a portfolio to include transfer of all legal authority for the planet to the creatures known as the 'fuzzys,' pending final certification of species sapience," Soltan said. "He is running the show internally and for anything directly involving the fuzzys, while I am tending to external matters involving the Colonial Authority. So if there's something you want regarding the planet, your people are talking to *him* now, because he's the one talking to the fuzzys."

"We'll be appealing this decision," Meyer said.

"Of course you will, Ms. Meyer," Soltan said. "But until then, you talk to Mr. Holloway. Are we clear?"

"Yes, Your Honor," Meyer said.

"Good," Soltan said. "And are you still planning to call witnesses to account for Mr. DeLise's whereabouts the day of Mr. Holloway's fire?"

"No, Your Honor," Meyer said.

"Then also, and independently, I find that there is enough evidence against Mr. DeLise regarding arson and destruction of property to go to trial," Soltan said. "This opinion will be published on the court's site, along with every other thing that happened today, and I'll set the date for the trial at a later time." Soltan lifted one of the folders Meyer had earlier placed on her podium. "Look on the bright side, Ms. Meyer," she said. "You'll be getting your change of venue after all."

Soltan stood. "This preliminary hearing is now finished," she said. "Thank God." She left the courtroom.

Holloway walked over to a visibly shell-shocked Meyer. "Ms. Meyer," he said. He repeated it again to get her attention.

"What do you want now, Holloway?" Meyer said.

"I just wanted to tell you," Holloway said. "Now you know what I wanted out of all of this."

• • •

The next afternoon, Holloway strode into the executive conference room in the ZaraCorp building, infopanel at ready, Papa Fuzzy on one side, Carl on the other. He took a seat at the center left side of the table. On the other side of the table sat DeLise, Sullivan, representing DeLise, Meyer, representing Aubrey and Landon, and Aubrey and Landon, representing Zarathustra Corporation's board. Holloway set down his infopanel, situated Papa Fuzzy in a comfortable position on the table, and had Carl lie down, which the dog did, happily.

"Well," Holloway said, briskly. "I slept like a baby last night. How about you folks?"

"Don't be any more of an asshole than you have to be, Jack," Sullivan said.

"Quite right," Holloway said. "I've spoken to Papa Fuzzy, who has spoken with its own people, and I've reviewed my own situation with Mr. DeLise, and I think we have an offer here that will work for everyone. Mr. Sullivan, I will settle with Mr. DeLise for damages relating to arson and destruction of property for the nominal sum of one credit. The fuzzys likewise will seek no damages against Mr. DeLise, Mr. Aubrey, Mr. Landon, or the Zarathustra Corporation for the deaths of Pinto or Baby. Additionally I will request to the Colonial Authority on behalf of the fuzzys that they drop all charges against DeLise, Aubrey, Landon, or ZaraCorp.

"Finally, while we will not request that Judge Soltan rescind her order rescinding ZaraCorp's E and E charter, we will request she instead amend it to allow the company an orderly drawdown of people and property over six months, and while not allowing ZaraCorp to additionally mine or extract resources from the planet, the company may complete processing of materials it has already mined or extracted as part of this extended drawdown. There are going to be fiddly bits to all of this, of course, but that's the general sweep of things."

"In exchange for what?" Aubrey said.

"That's simple," Holloway said. "In exchange for you walking away. First, the three of you specifically—you, Aubrey, you, Landon, and from my point of view especially you, Joe—leave the planet and never come back. Ever. But more generally, it means that Zarathustra Corporation doesn't appeal Judge Soltan's ruling, doesn't challenge the fuzzys' claim to sentience, and doesn't work in any way, shape, or form to stay on this planet. You all just walk away. Take what you have with you and go. That's it, that's all, it's done and over. Clean slates for everybody."

"I don't think we have any problem with that deal," Sullivan said.

"Well, of course you wouldn't," Aubrey said. "You're not being asked to walk away from decades' worth of revenues."

"I should note that this is an 'all in or none in' deal," Holloway said. "If you're not all on board, none of this is on the table."

"You can't ask this company to walk away from everything it's done here," Aubrey said.

"Sure I can," Holloway said. "I just did. And more to the point, Aubrey, while there's no doubt you could drag things out for years with filings and appeals, there are two fundamental problems. The first is that at the end of the day, the fuzzys are sentient. ZaraCorp has no claim on this planet anymore. You'll just spend millions prolonging the inevitable. The second thing is that you've been very bad men, and there's lots leading back to you."

"A whole lot," DeLise said. "Including that skimmer crash of yours, Jack. They were trying to get you out of the way early."

"Damn it, I *knew* it," Holloway said, slapping the table. "So that leads back to you too, Aubrey."

"It does," DeLise said. "I can guarantee that." Aubrey shot the man a look.

"So if you want to fight it, Aubrey, go ahead," Holloway said. "But *I* guarantee that if you do, at the end of it, you're going to be strapped down to a table, looking at a clock, and counting down the last few seconds before every neuron in your brain gets scrambled."

"I think you overestimate your abilities," Aubrey said, and smiled.

"That's a curious thing to say," Holloway said. "Considering that in the space of a month, I've managed to take a planet from you and cut out your company's heart." Aubrey stopped smiling. "You need to ask yourself what I could do if you gave me two months. Or a year."

"We'll take the deal," Landon said.

"Brad," Aubrey began.

"Shut up, Wheaton," Landon said, sharply. "You don't get a vote in this anymore. It's done."

Aubrey shut up.

Holloway looked at Landon, surprised. "So you're not actually his personal assistant," he said finally.

"God, no," Landon said. "As bad as this got, it would have been worse if he hadn't been supervised."

"I don't know about that," Holloway said. "This got pretty bad."

"But it's not going to get any worse from here," Landon said. "The rest of the Aubrey family has recognized there's been a brand value in having a Wheaton Aubrey at the head of the company. It connotes stability that's attractive to our B-class stockholders. But the last few generations have been going the route of the Hapsburgs."

Landon pointed a finger at Aubrey. "This one's grandfather nearly destroyed the company with *Greene versus Winston,* and if we didn't keep his father, our current glorious leader, in a state of constant alcoholic stupor, he'd probably try to reverse every single ecology-friendly policy the company currently has. We thought *this* one might be better. He showed at least some intelligence and actual interest in the business. So we gave him his head, permitted his schemes, and took him on a tour of the properties to see how he'd do. Now we know."

"That was an expensive lesson," Holloway said.

Landon shrugged. "Expensive now, yes," he said. "But the future is long. The family has faith that in time the fuzzys will come to realize the commercial value of their planet and might wish to exploit it in a way consistent with their needs and desires," Landon said. "When that day comes we hope they will consider us a valuable, eager, and considerate potential partner."

"That depends," Holloway said. "Will this one be in charge?"

Landon laughed. Aubrey glowered.

"Then we're done here," Holloway said. "And now, Mr. DeLise,

Mr. Aubrey, Mr. Landon, if you'll go out front, you'll find a skimmer waiting to take you to the beanstalk. A transport is waiting. Your personal effects will be sent along later."

All three men looked shocked. "You want us to leave *now*?" Aubrey said.

"Yes, you will leave now," someone said in a small, high voice. It was Papa Fuzzy.

The three men looked at the fuzzy as if they forgot it could speak.

"You said you would leave," Papa said. "You will leave. I do not want the men who killed my child to move in the same air or see the same sun that my child did. You are not good men. You do not deserve these good things."

Papa got up, walked across the table, and stood in front of Aubrey. "I do not know all the things you know. But I am smart," it said. It pointed to DeLise. "I know this man killed my child. Now I know that you told this man to kill my child. With this man, you killed my child. Jack Holloway told me that he would get the—" Papa looked up at Holloway.

"Son of a bitch," Holloway said, helpfully.

"Jack Holloway told me he would get the son of a bitch who killed my child and the mate of my child," Papa continued. "Jack Holloway did get that son of a bitch. Jack Holloway got you. You are the man who killed my child. Get off my planet, you son of a bitch."

Holloway set the detonation panel on the ground and looked at Papa Fuzzy.

"All right," Holloway said. "Just like we practiced."

Papa Fuzzy looked at him, and then looked back at Carl, who was going out of his little doggy mind waiting for the signal. Papa Fuzzy waited, and waited, and waited, and then just when Carl let out the little whine that said, *I'm going to pee myself if you don't do something,* opened its mouth. Holloway didn't hear the signal to fire, but Carl sure did. He skittered forward and dropped his paw on the panel.

A volley of fireworks went up into the sky, arced high above the watching humans and fuzzys, stationed as they were on the top of what used to be the ZaraCorp executive building, and then exploded into multicolors. Everyone cheered in their own fashion, except Carl, who decided there was just a little more *boom* in that explosion than he would have preferred. Holloway fed Carl the rest of his hot dog. Carl was satisfied.

And just like that, Zara XXIII was no longer Zara XXIII. It was now, officially, the fuzzys' planet.

To be sure, the paperwork for the final handover of the planet was performed earlier in the day, when the last of the Zarathustra Corporation people and heavy machinery were lifted up the beanstalk, and the Colonial Authority officially ceded authority of the planet to Holloway, whose official title was now Minister Plenipotentiary for the Nation of Fuzzy Peoples. Holloway signed forms, shook hands with the Colonial officials, and stood for photographs with Papa Fuzzy and the Colonials. From the point of view of the Colonial Authority, that was when the planet became independent.

But everyone knows you need fireworks to make independence official.

Fireworks done, the party resumed its cheerful chaos and mingling. Holloway reached down, picked up the detonation panel, powered it down, waved at Albert Chen, who was in an animated conversation with a pack of fuzzys, and then walked over to Isabel, who was watching him, amused.

"Here," Holloway said, handing her the panel. "I thought you might like a memento."

"Very funny," Isabel said, taking it from him. "I can't believe you actually performed that stunt again. As part of an official event. And roped Papa into doing it with you."

"Well, you know," Holloway said. "It's a good trick. And anyway, Papa is pretty much ruler of the fuzzys and I'm its Minister Plenipotentiary. It's not like we're going to get in trouble for it."

"Jack Holloway," Isabel said. "You always did know how to stay ahead of trouble. But it proves I was *right* about you teaching Carl how to set off explosives." Isabel poked Holloway in the chest to make the point.

"You finally caught me," Holloway said. "You win."

"It is a sweet victory," Isabel assured him.

"I'm sure it is," Holloway said. He looked around. "So where is your husband? He missed the fireworks."

"He's still on a conference call with Chad Bourne," Isabel said. "They're going around with that tourism group again about why its proposed jungle tour is a bad idea for anyone who doesn't like to get eaten."

"As long as the fuzzys get their cut of the tour fee, I'm perfectly happy to let tourists get consumed," Holloway said.

"It will cut down a bit on repeat business," Isabel said.

"Hey, I'm the idea guy," Holloway said. "Chad and Mark handle the details."

"Don't think I haven't noticed how you did that, by the way," Isabel said. "There's very little point in Mark and me being married if you keep him so busy that we never see each other."

"It's not just Mark who's busy, Dr. Isabel Wangai, Minister of Science and Exploration for the Nation of Fuzzy Peoples," Holloway said, employing her full title.

"This is very true," Isabel said. "But at least my work is interesting. The work you have Mark doing is pure drudgery."

"Being Attorney General is not pure drudgery," Holloway said.

"It is the way you make him do it," Isabel said.

"Building a nation is not all parties and fireworks," Holloway said.

"Said the man at a party, setting off fireworks," Isabel said. "I have an idea. Why don't *you*, Mr. Minister Plenipotentiary, go get *my* husband and drag him up to the party. So he might enjoy the fruits of his nation building. And then give him and me both a week off, so we might finally have our honeymoon. So he and I might enjoy the fruits of our marriage."

"An excellent notion," Holloway said. "And for the honeymoon,

I've heard that there might be a very nice jungle tour coming along."

"You first, Jack," Isabel said, and gave him a peck on the cheek. "Husband, please."

"On it," Holloway said. He headed off toward the roof exit, stopping only to extract two bottles of beer from a cooler.

Holloway found Sullivan in his office, formerly the office of Janice Meyer.

Holloway knocked on the open door. "Your wife sent me to retrieve you," he said. He walked into the office and handed Sullivan a beer.

Sullivan took it. "Good. I'm ready to be retrieved," he said. "Have I missed any thing important?"

"You missed the fireworks," Holloway said.

"I saw them out the window," he said. "Did you have Carl set them off?"

"Seemed fitting, since we changed the name of Aubreytown to Carlsburg," Holloway said.

"The universe's first planetary capital city named after a dog," Sullivan said. "We are truly a nation of firsts."

"To the Fuzzy Nation," Holloway said, raising his beer bottle.

"To the Fuzzy Nation," Sullivan said. The men clinked their bottles and drank.

"How did the jungle tour discussion go?" Holloway said.

"They settled down once Chad sent them some video of the zararaptors in action," Sullivan said. "Nothing like bloody predators to encourage introspection. Of course, a few minutes after we got off the call with them, one of them called up Chad and proposed a hunting tour instead."

"The entrepreneurial spirit is always restless," Holloway said.

"It's not always very smart, either," Sullivan said. "I'm tempted to let the hunting tour run, so long as it's only equipped with knives." Holloway grinned at this. "But I'm not actually concerned about the eco-tourists," Sullivan continued. "It's the mining companies who are bothering me."

"We've been pretty clear about it," Holloway said. "No commercial mineral exploitation of any kind for twenty years at least, and only minimal after that."

"There is always someone who thinks they're going to get around that," Sullivan said. "Particularly when it comes to sunstones. You know we've already caught a couple of freelance prospectors. They come down with the academics and then try to sneak off. One of them actually managed to liberate a skimmer and headed out to that seam you discovered, Jack."

"What did you do to him?" Holloway asked.

"It's not what *we* did to him," Sullivan said. "We found an arm next to the skimmer."

"That solves that," Holloway said.

"It's only going to get worse," Sullivan pointed out.

"I know," Holloway said. "Add it to the pile."

"What do you think, Jack?" Sullivan asked. "Is this worth all the trouble?"

"It beats the alternative," Holloway said. "For us and for the fuzzys."

The two men drank their beers in silence for a moment.

"Jack," Sullivan said. "You remember when I perjured myself at that preliminary hearing of yours. When I said I saw Chad talking to you."

"I remember it," Holloway said. "I remember thinking it probably took a lot out of you to do it."

"It did, and I still don't feel completely right about it," Sullivan said. "It's something that gnaws at me a little every time I think about it. You perjured yourself too, Jack, in the same way, at the same time. But I don't get the feeling it bothers you at all."

"It doesn't," Holloway said. "A while ago I said to you that sometimes it feels good to do the wrong thing. Well, this time it felt good to do the right thing. I just had to lie to get there first. We're lawyers, Mark. Lying is part of the skill set."

"Which reminds me," Sullivan said. "I've been reading your mail again."

"Somebody should," Holloway said. He took another drink of his beer.

"You'll be happy to know that you've been reinstated to the North Carolina Bar," Sullivan said. "In recognition of your work to make sure the fuzzys were recognized as sentient beings."

"It sounds so impressive when it's put that way," Holloway said. "I like it. It makes it sound like that was the plan all along."

"What *was* the plan all along, Jack?" Sullivan asked.

"I think I've made it clear that I never really had a plan, Mark," Holloway said.

"That's what you say," Sullivan said. "But I don't believe it. And I know *you* don't. Look, Jack. Today you took part in founding a nation. In claiming an entire world for people who couldn't have done it for themselves. In keeping them safe from the people who would just as soon kill them to get what was in the ground under them. You don't do that without a plan. And you don't do it without knowing why you're doing it. So, just between you and me, Jack. Tell me why you did it."

"At first I was doing it for myself," Holloway said, after a minute. "Because that's what I had always done, and it always seemed to work for me. Then later, I was doing it because I was curious to see what could happen, and how well that would work out for me. And then finally I was doing it because I knew what *had* to happen, and I knew that I was the only one who could make it happen."

"Why were you the only one who could make it happen?" Sullivan asked.

"Because Papa Fuzzy was wrong about me," Holloway said. "Papa Fuzzy said that I was a good man. I'm not, Mark. I'm selfish and unethical and I'm happy to lie and deceive to get what I want. You had a problem perjuring yourself. I did it without thinking twice.

"And that's what the fuzzys needed," Holloway said. "Don't get me wrong. They need good people like you and Isabel and Chad Bourne. They need the three of you more right now than they need me. But before you could help them, I had to get them to you. I was the only one who could. Because I'm the man who can hit a client to cause a mistrial. I'm the guy who can lie about his girlfriend in a corporate inquiry. I'm the guy who can make everyone think *they* are the ones who really know why he's doing what he's doing, and in letting them think that, string them along until he has them where he wants them.

"I'm not a good man, Mark," Holloway said. "But I was the *right* man. And for this, that was enough."

Sullivan looked at Holloway for a moment. Then he held out his beer bottle.

"To the right man, then," he said. "To you, Jack."

Holloway smiled, clinked his bottle with Sullivan's, and finished his beer.

Acknowledgments

Thanks to, in no particular order: Bill Schafer, Yanni Kuznia, Patrick Nielsen Hayden, Cherie Priest, Eliani Torres, Heather Saunders, Irene Gallo, Peter Lutjen, Kekai Kotaki, Wil Wheaton, Deven Desai, Doselle Young, Justine Larbalestier, Mary Robinette Kowal, Regan Avery, Karen Meisner, Cian Chang, Anne KG Murphy, and John Anderson.

Additional thanks to Penguin, in particular John Schline and Susan Allison, and the estate of H. Beam Piper.

I would like to once again single out for special appreciation my fiction agent, Ethan Ellenberg, who tackled a rather troublesome and potentially unprofitable project with enthusiasm and ingenuity. It's good to have a good agent.

As always, much love and thanks to my wife, Kristine, and our daughter, Athena.